SEVEN, EIGHT ... GONNA STAY UP LATE

REBEKKA FRANCK, BOOK 4

WILLOW ROSE

Copyright Willow Rose 2013
Published by Jan Sigetty Boeje
All rights reserved.

No part of this book may be reproduced, scanned, or distributed in any printed or electronic form without permission from the author.

This is a work of fiction. Any resemblance of characters to actual persons, living or dead is purely coincidental. The Author holds exclusive rights to this work. Unauthorized duplication is prohibited.

Cover design by Juan Villar Padron,
https://juanjjpadron.wixsite.com/juanpadron

Special thanks to my editor Jean Pacillo
http://www.ebookeditingpro.com

Connect with Willow Rose:
willow-rose.net

∼

I said, hey, girl with one eye
Get your filthy fingers out of my pie
I said, hey, girl with one eye
I'll cut your little heart out cause you made me cry

Girl with one eye by **Florence and the Machine**

PROLOGUE

She was drunk. Too drunk to walk straight. Too drunk to find her way back to the tent. But she wasn't alone. The festival grounds were crowded with people staggering around too drunk to know what they were doing. That was the way it always was, especially at this late hour on the festival's first night when people had been drinking all day, some for days in a row, living up to all the expectations of looking forward to seeing all the bands on stage and just drinking without a care in the world.

Amalie loved it. It was so real, so raw and the only time she would mingle with people that weren't from her part of the world, who weren't from her class. Here on the festival grounds, on the soil that was magically transformed every year from plain fields to this Mecca of vibrating music and people listening to it together. All boundaries were crossed. Rich were living in the same manner, in the same tents, as ordinary working class people. Being from the high-society jet-set of the Danish population Amalie always found it hilarious to mingle with people of lesser means, with the kind of people she never associated with during her daily life of horseback riding and golfing. The kind of people she wouldn't look at if she passed them on the street. But here, in these surroundings all walls were torn down. There was no rich, no poor, there was just people. People dancing, people singing, people peeing in all corners and people drinking and smoking. All were happy and talking to one another no matter where they came from or where they were heading.

While looking for her own group in the sea of tents she came across all kinds of people who, not knowing who she was, dared to speak to her like she was an ordinary girl from an ordinary middle class family. She found that amusing and laughed to herself just as a guy with wide eyes and a blissful smile greeted her and told her she was gorgeous. No one would ever dare to talk to her like that had they known who she really was. No one talked to her like that in her daily life and she enjoyed it. It was fun. But then again, she had always enjoyed playing with people. To Amalie people were like dolls. Dolls you could play with and get to do what you'd like them to, then throw them away afterwards. She was like that with her friends, the few she allowed to get close to her.

Amalie suddenly felt dizzy and staggered into a camp of people sitting outside of a tent smoking a bong. They all smiled and looked up at her when she tumbled into the side of one of their tents. Then they laughed.

She got up and laughed at herself as well. "Sorry about that," she said.

"No problem," one of them said. His eyes were red and bleary. "Do you want some?" he asked and pointed at the bong.

Amalie shrugged. "Why not?" Then she leaned over and

inhaled deeply from the bong. It made her body shiver in delight and the ground spun even faster than before.

"Best be on my way now," she said laughing like a mad man.

"See you around," the man holding the bong said.

"Sure," she said and staggered on. The dizziness increased and soon she found it hard to know in what direction she was supposed to walk. She tried hard to focus her mind on finding the right tent but they all looked the same. For miles and miles the area continued with nothing but tents all looked the same. It didn't help her much that it was in July and one of those clear bright summer nights when the sun would hardly set at all. She still couldn't spot her tent.

She was actually in a hurry to find it. Since she was going to watch The Mew play in about half an hour. She had told her friends that she was going to the restroom and that could usually take up to an hour because of the long lines.

"You're not going back to go to sleep are you? Are you caving in?" her best friend Camilla asked. She was the one who brought Amalie to the festival. Just like Amalie she came from a rich high-society family that didn't care for them being in such a place, but Camilla knew how to trick their parents, making arrangements for them to go sailing, paying off the captain of her father's yacht to tell her parents and Amalie's parents that they were both on the boat all four days the festival lasted. It was the second year Amalie and Camilla had done this. No one had ever suspected what they really had been up to.

"No. Are you kidding me? Amalie answered. "My favorite band is coming. I'm gonna stay up very late, maybe even make it an all nighter."

In reality she wasn't going to the restroom, she was going back for more colored pills that she had gotten from a guy earlier in the day. She had met him at a concert in one of the smaller tents where the lesser known artists played for smaller crowds. He stared at her from afar with a strange smile. He was handsome; she thought and smiled back shyly to the much older blond guy with slick hair and peculiar eyes, smoking a cigarette. She lowered her eyes and continued to dance to the music with her girlfriend feeling his eyes following her every move. She liked that. Him devouring her with his look. When she opened her eyes again he was gone. After the concert when she walked towards the restrooms he crept up behind her.

"Boo!"

She jumped, startled. Quicker than she could manage to turn her head, he was in front of her with a whooshing sound.

"Looking for fun, are we?" he asked with a whispering, almost hissing voice. His eyes stared wildly at her and her body. It made her feel warm. He was flickering his fingers in front of her face. At that time Amalie had been drinking since the same morning and yes, he was so right, she was indeed looking to have some fun. Lots of fun. She was determined to do all the things she had never been allowed to do. Do it before it was too late. Before she was all grown up and supposed to live the life determined for her since her birth. Before her birth, actually.

The man put his face very close to hers. She smiled and reached out to touch his soft, smooth skin. But it was like her fingers went straight through him. Either that or he was just moving really fast. Maybe she was just reacting slowly because she was drunk, she thought. Suddenly he was behind her. Whispering in her ear.

"I have fun in my pocket," he said. "Do you want to see? Do you? Do you want to see?"

Knowing how her father would be angry if he knew where she was and what she was really doing, she smiled at the prospect of really pissing him off. She nodded her head and felt the man put something in her pocket.

When she turned with the intent to pay him, he was gone. She looked for him while taking out the pills. Then she had decided to save them for tonight's big concert.

After several wrong turns and stumbling over a number of cords holding the tents, Amalie finally found her own tent. She crawled in and sat on her air mattress in the dark. She pulled out her backpack and found the colored pills in the side pocket. Then she found a half-empty beer bottle and flushed a pink one down with it. She enjoyed the taste of a common beer, like the ones ordinary people drank. Ah, she thought to herself while waiting for the pill to do its job. Ah, to finally be like normal people.

She looked up as she heard the whooshing sound of the wind. It was getting windier. She found a sweater in her backpack that she brought just in case. When she looked up she spotted a light outside the tent. A circle of light, like the beam of a flashlight was being shone towards her tent. It wasn't moving at all. Fingers appeared in the circle. Amalie tilted her head. Was it the drugs or was someone making shadow animals on the tent cloth? Amalie smiled when the fingers made a rabbit, she chuckled when they made what looked like a goat, and she even laughed out loud when they made a dog and pretended it was barking. But when they shaped a small devil with pointy ears, Amalie laughed no more.

1

"DID YOU GET a good one of him on stage?" I asked Sune. He stared at the display on the camera and showed me. I nodded my acknowledgement. It was an excellent picture of the guitarist my article was about. It was beautifully composed with the lights and colors on the huge stage. Orange stage, the biggest stage at the festival.

We were at the Roskilde festival, an event that every year attracted some of the world's biggest bands and around eighty-five thousand people from all over the world. It was one of the six biggest annual music festivals in Europe. It was a huge event for a small country like Denmark and naturally it was documented in all the media, and since it was within our area - also by my small newspaper, *The Zeeland Times*.

Sune and I didn't stay in the muddy campsite with poor sanitary conditions like all the paying visitors. As members of the press we had access to the secluded area of the festival where the press and musicians were treated more humanely. Sune and I saw this as an opportunity to spend some quality time together while working, with the added possibility of listening to some great music and meeting exciting people, like the guitarist we were doing a piece on.

"Happy?" Sune asked while I clicked through the photos.

Very," I said with a big smile. "It looks great."

Sune smiled back, and then he leaned down and kissed me. I enjoyed being alone with him for once. We hadn't had much time together lately, with work, taking care of my dad and the kids coming between us.

It wasn't that we didn't see each other. We actually saw a lot of each other every day. We had moved in together in Sune's small apartment and worked together on the paper, but still it was like there wasn't really time to be a couple, to be romantic. The kids were constantly there and if not, then it was something else.

It was July. Four months had passed since our disastrous winter vacation in Arnakke and Denmark was showing itself from its most attractive angle. The forest was in bloom and even if it did occasionally rain now and then, the weather was behaving nicely for the festival and kept the ground from turning into a pile of mud like it usually did.

The sun peeked out every now and then and warmed our faces and made it all just really nice. Along with the great music and the wonderful vibe from the happy, almost ecstatic people all over the festival grounds, it was an assignment we both really enjoyed.

Peter had taken Julie the four days we were gone. She was on her summer break and I gave him permission to take her with him to Aarhus where he lived in our old house from back when we were still together. He had been back in our lives all spring now and it seemed to be going well. He had been in therapy and I was beginning to see a huge change in him. The anger issues were gone, or at least I didn't see them anymore, and neither did Julie. He seemed to have that part under control. So I slowly allowed him to come back into our lives little by little, and I enjoyed seeing how happy Julie was to spend some time with her dad. I never asked about his business, if he still worked as a mercenary for so-called "security" companies operating in Iraq and Afghanistan, but I figured he still did since he never told me otherwise. I still didn't care much for it and hoped he would never talk to Julie about it. So in the beginning I allowed him to stay in Karrebaeksminde at a hotel and take Julie out on weekends, later she was allowed to stay in his hotel room with him the entire weekend. Julie was ecstatic naturally to finally have her father back in her life and I didn't mind to occasionally have a weekend of my own. The problem was that Sune didn't have any possibility of someone taking Tobias out of the apartment, so it wasn't that we had time to ourselves even if Julie was out of the house.

But we managed okay, I thought to myself as I kissed him back. Living together had made everything a lot easier. If only I wasn't so guilt-ridden about leaving Dad. He hadn't been feeling well lately, if it was due to the exposure to radiation four months ago or if it was just him getting older and missing us in the house, I didn't know. Maybe it was all of it. We tried to visit several times a week, but it was getting increasingly difficult to find time in our busy schedules. Julie had gotten really serious about horseback riding and went there three times a week, and I, well I had my job and my editor had begun demanding more and more from me. The newspaper had expanded and I had been promoted to cover more than just Karrebaekminde-stuff. I traveled all over Zeeland now and did stories. It was great for me career-wise, but left me with less time on my hands. Dad was the one who suffered because of it. He would never say it to my face, but he was disappointed that I chose to move out of his house. I knew it, I could tell on his face. I knew he had enjoyed having us in the house, especially after Mom died, but I had a life to live too. Julie would occasionally spend the night at his house and let him spoil her rotten, but she too was growing older and getting a life of her own. She had made a lot of new friends who were also into horses and riding and along with Tobias they could spend hours and hours on the riding school.

"Where did you go?" Sune asked and kissed my nose.

I chuckled. "I'm sorry. I was just thinking about Dad. I hope he's alright alone in that big house. I won't be able to visit him until Tuesday."

"He'll be alright," Sune said.

A couple of young guys staggered drunk past us, yelling happily. Sune greeted them with a friendly nod. "Don't do this again," he said.

"Do what?"

"Don't turn what is supposed to be a great couple of days for us into a guilt-trip so you can't enjoy us finally being alone together."

I bent my head in shame. "You're right. I always do that, don't I?"

"Over thinking everything, yes," he said and removed a lock of hair from my face.

"I'm sorry. I'll stop right away."

Sune chuckled and kissed my forehead. He knew as well as I, that I wasn't capable of leaving it alone after the thought first entered my mind. But I was determined to not let it destroy my trip with Sune. "I can't do anything about it anyway, right?" I continued. "Well, maybe I could call him and ask if he's alright." I looked up at Sune. "Later," I said. "I'll call him later."

Sune smiled, and then kissed my lips. "Wonderful. 'Cause

we have a schedule. There are a lot of smaller bands that I really want to see, but I have two big ones that I am not going to miss. Björk is on in half an hour and Saturday night is the big night."

"Springsteen?"

Sune nodded eagerly. "The Boss himself. I've been looking forward to this for months. Nothing's going to keep me away. I don't care if the world comes to an end; I'm watching him on stage."

"Well we better hope the world stands a little longer, then," I said and patted his stomach. "Let's grab something to eat first, and then head over to see the eccentric Icelander."

2

Amalie was still groggy when she woke up. Her head was hurting badly. She tried hard to remember what had happened. She remembered taking the pill, then seeing the shadow fingers on the tent and then ... then what? A face, a set of eyes. She recognized him right away when he stuck his head in the tent. He was the same guy who had given her the pills. Had she pushed him? Yes, that was it. She had tried to push him out, thinking he came to reclaim his payment for the pills, thinking he thought he was going to get lucky with her because he had treated her to a little something.

She had pushed him amicably to let him know that he wasn't getting anywhere near her. Even if he was handsome, he was way too old for her and she was not about any of that. She made it very clear to him. Then she had told him, that her friends were on their way. They would be here any moment now. That was when he began laughing. Then what? Amalie touched her head, there was a bump, several actually. He hit her with something. Something big and hard. It had hurt like hell. Still did. He had swung what she now believed was a big flashlight again in the back of her head, smashing it against her skull, and again, this time behind her ear, then a succession of blows followed. She had tried to scream and drag her body towards the entrance of the tent, but she knew the noise from the concerts and the drunken people walking to and from the stages, yelling and screaming in joy would drown out her cries for help.

Amalie touched the back of her head again and thought about her dad. He would kill her once he found out where she had been. When he came to get her. He was going to get her, wasn't he? she thought suddenly with desperation. Of course he was. He always found her. But what if he didn't this time? What if he couldn't?

Amalie stared into the empty darkness in front of her. She had to find a way to get home before he found out she wasn't on the boat with Camilla. Where was Camilla anyway? She had to find her in a hurry, so they could get their stories straight. She felt sick to her stomach, probably from the drugs. Her pants were wet. Had she wet herself while unconscious? How gross. How humiliating.

But where was she? She wasn't in her tent; she thought and felt underneath her body. It felt like she was lying on some sort of plastic. It wasn't her air mattress, and it certainly wasn't a bed. She couldn't be in a hospital.

"I have to get out of here," she said and tried to sit up. Her head hit something hard that forced her to lie down again. What was that? She moaned and touched her forehead. Then she reached up her hand and touched what it was her head had hit. It was like a ceiling; she thought and patted along it. It felt just like the floor she was lying on. Could she be in some sort of bunk bed? Had that creep taken her somewhere? Had he taken her back to his place or something? Amalie shrieked at the thought of what he could have done to her while she had been unconscious. Who the hell did he think he was? Didn't he know who she was? She could destroy his life for doing this. Her father would make sure he was properly punished. For many that was a fate worse than death.

Amalie tried again to sit up, but it was impossible. Then she turned her body with the intent of sticking out her legs and crawling out. But her arms and legs hit a wall as well.

With her heart pounding in her chest she turned to the other side, only to hit another wall of plastic here as well. Slightly panicking, she tried to slide with her feet first, but they too hit a wall right away. Then she stretched her hands upwards above her head. Her hands hit yet another wall of plastic.

She began gasping for air while patting the walls surrounding her very close to her body. Then she screamed.

"HELP! HELP!"

She kept patting the plastic until she realized it surrounded her completely, without an opening anywhere - at least not one that she could find. Then she put her hands on the ceiling and tried to push it with all of her strength, but it didn't move at all. In desperation she began hitting it with her clenched fist, trying to smash it, and then kicked it while screaming, but nothing helped. She gasped while panic grew inside of her. The realization felt catastrophic.

She was trapped.

3
___

HE LISTENED WITH pleasure to the screams coming from the basement of his three story house in Hellerup overlooking the ocean. A smile was planted across his face. She was awake. Allan licked his lips to moister them, while he sat in the black chaise longue designed by Le Corbusier with his iPad in his lap. He turned up the music from his B&O and enjoyed the tunes emerging from his built in speakers. This was indeed a *great moment*, he wrote on the iPad with the five hundred dollar Balenciaga iPad folder made from vintage lambskin that his annoying boyfriend Sebastian had bought him on one of his trips to Florence.

Have fun and enjoy the ride, a man calling himself Michael Cogliantry answered. It wasn't his real name, Allan knew that much. Like himself they all used aliases.

Oh I intend to, he wrote back.

Don't forget to post pictures and tell us all the dirty details, a guy who called himself Karl Persson answered.

I will, Allan wrote. *She is still screaming.*

Ah, that's the best part, Cogliantry wrote. *I love it when they scream like that. I love listening to the desperation in their voices. How I miss it.*

Why don't you go out and get a new one for yourself? Allan asked. *It's been awhile. You must be getting thick behind the ears. Lol.*

I am. It's like I'm itching all over for the thrill. I badly need to kill again soon. But I have to lay low. At least for a few months more, he answered.

You don't think the police still suspect anything? After they grabbed the ex-boyfriend for killing her? I honestly think they have moved on by now, Allan wrote.

Yeah. You might be right. But they came to my door, remember? Scared the shit out of me. Asked me where I had been on the night she disappeared.

That's what you get from picking a girl from your neighborhood, Persson wrote. *You don't shit where you eat, remember? That's the first rule. You don't mess with the rules, man.*

I got to go, Allan wrote. *She just went quiet.*

Losing strength already? Persson wrote. *Good luck, Einaudi.*

Thanks. Will be posting again soon, Allan wrote, and then logged off. He raised his head from the screen and looked at the painting on the wall, made by the artist, the real Fred Einaudi himself. It showed a boy above a lake looking down at the body of a dead girl floating in the surface while he was trying to poke her with a stick. The title was the mermaid, and visitors to Allan's house thought that was what the painting was all about, but Allan knew the girl was no mermaid. The title simply referred to what the boy thought it was, but in reality she was as dead as they come. She was never going to swim anywhere again. Allan chuckled to himself remembering the first time he had drowned a girl. That was what he enjoyed so much about this painting and why he had desired it so much the first time he had seen it in an exhibition in New York that he was willing to pay the enormous sum the artist was asking. He had been that boy once. The first time he had killed. And the painting reminded him of that beautiful time when he had stared at her floating dead body in the water, looking back at him with her empty eyes. She was nothing, meant nothing to him before that second. But once she was in that water she was eternalized in his memory as the one who took his virginity. That's why he bought the painting, and that was why he used the artist's name on the chat. It seemed appropriate somehow. Like there was a supernatural connection between him and the real artist. Allan was after all sort of an artist himself. At least that was how he viewed himself. They all did.

But he too had broken the rules now, hadn't he? That was why he had left the chat in a hurry. It wasn't because the girl had stopped screaming, no she was still at it much to his pleasure, since the feistier they were the funnier it was to kill them. No it was because of what one of them had said. Allan knew it was bad to pick someone that close to you, someone who might know you. He had played it very safe for years and years and never made one mistake. He couldn't tell the others about it, they would think he had lost it. But he knew that he could easily do this without endangering himself. He knew he could. He was the best at everything he did, especially killing. Superhuman even. This one wasn't random, it wasn't just another one. She was nothing like the others. She was special, and this was something he needed to do. Yes, he was probably going to break some of the rules from now on, but so be it. It was something he had planned for a long time, and he had been thrilled to realize that the pretty little thing hadn't recognized him when he stared at her in the tent at the festival. She didn't know who he was. After all it didn't matter.

She would be dead soon anyway.

4

"We're here to see a lot of naked people," the young man with the cap said. His friend standing next to him nodded.

"It's true. It's only here on Roskilde Festival that they have a race like this. It's a tradition. We've been standing in this line for forty minutes in order to see it. You have to get here early to get a spot in front," he laughed boyishly. "The best view is in the front."

I wrote his comments down on my pad along with their names, then Sune took their pictures and we left them. There were only a few seconds till the annual naked-race was about to start at the festival. It was always a fun event that the entire media covered with lots of pictures of the naked people racing each other to the finish line. Even TV crews were in place, ready to broadcast video of the naked contestants all over the country. It had been going on for fifteen years now, and was arranged by the festival's own radio station that was only on air once a year during the four days of the festival.

This was day three. It was Saturday and as tradition had it also the day when hundreds of festival participants took off their clothes and ran across the mud stark naked. Thousands of spectators would cheer them on. It didn't matter what they looked like, the runners came in all sizes and shapes. It was quite a show and so very, very Danish, I thought to myself as the white bodies wearing nothing but boots ran past me splattering mud into the air and Sune took a series of pictures. The winners were announced and displayed on the podium while the crowd cheered happily. One man and one woman. I chuckled while I wrote down the two winner's names on my pad. Their pictures would probably be on the front page of the newspaper, since nothing much else was happening in our small country at this time of year.

We went back to the media-center to write the story and send it. The room was soon packed with journalists who came to do the same. Radio people were editing their pieces, reportages and sending them home, the TV crews worked their equipment with precision. It didn't take me more than half an hour to finish it up and send both article and Sune's pictures back to Jens-Ole, who was sitting at the editor's desk at our main office, waiting for something to happen, waiting for the perfect story to break, so he didn't have to display two naked people winning a race for the third year in a row on the front page. I pressed "send" and looked at Sune.

"Now we just have one more thing to do before the big concert tonight," I said and got up from the chair. I grabbed my laptop and put it in my bag. We had promised the paper to report from the Springsteen concert that same night. He wasn't doing any interviews this time, his manager had told everybody, but we had been allowed to write a piece about his wife, Patti Scialfa who was also playing guitar in the band. She agreed to do a brief interview. So now we walked towards the huge Orange stage where they were going to play the same night. She had agreed to meet us there so we could get some nice shots of her and her guitar.

I noticed the posters for the first time while walking across the area in front of the stage, where thousands of people would gather in a few hours to the biggest concert of the entire festival. Everybody was going to be there, that was for sure. People wanting to be in front had already arrived; some were sitting on the ground smoking cigarettes, talking, drinking beer, and waiting. I passed a group of young punk girls dressed in black, sitting on the muddy ground. That was when I noticed they were each holding a piece of paper in their hands, intently reading it. I didn't think more of it until a few seconds later when two men passing us were holding the very same pieces of papers while talking loudly.

" ... Happens every year, you know."

"... probably just passed out in a tent somewhere."

They looked at the paper, and the photo displayed on top of it.

"Good looking, though," the one guy said just before he crumbled the paper up and threw it through the air.

I kept walking while suddenly noticing everybody around us holding the paper posters in their hands. As we walked on I spotted a girl in the center of area, right in front of the stage. She was handing out the papers while talking. There was something about her that made me stop, something in her frantic way of pushing the pieces of paper at people. It was an air of desperation that drew me towards her.

As I came closer, she looked at me, then handed me one. "Please, help me. I'm looking for this girl," she said and pointed at the picture. A beautiful blond girl about the same age as she was stared back at me. What were they, fourteen?

Fifteen? "She disappeared Thursday night and hasn't been seen since," the girl said with shiver in her voice. "Her name is Amalie."

I looked at the girl handing out the papers. She was biting her lip. "What's her last name?" I asked. "It doesn't say."

The young girl stared at me, and then shook her head. "I'm afraid I can't tell you."

"She is very young and so are you, have you contacted her parents?"

The girl shook her head heavily. Then she smiled insecurely and turned her back to me. She started walking away. I followed her. "Hey. I was talking to you," I said. I caught up to her and grabbed her shoulder. She tried to walk faster. "Hey. I'm a journalist. I might be able to help you," I added. "I could put her picture in the paper and write a small note about her disappearing. Have you contacted the police?"

The young girl stopped walking. She turned and looked at me. She grabbed my paper and pulled it out of my hands. "Just forget it," she said shaking her head. "I'm sure she just found some guy and stayed with him."

"But you don't think she would ever do that, do you?" I asked. "You're her best friend and you know she would never do anything like that, right? You wouldn't be out here with these homemade posters, if you thought that, am I right?"

The young girl sighed deeply, then bowed her head and shook it slowly. "She said she was just going to the restroom. I knew she was drunk, but we all were. I thought she would be back. She had been looking forward to seeing The Mew. When she didn't come back I began searching for her, we had promised to stick together. We always make a deal to stick close together and never go with anyone. I was mad at her at first for breaking our deal, but when she didn't come back to the tent all night, I became scared that something had happened. I searched for her all day yesterday and today, passing out these posters. Someone that I know in the festival's radio station helped me make them and print them. I keep checking my phone thinking she is going to call soon, but ... " The girl turned away from me. "The festival is closing tomorrow and if I haven't found her then ..."

I grabbed both of her shoulders and turned her. "Look at me," I said. The girl lifted her head and looked me in the eyes. "I can try and help you, if you'd like. My name is Rebekka Franck. I'm a reporter at *The Zeeland Times*."

The girl sniffled. "I'm Camilla."

"Okay, Camilla. Now tell me, why haven't you called her parents yet? Is it because they don't know you're here?"

Camilla sniffed and nodded. "They would never let us go. They'd kill us if they found out."

"Okay, so that's why you're trying to find her on your own first. I get that. I know that people disappear from the festival every year and once the festival is over they turn up again. Most of them have just been too drunk and then fallen asleep somewhere. It happens. But they are not as young as you two. How old are you?"

"Fourteen."

"And your friend ..." I stared at the paper and read the name. "Amalie? Is she fourteen too?"

Camilla nodded.

"Okay. Well you're not the first fourteen-year olds at this festival, but you are definitely among the youngest. Is it your first time?"

"No, we were here last year too. But nothing like this has ever happened before."

"Have you thought about having the festival radio broadcast an alert for people to look for Amalie?"

Camilla nodded. "They say they need her last name for it, and I can't give them that."

"Why not?"

Camilla exhaled deeply. "It's complicated, okay. Let's just say that I'm afraid the entire hoard of press will come running after me. It would be all over the news."

5

She was still screaming. Amalie scratched her fingers at the slippery plastic and felt how they had begun bleeding. Then she clenched her fist again and began hitting the thick plastic. She continued until her hands became numb and she couldn't feel her fingers. She tried to use her nails to grab a hold of an edge or a crack or at least something to grab on to. There had to be an opening somewhere, where she had gotten in, she thought and searched frantically. But she found nothing. No cracks, no sharp edges. It was all smooth and so very, very close to her. When she could feel her fingers yet again, she started scratching with her nails. Blood dripped in her face and hit her lip. She recognized the taste from her childhood. Her fingertips were hurting badly and the pain forced her to stop. Then she opened her mouth and let out another scream. Her heart pounding, she screamed until her voice became hoarse and she almost lost it.

Then she stopped. Breathing heavily she tried to calm herself down and use another weapon. Her brain. She began to think.

The darkness still surrounded her and Amalie had lost

track of time and space. She knew she had been attacked Thursday night, but how long had she been unconscious? A day? Two days? How long had she been lying awake staring into the void, the darkness, seeing nothing, just feeling her way around and screaming and kicking? She didn't know. All she knew was that she had gone from utter panic, knocking, kicking, screaming to finally calming herself down, trying to think of a way out. But the panic was still there, wasn't it? It was lurking underneath the surface constantly. She tried to control her breathing again, not thinking about the hard plastic surrounding her, just imagining herself in open places, on her father's yacht, out on the open sea, breathing in the fresh sea air. That was when a thought occurred to her. If she were in fact in a closed box of some sort as she suspected, and then she would eventually use up all the air, wouldn't she? The thought brought the panic back. The feeling of suffocating overwhelmed her and she gasped for air. But that was just it, she realized. There seemed to be air enough for her. That meant that there had to be an opening somewhere. The air had to come in somewhere.

Amalie began patting the plastic above her meticulously. Putting one hand next to the other and by that way covering all of it eventually. She took in a deep breath. It smelled like old urine. But it also confirmed her theory. Yes, there was indeed enough air, no doubt about it. She wasn't supposed to suffocate. She was supposed to be able to breathe. Her fingers examined the ceiling but found nothing, then she moved on to the sides. First the one to the left. After a few seconds she felt something close to the upper corner. She put both of her hands on it and felt it closer. It was a hole. A circular hole in the plastic big enough for her hand to almost fit in it. But it didn't lead outside of the box, she realized as she tried to push her hand through it. It seemed to lead into a tube of some sort. A tube going upwards. But where? She speculated while examining it more closely. Where did it end? What was on the other side of it? And most importantly, *who* was?

What were their plans with her? Why had they put her in this awful thing? They were determined to keep her alive, but why? For what? Money? Her dad would pay them in a heartbeat. Of course he would.

And afterwards he would hunt them down like the beasts they were.

They had to know who she was, she thought calmingly to herself. That meant she wasn't a random victim to some psychopath. This was arranged. This was a kidnapping. Of course it was. They wanted money. The bastards.

Amalie chuckled to herself. They had to be very stupid bastards. Most people would know to pick a different target, she thought grinning. Most people would have sense enough to never dare touch her. She amused herself by imagining how they would get what was coming to them.

Amalie kept thinking about what her dad would do to them, imagining the worst things she could come up with, and decided to not give her captors what they wanted. She wasn't going to cry, she wasn't going to be weak. Instead she began planning her revenge.

Once my dad gets to them. They won't know what hit them.

6

Allan was preparing dinner for himself and Sebastian. He stared at the butcher's knife and turned the blade to make it catch the light. Such a marvelous instrument. Such beauty in its simplicity. He touched the blade and cut his fingertip slightly. A drop of blood landed on the raw meat. Allan smiled, then found a paper-towel and wiped the blood off. The meat looked fresh even if it had been in his freezer for months.

Allan lifted the knife in the air, then stabbed the meat. He exhaled satisfied as it penetrated the raw meat, as it cut through the flesh. He cut it into big slices that he placed in a baking dish, then sprinkled herbs on it and covered it with a sauce he had been cooking for hours on the stove. He smelled the dish just before he sent it into the hot oven. It smelled heavenly.

"The secret's in the sauce," he said to himself while chuckling at his own reference to one of Sebastian's all-time favorite movies *Fried Green Tomatoes*.

Allan loved cooking for his boyfriend even if he never enjoyed his company much. Allan wasn't really gay, to be frank he wasn't anything really. Not homosexual, not heterosexual, not bi-sexual either. Allan really wasn't any of those things. He was more sort of ... well the word psychopath would be closer to the truth, but it had such a negative ring to it, didn't it? That's why he liked to see himself as more of an artist. Like other artists, he created things. And like most artists he would never be recognized by his time, but he would be remembered for many years to come. People would talk about him and discuss his work. Most of them with repulsion, but that was always the risk one took as an artist. You had to not care what people thought about it. An artist had to create what his heart longed to tell the world, didn't he? Whether they liked it or not. That was the blessing and the curse of being a true *artiste*, as they liked to pronounce it. And Allan was a true *artiste*, he thought to himself as he looked inside of the oven and stared at the herb-covered meat boiling in the hot sauce.

"Another *creazione* by the marvelous Allan Witt," he said to himself lifting up his fingers pretending to be artistic, then blowing finger kisses and bowing like he was receiving applause. Standing ovation, naturally.

Oh, they would get to respect him and admire his work. One day they all would speak his name in awe and admiration. They would write about him everywhere and people would shiver in fascination. *Ah, yes*, Allan thought to himself as he closed the door to the basement and shut out the screaming. Then he turned on the music to drown her out completely. *One day they'll understand my genius.*

Allan was ripped out of his daydream by the sound of the bell. He jumped with anticipation, then ran to open the door. Sebastian stood on the outside steps wearing a short-sleeved white silk-shirt from some overly expensive Italian designer. He smiled showing pearly white teeth.

"Right on time," Allan said.

Sebastian stepped inside and kissed Allan on the lips. "Smells absolutely fabulous," he said and looked at Allan. "Are you about to spoil me again?" He tapped his well proportioned six-pack stomach. "I know what you're up to," he said. Then he leaned over and grabbed Allan's face between his hands and kissed him again. The kiss left Allan feeling nothing.

"You just want to fatten me up, don't you? Fatten me up so no one else will want me, and you can have me to myself? Ah, don't think I haven't noticed how you put extra cream in the sauce to make it so good I can't resist it. I'm on to you, sweetie-pie. I am so on to you."

Then Sebastian clicked his tongue which made him sound gayer than ever and walked towards the kitchen. Allan closed the door.

"You got me there," he said.

Sebastian looked inside of the oven, then drew in a big breath and looked back at Allan. "Oh, that is so good," he said. "What are we having?"

Allan smiled widely. "Just a little something I pulled up from the freezer."

7

I ASKED CAMILLA to meet me after I finished the interview with Patti Scialfa. Sune stayed behind to take some more photos while I hurried to our meeting place. Camilla was waiting when I arrived. She stood in front of a stand that sold vegetarian dishes. Her face seemed strained and her eyes showed she hadn't slept much. It wasn't unusual at a festival like this, but in her case it wasn't because she had been partying all night. Her eyes were flickering like they were constantly scanning the area surrounding her, on the lookout for her friend, anxiously hoping that she might catch a glimpse of her somewhere in the crowd of hundreds and hundreds of people constantly passing by.

"I keep thinking I see her," she said as I approached. Camilla kept sweeping the area with her eyes and spoke without looking at me. "But it's just someone looking like her. Like that girl over there. Her hair looks just like Amalie's."

I put my hand on Camilla's shoulder. She turned and looked at me. Then she exhaled deeply. "Do you think she's still out there somewhere?" she asked.

I nodded. Not because I knew anything about it, but

because I wanted to comfort her. Plus it was very unlikely that she had left the festival. I wasn't afraid of that. But I was afraid that something had happened to her inside the fences, on the festival grounds. I was afraid that she might have been hurt somehow and unable to contact Camilla.

"Does she have her phone?" I asked.

Camilla shrugged. "I think so. It wasn't in her backpack anywhere." Camilla pulled out her phone and looked at the display. "My own is running out of batteries soon."

"I can help you charge it. I can bring it to the media area and plug it in," I said.

"Thanks," she said with a sad voice.

"But you're thinking that if your phone is almost dead, then hers might be running out of batteries soon too?"

Camilla nodded.

"What happens when you try and call her? Does it go directly to the voice mail?"

Camilla shook her head. "No."

"Okay. That means it's not dead yet," I said.

Camilla looked up at me. "But it could also mean that she can't answer it."

"Let's not get ahead of ourselves," I said. "She might have dropped it somewhere, have you thought about that? It could have fallen out of her pocket somehow." I looked in the direction of the campground with thousands of tents. "It happens that people get lost here. Maybe she is simply lost. Did you make a plan for what to do if any one of you got lost?"

Camilla shook her head. "No. But she is smart enough to find the paramedics or some officials working here and have them help her."

"Well maybe she has done just that. Maybe we should go and talk to them? Ask them if they have seen her?"

"I did that yesterday. I wondered if Amalie might have

been hurt. She was pretty drunk when she left me, so she might have fallen or something, or maybe gotten sick. So I went to talk to the paramedics but they hadn't seen her."

"Maybe they've seen her today?" I said. "Let's go ask them."

Camilla nodded, then began walking. I looked at my watch. "I think I have about half an hour before I need to get back to write my article."

We walked in silence. Camilla kept handing out papers with Amalie's face on it to people passing by, while I continued to wonder who Amalie really was and why Camilla didn't want her last name out. Was it just because she was afraid of the parent's reaction, or was it true that her name would make the headlines? I kept wondering what kind of name would trick such a reaction.

I received a text from Sune telling me he was done and on his way back to send the photos. I texted back that I would meet him there. I looked at my watch, then sensed the pressure of my deadline. I began walking faster. I didn't have much time.

We spoke to the paramedics. They recognized Camilla from yesterday and told her they unfortunately hadn't seen Amalie today either. They had had many patients with minor injuries, mostly blisters on their feet from walking and dancing in boots for too many hours and Amalie might have been among them. Since they saw so many faces for only a short period of time it was possible that she could have been there without them knowing it.

"I tell you what," the guy said. "Hang your little poster on the wall over there and I'll make sure to keep an eye out for her, okay?"

Camilla did as he told her. The paramedic watched her closely. "And remember. This happens all the time," he said. "Every year someone disappears but they always show up eventually. She's probably just having fun with some guy in a tent somewhere, forgetting that she has people caring for her and worrying about her. It happens all the time."

Camilla sighed, then nodded. I put my arm around her while we left. "See," I said. "I told you it's common. I don't think you need to worry this much. Try and enjoy the festival. Amalie will show up eventually. Just wait and see."

Camilla seemed to lighten up slightly. "Okay," she said. "I really wanted to go see *Suicide Silence*. They're playing now. Some friends Amalie and I met here at the festival are over there."

"Then go join them. Try to have a little fun. Forget about Amalie for a little while."

"I think I will," Camilla said with the hint of a smile.

I hugged her. "Let's meet tomorrow in the same place," I said. "I'll charge your phone and bring it back to you, okay?"

"Okay."

8

There were people upstairs. She heard the doorbell, then footsteps, then voices, people talking and lots of laughing.

Here is my chance, Amalie thought to herself. *If I make myself heard, then they'll certainly come to my rescue.*

So once again she screamed all she could and banged on the plastic surrounding her. With great strength she banged on the sides, on the top, even kicked her feet at the bottom as hard as she could to make as much noise as humanly possible.

"Help me! I'm down here!" She yelled. "I'm being held hostage down here! I'm right here! I'm down here!!"

She realized she still didn't know where "down here" was. If it was the basement of a house, or maybe she was in an apartment and what she heard were the voices and footsteps of people living upstairs. She had been in the darkness for so long that she hardly knew what was up or down. But somehow she had to alert those people, let them know that she was there, and was being held against her will. Someone had to hear her, someone had to be able to help her.

Her voice soon became hoarse from the yelling. Her mouth was so dry by now and she was so, so very thirsty.

"PLEASE!" she pleaded one last time, then gave in to the sulking and tears that had been wanting to get out for many hours. She sobbed and cried in agony and anguish, feeling sorry for herself and finally admitting she was terrified that she would never get out, never see her beloved horse again, never breathe the fresh air or see the open ocean again.

The very thought arose something in her, some kind of strength to lift her head and put her mouth to the hole and scream into the tube.

"HEEELP!"

Then she sunk back into her own feelings of misery and pity. She cried and howled and let her tears wet the floor of her cage. Her body was beginning to hurt from being in the same position for so long and from the hard material she was lying on. She tried to move, to turn her body, but there wasn't enough room.

She was afraid to lose her mind while wondering why this was happening to her, what she could possibly have done to deserve this? She hadn't been a good person, she knew that. She was spoiled, a typical rich-girl with an attitude that she expected everybody to wait on her. Yes, she knew that. And it was bad. She was bad. She knew she had not treated people well. Was God somehow punishing her for that? She had been mean, acting superior towards even her best friends, even towards Camilla. Oh, Camilla. How worried she had to be. She at least had to know that Amalie was gone, didn't she? Had she told her father by now? Amalie hoped she had, cause then this would be over soon. But what if Camilla didn't care? What if she thought that Amalie had deserved what she got? Deserved it for treating her poorly?

Amalie had brought so much pain to others, she thought

and regretted each and every thing she had ever done. She had hurt so many people especially her own mother whom she didn't care much for, since she left four years ago for some Spanish man named Pedro and moved to Spain to get away from Amalie's father. Amalie detested her for that. No, she loathed her for leaving. The few times she had been invited to Spain to visit, Amalie had acted like a spoiled brat, slammed the doors, refused to spend time with her mother and constantly told her how much she hated her and how she hated Pedro even more. In the end her mother had stopped inviting her to come. It was her own fault, she had said to Amalie's father on the phone. And her dad's fault.

"You have turned her into this cold beast with no emotions," Amalie heard her say while listening in on the conversation from a phone in another room. "She's all yours."

Now Amalie missed her mother more than ever. She missed the mother she remembered from her childhood, the one who had enjoyed her company and loved her like a mother should love her child. But something had happened. Something that had made her mother angry and resentful toward her father. Suddenly they barely spoke and her mother started drinking before noon. In the beginning it was just a glass of white wine now and then when only Amalie noticed it, but later her mother would lie in her bed upstairs in the middle of the day when Amalie came home from school. She would be asleep, an empty bottle on the floor and several pill bottles on the nightstand. In the end Amalie hardly saw her mother anymore. Her father took over the education of his daughter and soon he had taught her all she needed to know. All he had learned about life. When Amalie's mother came back from her third stay at a rehab center, she came home only to pack her stuff. She was leaving, for good, she told Amalie. She had met someone else,

Amalie overheard her tell her father. She also heard her father laugh and send her away with the words: *Get out. I'm busy.*

Amalie's father had told her that he didn't care, but Amalie knew he did. He cared so much he had sent a pack of his reservoir dogs to beat the living daylights out of this Pedro and send him to the hospital for several weeks. He was attacked in his village in Spain by what seemed like a random gang only out to rob him, but both Amalie and her mother knew who sent them and they also both knew that this was just the beginning of it.

On the day the mother told them she was leaving, Amalie's heart was torn to pieces. Still she managed to keep her calm like her father had taught her. *Never lose it*, he said. *Never show emotions in front of people. They'll think you're weak.* So she stood proud and stoic, not moving a muscle in her face while watching her mother pack her bags. Her mother looked at her just before she went out the door.

"Not even a tear, huh? Well you certainly are your father's daughter," she said, her last words before she went out the door.

Amalie hadn't shed one single tear for her mother. She decided she wasn't worth it; she didn't want to give her the satisfaction. Instead she made her life a living hell every time they were together. That was her way of getting her revenge. But it had failed. Now she needed her mother more than ever. Now she was shedding all her piled up tears for her mother and for herself.

But it was much too late.

An hour later, maybe two, she heard a noise above her. She was sniveling and gasping for air. Suddenly she saw a light somewhere. It almost blinded her eyes since they had gotten too used to the darkness. She blinked fast to force her eyes to work properly. More light emerged as she realized a door had been opened. Someone was coming!

She heard a voice. Someone was talking! A face was revealed in the door opening. She gasped and saw for the first time her cage. It was a small box, not much bigger than her, made from see-through plastic.

"Help!" she said from inside of the box. "I'm in here." She repeated it a few times, then stopped. The face in the doorway smiled and winked at her. Seeing the face and especially the peculiar eyes made her stop yelling. It was him. The guy from the festival and he was walking towards her small plastic cage on the stone floor. Then he winked again and took a turn towards the racks of wine that covered the entire wall to her right. He grabbed a bottle and pulled it out.

"Got the wine," he yelled towards the open door.

Then he winked at her one last time and ran for the stairs. Startled Amalie saw him disappear up the stairs. She wanted to yell at him, she wanted to scream to let whoever was upstairs know where she was, but she couldn't. She was simply paralyzed. Paralyzed by something she had seen. Right there, right next to her was something hanging from a hook under the ceiling. It was the remains of a human body. The hook was pierced through the neck and the head fell to the side, the eyes staring wide and empty into the air. The skin was smeared in dried blood. One leg was missing and pieces of the flesh on the back had been removed.

Then the lights went out as the man closed the door. Everything went quiet except for the low shrieking sound coming from Amalie's mouth.

9

When they were done eating, Allan walked into the basement to get a second bottle of wine. Not because he intended to drink much of it, but he wanted Sebastian to. He had been chatting and blabbing on and on all night about his last trip to Milan. Allan couldn't care less about the designers or the fashion-week or any of all that Sebastian talked about. To be honest he didn't care much about Sebastian at all. But he did care about having an alibi for tonight and as usual Sebastian could deliver just that. He was the perfect cover completely oblivious to what was going on behind his back, mainly because he was so self-involved that he hardly noticed anything, not even the distant sound of the muffled screaming coming from the basement, that Allan tried to drown by turning up the music. Nor did he suspect that he had once again enjoyed part of Allan's latest victim in a delightful sauce.

In his defense Allan was a great actor. He knew to nod at the right time and knew how to sound truly interested in what Sebastian told him.

Allan opened the next bottle and poured the wine in the

glasses in the kitchen. Then he pulled out a small sleeping pill from his pants, crushed it between his fingers and threw the remains into Sebastian's wine. He rotated it with his finger, then brought both glasses with him into the living room where Sebastian was waiting in the white couch. He looked great, but not as handsome as Allan, he thought as he spotted his own reflection passing a full-length mirror on the wall.

When he sat down and gave Sebastian the glass, Sebastian put his hand on Allan's thigh.

"I missed you while I was gone," he whispered.

"Well I was right here, waiting for you to come home," Allan answered with a smile.

Sebastian's hand caressed Allan's leg, then became a little too comfortable. Allan didn't particularly enjoy having sex with Sebastian. He didn't hate it either. It just left him kind of numb. Usually he would enter him from behind imagining that Sebastian was the lifeless body of someone he had just killed. That would do it for him. He wasn't into intimacy, he didn't care for anyone's eyes or face, but the body, the flaccid body of someone whom he had deprived of the very gift of life, now that was something that would turn him on. He didn't care if it was a boy or a girl. It didn't matter. As long as they didn't have a pulse.

But Sebastian did very much have a pulse and his blabbing was annoying Allan particularly this evening. He kept looking at his watch, while Sebastian spoke about some guy, a designer he had met in Milan who helped him get backstage at his fashion-show. Sebastian only told Allan this story to make him jealous. Allan knew that so he played along.

"You didn't do anything bad while backstage, did you?" he asked, pretending to care.

Sebastian was clearly satisfied to hear the jealous tone in

his boyfriend's voice. He chuckled, then slapped Allan gently.

"Ah, you naughty boy. Is that all you can think of? No, you silly. He showed me his passion. Not that kind of passion. His fashion-passion, of course, heh heh."

Allan laughed pretentiously. "Boy, am I glad to hear that," he said.

While Sebastian continued his story, Allan drank from his wine staring at Sebastian's glass. Then he looked at his watch. It was getting late. Allan hoped the pills would kick in soon.

"Let's toast to you coming back," he said and raised his glass.

Sebastian followed. "And to naughty boys," he said laughing.

"And to naughty boys," Allan repeated.

Allan's eyes followed Sebastian as he put the glass to his lips and drank. When he was about to stop, Allan pushed it towards his mouth again.

"Oh, my," Sebastian said. "You're trying to get me drunk. Well, I'm not going to refuse you that pleasure. Just promise me one thing; when you use my body sexually later tonight and exploit me ..." Sebastian leaned over and whispered. "Please ... don't be gentle." Then he burst into laughter that echoed in the high-ceiled living room.

Allan clinked his glass against Sebastian's.

"I promise I won't," he said and watched as Sebastian finished his.

As Sebastian dozed off in a matter of seconds Allan smiled widely. Then he slapped his boyfriend a couple of times across the cheek and when he got no reaction, he carried him upstairs and planted him in his bed. He pulled off all of his clothes to make him think they had had sex if he woke up while Allan was still gone.

"Now if you'll excuse me," he said and bowed in front of Sebastian's lifeless body, looking exactly the way Allan preferred him.

"I have somewhere to be."

10

I couldn't quite forget about Camilla while writing my story in the press-room. The poster with the picture of Amalie was lying next to me on the table, her eyes staring at me like they wanted something from me. I turned the paper upside down, then focused on the screen in front of me. I had only written one paragraph of the interview. I looked at the big watch on the wall in front of me. There was only fifteen minutes till the concert started. Sune was standing next to me with a cup of coffee in his hand. He had packed his gear and was ready to leave. I, on the other hand wasn't even half done with my article.

"Maybe you can write the rest after the concert," Sune said.

I shook my head. "I promised Jens-Ole he would have it for tomorrow's paper. I have a deadline at midnight."

Sune finished his coffee and put the cup on the table. "Well I'm not missing out on The Boss." He lifted his bag and swung it over his shoulder. "I'm going to be in front and get the best pictures."

"Just go," I said. "I'll find you there. Get some great shots."

"Okay," he said and kissed my forehead. "I'll be easy to find."

"I know," I said chuckling. "Just look for the guy who sings and yells the loudest."

"You got it."

I heard Sune leave and returned to my laptop. It was like the article laughed at me to my face. Why couldn't I just get it done? It was a great interview, Patti Scialfa was an interesting person with interesting things to say. It should be the easiest thing in the world to finish up in a hurry. I got up and grabbed another cup of coffee from the pot, then sat down next to the computer. We were only two people in the big room. The other journalist closed his laptop and put it in his bag. He nodded and smiled at me as he hurried out the door. Now I was alone, not something you experience often at a festival with more than eighty thousand people attending. It felt kind of nice. I wasn't a fanatic Bruce Springsteen fan like Sune, so I didn't mind missing out on some of the concert. He probably saved the best songs for last, like they always did anyway. And I had my press badge which meant I could get in front at any time I wanted to. I sipped my coffee while staring at the paper I had turned and placed with Amalie's face down. I grabbed it and turned it upwards again. Amalie stared at me. I sighed and put the paper on the table.

"Where are you little girl?" I mumbled while wondering where I had seen her before. I knew her face from somewhere, I just couldn't quite place it.

I shook my head and returned to my screen. I sipped my coffee again and continued writing my article. In the distance I could hear the music from the concert begin. It was the biggest concert at this year's festival and it was one everybody wanted to go to. Well everybody over the age of twenty-five at least. I looked at Amalie again. Camilla had said that they were going to the Suicide Silence concert tonight. It took place on one of the smaller stages. Maybe Amalie would show up? I truly hoped so, mostly for Camilla's sake. She was so worried about her friend. Meanwhile Amalie was probably just with some guy in a tent forgetting all about letting her friend know where she was either because she was too drunk or because she just didn't think about anyone else but herself right now. At age fourteen you could easily get lost in some guy that you thought was going to be the love of your life.

I decided to remove Amalie's distracting face and put the poster in my pocket. Then I returned once again to my article and wrote another paragraph. Suddenly a phone started to ring. I looked at my own. The display remained black. It wasn't mine. The ringtone was different. I shrugged. Probably just some journalist or photographer who had forgotten his phone when he went to the concert. I stared at the screen again and wrote a few more words. The ringing continued. It played a melody. The tunes of One Direction's *You don't know you're beautiful*. A thought caused me to look up from the screen. What grown-up in their right mind would have such a ringtone? I got up from my chair and walked towards the corner where I had put Camilla's iPhone in my charger. There was light in the display. It said 'Amalie.'

I gasped and picked it up happily, thinking now I could tell her where Camilla was and they could be reunited.

"This is Camilla's phone," I said. "Is this Amalie?"

There was a silence on the other end. Nothing but a whooshing sound. It sounded like someone breathing heavily.

"My name is Rebekka," I continued thinking that Amalie might be drunk and therefore slow to answer. "Camilla is not here right now, she went to see Suicide Silence, you can find her there. She has actually been looking for you, she'll be very happy to see you."

A deep male voice startled me when it answered. "I bet she will. She'll be thrilled," the voice said, rolling the tongue on the l's.

Then he hung up. I looked at the display with the text *call ended*. My heart was beating fast in my chest. Who was that on the other end? Frantically I touched the display and tried to call back. No answer. The phone went directly on Amalie's voice mail. He had shut it off. I put the phone in my pocket. I could still hear the voice in my head. Something was really wrong here, I thought to myself. This man, who was he? And why did he call from Amalie's phone? Suddenly it struck me like a punch in the stomach.

It had sounded like he was in a car. He was coming here. *He was coming for Camilla.*

11

The package arrived just before midnight. The man who called himself Thomas De Quincey opened the big gate himself and let the black hearse into his property. As the car passed he carefully closed the gates and carefully scanned the area to see if there had been any cars on the road to see the black hearse arrive. But the road was empty. Nothing but fields stretching as far as the eye could see. It wasn't completely dark, since it never got dark at this time of year and he spotted light in the horizon almost like bluish waves across the sky. It was beautiful, he thought to himself. But nothing compared to what was in that package he was about to unwrap. Truly a masterpiece to complete his collection.

Thomas De Quincey ran across the gravel to catch up with the hearse, butterflies in his stomach, and butterflies of expectation very like the ones he had experienced as a child and again as an adult just before his next kill. There was nothing like the joy of expectation, just like Kierkegaard had put it. Even if he wasn't the first to say it, like many Danes believed, he was a wise man, Thomas De Quincey thought to himself.

A man Thomas De Quincey knew as Alex Andreyer stepped out of the black hearse with the drapes shut in the back. The two men greeted each other silently. Alex Andreyer opened the trunk. In the back of the car lay a big rectangular box covered with a heavy black blanket.

Thomas De Quincey couldn't help clapping his hands in joy. He was so excited he could almost burst.

"Where do you want it?" Alex Andreyer asked.

"Let's put it in the cellar with the others," Thomas De Quincey said.

"As you wish."

Alex Andreyer pulled the box out and the two men grabbed it on each side and carried it towards the main building. Carefully they lifted it down the stairs and into the big room where a sea of boxes just like it stood covered with white sheets. Most of them were rectangular like the one they now placed on the stone floor in the center of the dark room, but some were tall and cylindrical-shaped. Thomas De Quincey saw the curious look in the eyes of his helper and grabbed him by the shoulder.

"Soon my dear friend," he whispered. "Soon it will be complete and ready for you to see. But not yet. It has to be perfect."

"Naturally," Alex Andreyer answered. "Patience is after all the finest virtue of them all."

Thomas De Quincey smiled widely while turning his helper around and escorting him up the stairs. "I do believe you're right," he said with a smirk.

As they reached the top of the stairs, Thomas De Quincey sensed that the good Mr. Andreyer had a hard time pulling away, letting go of his huge curiosity. It thrilled Thomas De

Quincey and it worried him at the same time. Because no one, and that meant *no one* was to see it all until it was ready, until his work was done.

"Now, you hurry up and get me the rest of the packages that I asked for, alright?" Thomas De Quincey said and pushed Alex Andreyer towards the hearse.

"They are not that easy to provide," he said.

Thomas De Quincey patted him on the shoulder. "That's why I have asked you to do it, right? Cause you are the man for the job, aren't you? Or should I have to ask someone else?"

Alex Andreyer shook his head fast. "No. No. Oh please don't. I can do this. I'm the best. Please *Master* allow me to do this."

Thomas De Quincey smiled again and patted the man on the cheek. "Good. That's what I wanted to hear. Now get out of here before someone sees you."

Alex Andreyer nodded then hurried back into the car. He started the engine then drove towards the gate. Thomas De Quincey waited a couple of heartbeats, then started running and caught up with him before he reached the big iron gate. Thomas De Quincey laughed loudly as he stuck his head into the car and saw the surprised face of Alex Andreyer who hadn't expected him to be that fast. Thomas De Quincey had always enjoyed a little run. Keep the old ticker working, keeping the body in shape.

"Let me get the gate for you," he said and pulled it open.

12

So she didn't have her phone, Allan thought to himself as he took the exit towards Roskilde. Well it didn't matter much. The woman answering had been stupid enough to tell him exactly what he wanted to know. The whereabouts of Camilla Langstrup. It was going to be easier than ever to just waltz right in there and find her. Best of all, she didn't suspect a thing. If she had, she wouldn't be at the festival at all. That was why Allan had called in the first place. He was certain Camilla would answer her missing girlfriend's phone. Allan wanted to make sure Camilla was still at the festival and hadn't gone home instead after her friend's disappearance. It would have made it increasingly dangerous for Allan to fulfill his mission, but not impossible. Now it was almost too easy.

He parked the car outside the festival grounds and showed the guard his admission bracelet. The guard nodded him through and now he was once again surrounded by sweaty, drunk and very loud people walking with their muddy boots, beers in their hands, smoking cigarettes, singing, cheering, having the time of their lives.

"The Boss" was playing on the big stage and Allan knew that most people were there. He chuckled as he walked away from the crowd in front of Orange stage, where Bruce Springsteen opened the show with *No Surrender* and the crowd were dancing, smiling and looking at each other with an *ah this is so cool* look in their eyes, while everybody joined in and sang along.

He left the area and entered another where more music emerged from a big tent. The area outside was almost empty. A man selling chicken tartlets was bored to death outside. Allan approached him. He smelled the warm tartlets and the scent brought him back many years. The maid had served tartlets to him on the day they had told him, on the day his world changed forever. He had been sitting alone in the dining room enjoying the delightful taste of the warm and crispy tartlets. He had just cracked one open and the chicken sauce had begun running out on the plate, when they had entered.

"We have wonderful news," they said.

Allan remembered staring at the plate where all the delicious sauce now ran out on the plate and wetted everything, soaking it. Now was the best time to eat it. In a few seconds it would all get too moist and the sauce would have ruined everything. He picked up the fork and began eating before it was too late. The woman he had loved like a mother grabbed his hand and forced him to put the fork down.

"This is important, Allan," the man said. "More important than your food."

And then the words came, those words that at the moment seemed so innocent, so indifferent to the young boy, but later he would look back on as the worst words of his life.

"We're having a baby."

Allan was eight when it happened.

Allan took in a deep breath while staring at the man with the tartlets back at the festival. The man stared back at him. "So you want one or what?" he asked irritably.

Allan clenched his fist hard, then lifted his hand in the air and knocked the man down while yelling "*No!*" The blow was so hard he knocked him out. He was bleeding from his nose.

Allan snorted irritably. This wasn't part of the plan. He scanned the area to see if anyone had seen him, then grabbed the man by the arms and pulled him behind the tent. The music coming from inside was so loud no one heard Allan grunt or the sound of him beating the unconscious tartlet-selling man senseless. Once he was done, he came out from behind the tent, straightened his expensive pants and slicked his hair back with his hand.

He walked to the stand, grabbed an empty tartlet. With his pulse still pumping wildly, he put it on a plate and filled it with the white chicken-sauce with carrots and peas. Allan took in a deep breath to calm himself down, then found a plastic fork. He closed his eyes enjoying the creaking sound of the crispy pastry as the fork penetrated it. He ate with great joy thinking yet again of the day when he had been told about the baby. It was the first time since then he had been able to stand the taste or even the smell of tartlets. If it was the anticipation of what he was about to do or just the time he had put between him and what happened back then, he didn't know, but the taste was intoxicating.

13

Camilla was usually a very confident girl. She had good reason to be. She had grown up in a very wealthy family living in Klampenborg, one of the most prominent and expensive addresses in the country. She had gone to some of the best schools in the country and always hung out with people of her own class. She had lived a very protected life and never met anyone who wanted to harm her in any way. Everybody wanted to please her, since they knew that the way to her father's heart went through his daughter. She always considered her parents to be smothering and too overprotective when they told her to not go out on her own at night, when they told her to be careful of whom she talked to. She didn't consider the world a dangerous place.

But during the last two days Camilla lost a lot of that confidence and trust in the world surrounding her. She was used to doing what she wanted to, since her parents were never home and when they were they hardly noticed her anymore, so she had done pretty much exactly what she wanted to the last couple of years. But for the first time something had gone wrong. Terribly wrong, she now realized standing with her friends listening to the band on stage, drinking the beer a guy named Kasper bought her, hoping he'd get lucky later. Camilla's eyes scanned the tent nervously. Maybe a hundred teenagers were present, the rest of the festival was at the big stage listening to that old guy with the guitar, Camilla had hardly heard of. She hadn't heard of Suicide Silence either, but two boys they met on the first day had told them that they "just had to be there." Camilla was a party-girl, she enjoyed to get drunk and dance, but she was more a fan of pop-music than this death core. She hardly noticed the music right now, though, since all she could think of was Amalie and every time someone entered the tent, she would gasp and look to see if it was her. The band had been playing for almost half an hour now and there was still no sign of Amalie.

Camilla had begun wondering if she should just pack her belongings and go back home, but how was she supposed to explain it to Amalie's father? That she lost her? He thought they were both on Camilla's dad's yacht sailing protected and guarded on the ocean around Zeeland, just like they did every year at this time. Was she supposed to tell him that they hadn't done it the last two years? That they instead had gone to the festival, smoking, drinking, dancing, out among "ordinary" people? Camilla shivered at the very thought of having to face Amalie's father. She was afraid of what he would do, to her, to her father. The man could ruin her father's life and career in a matter of seconds. He could ruin their entire lives. And he would. In his anger, he would. That was the nature of Amalie's father. That was his way of dealing with things.

Camilla felt an anger rise inside of her as she drank more of her beer. Damn that Amalie, she thought. She was so selfish, always so egocentric. She was probably with someone else, someone she had just met, maybe even a guy and never thought to contact Camilla. She never cared about her emotions, about how she felt.

Camilla sighed deeply feeling the tears press on from behind. Camilla loved Amalie. She loved her more than you love a friend. She was *in love* with her. She had been for many years, almost as long as Camilla could remember. Amalie of course didn't know. The very first time Camilla kissed her at a party at a friend's house, she had laughed and kissed her back, whispering *Great idea, let's stir things up a little, let's give them something to talk about.* Thinking Camilla had only done it because she was bored and wanted to shock the dull rich kids at the party, Amalie grabbed her face and kissed her passionately. Camilla enjoyed it more than anything in her entire life and to this very day she still remembered the way the kiss had tasted. The second time Camilla kissed her, Amalie hadn't taken it nearly as nicely. They were at Amalie's house watching a movie in the living room, when suddenly Camilla couldn't resist her lips any longer and had to taste them once again.

"What the hell?" Amalie had screamed.

Camilla had blushed, then pulled away not knowing what to say. Her desire to kiss her again and hold her tight, their naked bodies pulsating against each other, was overwhelming, almost overpowering.

"Why did you do that?" Amalie had asked. "Are you a fucking dyke?"

At that instant Camilla wanted to hit Amalie. Knock her down for not wanting her as badly as she wanted Amalie. For not loving her in the same way she loved her.

"No," she said, instead insinuating with her tone that a dyke had to be the worst thing in the world to be. "Are you?"

"Hell no," Amalie said while wiping her mouth with her sleeve.

"Just checking," Camilla had said.

Amalie stared at her for a long time. Then her facial expression changed. Then they both burst into laughter. Camilla had forced it through the feeling of her heart being ripped open. Since then she never tried to kiss Amalie again.

While standing in the tent listening to this infernal music, staring at the entrance like it was some sort of secret gateway to a magic place where they kept beautiful women who mysteriously vanished, Camilla slowly lost hope of ever seeing her beloved friend again. She tried hard to remember that soft kiss they once shared at the party, the salty taste of her red lips. Staring at the entrance she felt the tears beginning to run down her cheeks when her eyes suddenly met those of someone who had just entered the tent. He was wearing shiny shoes and expensive pants and a white shirt. That alone made him stand out. But that wasn't what caught Camilla's eye and made her keep staring at him. It wasn't his good looks either. It was what he was holding in his right hand. She immediately recognized the five thousand dollars cover with its twenty-two VVS1 diamonds, a total of three and a half carats.

It was Amalie's phone.

14

Allan loved the band. The music was intoxicating as were the lyrics to their songs, he thought as he entered the tent and walked directly towards the stage. This was wonderful, he thought. The perfect setting. He couldn't have chosen it better himself.

He marched right up to the stage and pushed aside some drunk longhaired dancing fans, just a small push was enough to make room for himself. He had come for Camilla, yes. But there was time enough to enjoy the music as well, he figured. Everything in its proper time. It was after all one of his favorite moments to it all, finding the girl and figuring the proper way to snatch her without anyone seeing it. Just like everything else about killing, it was an art form, really. Unfortunately not very many like him were very good at it. It aggravated him how loosely some would take this part of the killing. Like it wasn't of importance. They didn't understand that if you were ever to be taken seriously, if you were to go down in history and be admired properly for your work, you needed to attend to every little detail. Everything you did, how you comported yourself was of the utmost importance. Only the true artists understood that. There was no easy way to become something in this life. It was all hard work and talent. Allan was very talented. He was great at staging it, at orchestrating the disappearance of yet another poor innocent victim.

He clapped when the band stopped singing and a new song started. He felt her eyes on him and her slowly approaching as he knew she would once she spotted the extremely expensive phone cover in his hand. No one else would notice, since Allan was the kind of guy who would buy such a cover, or at least Sebastian would buy it for him, but it didn't look strange in his hand. His appearance, his clothes matched it even if he did stand out in this crowd. But Camilla would notice. She was the only one who knew. She would come to him. Allan chuckled while singing along very loud.

"*The ragged they come ... and the ragged they kill! You pray so hard on bloody knees ...*" the band sang.

Allan closed his eyes while sensing her moving closer and closer. He kept his eyes closed and imagined her face, her eyes full of fear and dread. Oh the joy, oh the expectation. He opened his eyes and looked at the lead singer while he sang: "*The ragged they come and the ragged they kill ...*"

She was right behind him now. "*I'm the one you wanted. Hey. Yeah. I'm your super beast,*" he continued to sing.

He was so certain she was there. He could almost hear her breath. She was probably wondering now. Debating within herself. Should she disturb him? Poke him on the shoulder and ask him outside and then ask how he got a hold of her friend's phone? Or should she wait a little longer? Observe him a little while longer before she confronted him? Ah a difficult dilemma, Allan thought to himself while dancing slowly to the music. He was waiting with great anticipation. What was she going to chose? Did she dare to talk to him? He could after all be dangerous. You never knew these days. Her parents had always warned her against strangers, and warned her not to go out on her own at night. But the parents weren't here, were they? And she was desperate now. She had to know what happened to her friend. She had only one day to figure it out before she would have to come clean. She was in a hurry to find her friend. Allan chuckled happily while thinking of Amalie in the plastic box in the cellar of his house. It had been many years since he had enjoyed something that much. Well come to think of it, maybe he never enjoyed anything as much as this. This was like the frosting on the cake. He had been preparing for this for years and years, eating the dry cake underneath and now he came to the best part. It was so sweet, so delicious even more delightful than he had dared to anticipate while dreaming of it, while fantasizing in the bed at night in the dormitory at the boarding school, when being raped again and again by the older students who thought of him as a freak who needed to be kept down. It was back then he had begun planning this masterpiece of his. It was going to be absolutely perfect.

The song ended and she still hadn't poked him on the shoulder. *Chosen to wait, huh?* He thought to himself. It told him a lot about her as a person. She was smarter than he thought. More calculating, even under pressure.

Allan clapped his hands, then turned around on his heel and looked directly into the eyes of Camilla. He noticed how she gasped as their eyes met. He felt a chill of pleasure across his skin and had to restrain himself from giggling with joy. Instead he pretended he didn't know her, gave her one of his most endearing smiles, then walked right past her.

He felt her eyes on his back as he walked out of the tent.

"Come on, little girl, follow the yellow brick road," he mumbled while walking, quoting one of his favorite childhood movies.

15

CAMILLA FELT INDECISIVE. She had been looking at the man's back through an entire song now, not knowing what to do. He had Amalie's phone, there was no doubt about it. Once she had gotten a little closer to it, she was certain. Even if the guy looked like someone who could afford a phone cover like that, it wasn't his. Camilla knew Amalie's phone enough to also know that there was a diamond missing in the right corner on the back. This was also the case with the one the man was holding. That was hardly a coincidence. But then the man turned and looked directly at Camilla, smiled and walked out of the tent. It had taken her completely by surprise. His smile was nice and warm and as she stood watching him leave the tent, she felt compelled to run after him. He didn't seem like the type who could in any way hurt Amalie or even stolen the phone from her. But how come he was holding it? Had he found it somewhere? Whatever the reason, Camilla knew she had to talk to him. She had to ask him if he knew anything about where her friend could be. So she followed him outside. She walked a few steps behind him as he crossed the area and walked towards the Orange Stage where that old guy played his guitar. The man wasn't walking very fast and Camilla didn't find it hard to follow him without him realizing it. She had always been good at sneaking around.

The man jumped elegantly over a huge mud pile and Camilla did the same. The music from the big stage became louder. She had to react now, before he disappeared in the crowd of people and while she was still able to talk to him without her words drowning in the music.

"Hey!" she yelled.

The man kept walking. Was he pretending to not hear her? Or didn't he think she was talking to him. "Hey, you in the nice pants," she yelled and began to run to catch up with him.

He seemed to slow down a little. She ran towards him. As she was almost there, he turned his head like an owl and stared at her. Camilla stopped. Then he smiled widely.

"Are you following me, little girl?" he asked. "You shouldn't be running around out here all alone."

"I need to talk to you. I need to ask you something," Camilla said.

"How delightful," the man said. "To have the pleasure of such beautiful company. How may I be of service to you?"

Camilla smiled and blushed at his comment. Nobody ever called her beautiful before. Amalie was the beautiful one. Camilla was just, well more just the awkward friend. At least that was how she viewed herself. She relaxed slightly. The man seemed nice. Then she approached him. "It's just that ... well I couldn't help but noticing that you have my friend's phone in your hand."

The man looked at the phone in his hand. "Ah, you mean this?" He held it up so she could see it better.

Yes, that was Amalie's phone for sure. "That's my friend's phone."

"Well that's good then," he said. "I was wondering who it belonged to. I found it just before over there by the campground. It was on the ground between two tents. I thought with such an expensive looking cover that someone would be missing it. You say it's your friend's?"

Camilla sighed deeply. The man didn't know what happened to Amalie after all. But at least she now had an answer to why Amalie hadn't called her back or even replied when she called her. She had lost her phone. Maybe she was with someone she had met after all, but had no phone to call her friend and let her know where she was? The thought gave her some relief.

"Yes. She must have dropped it. I haven't seen her since Thursday and I have to admit that I have been a little worried about her."

The man tilted his head. "You say that you haven't seen her since Thursday?"

"Yes. I mean no. I haven't. I'm beginning to fear that something happened to her. That's why I needed to ask you about the phone. You said you found it at the campground?"

"Yes. Just a little while ago. I was walking across the grounds to get here."

"Can I see it?"

The man smiled, then handed her the phone. "Well of course. Here you go."

Camilla held the phone for a while then looked up at the man. He was still smiling. He was very handsome, especially when he smiled.

"Why is there blood on it?" she asked.

"Is there? Oh my. I hadn't even noticed. You don't think ..." The man gasped. "You don't think it's *her* blood, do you?"

Camilla felt the tears pile up, then swallowed hard to try and hold it back.

"Oh my, little girl. You're getting upset now." The man wiped away her tear with his thumb. "Here let me help you ..." he said and fumbled in his pocket. He pulled out a silk handkerchief and wiped her tears with it. It smelled bad, Camilla thought and tried to pull away. Then the man grabbed her neck and pulled her closer, she let out a small shriek before he covered her mouth and nose with the handkerchief and soon Camilla saw nothing than the stars of a deep dream.

16

I RAN AS fast as I could across the festival grounds. I didn't care that mud splattered on my pants or that I accidentally pushed a guy to get him out of my way. I didn't even bother to yell that I was sorry when he yelled after me. There simply wasn't time. Camilla was somewhere out there and she was in danger. This man who called on the phone didn't want to do her any good, I just knew it. And I had given him exactly what he wanted, what he needed. I had told him exactly where she was. I could only hope I wasn't too late. Bruce Springsteen was singing *Two Hearts* from the big stage. The song all of a sudden woke an eerie feeling in me.

I went out walking the other day. Seen a little girl crying along the way. She'd been hurt so bad she'd never love again.

He was singing behind me as I ran towards the area with the smaller stages, where the smaller bands were playing at the same time. I stepped in another mud pile and soaked my shoe and socks. I cursed and pulled my leg free from it. Then I heard music coming from inside the tent where Suicide Silence playing. I turned and ran towards it. A stand selling tartlets was empty next to it.

I entered the tent and scanned it quickly. It didn't take long since there weren't that many people. A flock of teenagers were gathered in the corner, nodding along to the music while drinking beers. I approached them while the band sang on stage:

Make sure you take the time ... to put them down on their knees ... Make sure you take the time and listen to them beg and plead. We are violence at its finest! So take your precious time and pick your enemy, then you take the time to put them down on their knees. Now take a second look into their worthless eyes, now pull the trigger back, click, surprise! Now you are the victim of, my, my two hands. Now you are the victim of more violent circumstance. We are violence.

The guys listening were muttering along, some closing their eyes while enjoying the music and singing along on the lyrics.

Now we're vengeful and war is what we all crave. And I know exactly what this is! More! Human violence at its finest and I want more.

One of the boys looked at me as I came closer. I tried to talk through the loud music.

"I'm looking for a girl named Camilla, have you seen her?" I yelled.

The boy shook his head and pointed at his ears to signal me that he couldn't hear anything. I tried again, but it was drowned by the loud music. I felt desperate. Frantically I scanned the area again to see if she might be sitting in a corner somewhere on a bench where I hadn't been looking. The area in front of the stage counted maybe ten to twelve devoted fans dancing, singing, lifting their hands in the air, some even head banging to the music. None of them were Camilla. A group were standing in the bar ordering beer, some just hanging out while enjoying the music. She wasn't there either. Where could she be? My heart beat faster and faster as I looked around. Then my eye caught something. In front of the teenage boys, on the table they leaned up against, was a beer that seemed to have no owner. It was almost full. I walked closer and picked it up. It had lip-gloss on the side. Pink lip-gloss.

"Where is she?" I yelled.

The boy from earlier shrugged while pointing at his ears again. I lifted the glass and showed it to him.

He seemed to understand. "Where is she?" I yelled again.

He shrugged while shaking his head. Then he leaned over and as the music became slightly slower, there was a small break in the song and I just managed to hear the words:

"She left ... some guy ... Don't know where."

It felt like my heart stopped. I stared at the boy as the music became loud again and the band started a new song. It was like the entire tent started to spin. I looked towards the entrance, then stormed out. Outside I stopped myself. There were so many directions they could have gone. I pulled my hair. How was I ever going to find which one they took?

I began spinning around myself, walking first in one direction, then in another. The music from the tent quieted down while they got ready for a new number. That's when I heard the groaning. A deep moaning was coming from behind the tent. I walked around it and stopped. Someone was lying in the mud, he was barely moving.

"Hello?"

I walked closer as he didn't seem to respond. Probably just some drunk guy who had passed out, I thought. But instinct made me walk closer. A feeling, a sense that this was something else. This wasn't just your ordinary drunk-passing-out-in-the-mud kind of thing. This was something else. As I approached him I realized I was right. The man lying on the ground was severely bruised.

"Please help me," he muttered. "Please someone help me."

17

I HELPED THE man get on his feet and had him hold on to my shoulders. He was mumbling incoherently while I helped him walk. I still had no idea what happened to him or how he ended up like this, but he was badly bruised and I knew I had to get him to the paramedics right away. But he was heavy and barely conscious, and I couldn't carry him far. I got him out in the open then I had to let go of him and place him on the ground. A couple strongly entangled in each other walked by and I stopped them by yelling.

"A little help, please? This man has been hurt."

They stopped walking and approached us. The young woman kneeled down next to him. "I'm a nurse. Let me have a look at him. What happened?" she asked.

"I have no idea. I found him like this. He's severely bruised."

The woman leaned over him. "Looks like he has been beaten," she said.

I nodded. "I think so too."

The woman checked his pulse, then lifted his eyelids to

look into his eyes and see the pupils. "He doesn't seem to be affected by drugs or alcohol," she said. "Who did this to him?"

"I have no idea. I found him in there," I said and pointed. "I don't even know who he is."

"We need to get him to a hospital as fast as possible," the woman said. Then she turned her head and looked at her boyfriend. "Mads, could you run and get the paramedics?"

Mads nodded. "Sure," he said and began to run.

The man on the ground moaned and the woman spoke to him. "We'll get you to a hospital soon, don't you worry."

I felt my heart racing in my chest. I still had no idea in what direction I was to look for Camilla. I was confused. Had she gone with him willingly? Had he lured her to go with him, maybe told her he knew where Amalie was? No, Camilla wasn't that stupid, she wouldn't fall for that, would she? I breathed heavily. I realized I didn't even know either girl's last name. I wouldn't be able to file a missing person's report for Amalie nor Camilla. I wouldn't even be able to call their parents. I felt suddenly helpless. I received a text from Sune.

YOU'RE MISSING OUT ON A GREAT CONCERT. COMING SOON?

I touched my face. I had no idea how to begin to explain the whole thing to Sune, and I certainly didn't have time to answer now. So I put the phone back in my pocket, as Mads arrived with the paramedics. They got the man on a stretcher, then looked at me. "Did you see anything?" one of them asked.

I shook my head. "No I just found him." I reached inside of my pocket and found a card, that I handed them. "Here in case the police want to talk to me."

"Good," the paramedic said. Then they carried the man away. I sighed and thanked the young nurse and her boyfriend. They left me and suddenly I was back to chasing Camilla and the mysterious man. I stomped my feet in irritation. Where the hell could she be?

That was when I heard a scream. It sounded like a small shriek and then it was suddenly gone. Convinced that it was Camilla I ran towards the sound, but soon found myself at the area in front of Orange Stage. Bruce Springsteen was still going at it on the stage and people were dancing and singing in a daze of ecstasy. No one would have noticed anything let alone heard Camilla scream. What now? I thought. He had Camilla somewhere, but where? Where would I go if I had just kidnapped a young girl? I wouldn't stay here on the festival grounds would I? No of course not. I would take her away from here to a place where no one would find her. I turned and spun around myself. There were several entrances and exits. The ones leading to the stages were all guarded. He could pretend that she was very drunk and use one of those exits since they were closest. Or he could play it safe and use one of the exits by the campsite that weren't guarded. I started running towards the campground when I realized something. You only had to show your bracelet going *in* on the festival grounds. Not out. It didn't matter what exit he took. No one ever noticed anyone exiting. The smart person would choose the closest, I thought and spotted one not far from where I was standing. The big concert on Orange Stage was almost over and people had already begun walking towards the exits. In a matter of minutes it would be overly crowded when all the people who didn't stay in tents on the campsite were about to leave.

After that it was going to be very easy for him to escape in the crowd.

18

Chloroform always did the trick, Allan thought as he went through the exit to the festival. He quite enjoyed himself walking with Camilla tightly wrapped around his shoulder, carrying her by holding her around the waist. To people passing by it looked like she was just wasted and clinging on to him to not lose her balance. Allan found this part amusing because it was always so exciting to see if anyone would even notice. He had found that he could walk around with his victims even bleeding from their heads and yet with his appearance and charming smile no one would even blink. If they did notice something was wrong with the girl, they would assume that he was taking care of her. Allan knew it and often found himself taking chances that no one else would dare, just for the fun of it, just to feel the thrill of excitement of possibly getting caught.

Just like all the other times, Allan managed to walk all the way to his car without anyone even asking him if the girl was alright. Of course he knew perfectly well to tell them that she was his younger sister and that she had called for him to come and get him because she was too drunk to get home on her own, of course he was prepared for questions, but they never even came. Not a single person turned their head to look or addressed him. It was too easy, he thought slightly disappointed. It was always more fun when he had to fight for it, it wasn't as fun when everything went too smooth. That was just plain boring.

Allan opened the door and put Camilla in the backseat while talking to her like she was awake and could hear what he said.

"I'll get you home now safe and sound," he said and closed the door.

Just as he had shut it, the scene became slightly more interesting and exciting when he spotted a woman run out of the exit, scanning the area, looking desperately around her. In her hand she was holding a phone tightly. Allan laughed. He knew perfectly well who she was. He was happy to see that he had in fact underestimated her thinking she wouldn't care who was on the other end of the phone asking for Camilla. She had known somehow that he was going to get her and somehow she had found him.

Allan studied the woman for a little while. He watched her as she talked to people passing by, probably asking them if they'd seen a young girl with brown hair with a man, maybe he was carrying her. However she had no idea what Allan looked like, how old he was or how he was dressed. If she had at least known that it would have been easier for her, he thought. *I should at least have given her something to make it a little more interesting,* he thought. *Throw the woman a bone.* He chuckled while watching her desperately asking everybody in the parking lot, explaining to them that she was looking for this girl, only fourteen, brown hair, etc. Oh how fun, Allan thought and for a few seconds wanted her to come to him and ask. She was pretty, the woman. In her mid-thirties, probably had a kid or two, but still gorgeous. Would make a beautiful corpse. He started imagining what he could do to her body after he had strangled her. He would definitely have sex with her. That would be perfect. Then he would cut out her organs, maybe boil her tongue and eat it. With a great Chateau La Garde from 2009 or maybe even a Castello Fonterutoli Chianti from 2006.

The woman came closer and Allan shivered with pleasure. This woman triggered something in him. A lust, a desire to do something, to deviate from the plan. He could put her in the car with Camilla, then hang her from a meat hook in the cellar, maybe have sex with her while she was hanging there, her feet scraping across the ground. Maybe kill her in the car before he took her inside. No that was no fun. It was better to have Amalie watch him. Maybe kill the woman while she was looking at it. That sounded like more fun. Allan licked his lips while watching the woman approach.

"Excuse me," she said.

Her voice was like music in Allan's head. Like promises of spring. He smiled and their eyes locked for a second. The beautiful second when two souls meet. He could smell her, smell her blood. It drove him insane. The lust for the kill, tasting her, sinking his teeth into her flesh. Oh how he craved the kill. He yearned to look into those eyes and see the fear, the anxiety when she realizes it's all over.

"Excuse me?" she repeated.

"Yes?" Allan smiled endearingly.

"I'm looking for a young girl. She is possibly with a man. I'm afraid that he is forcing her to leave against her will. I don't know ..." The woman sighed resignedly. "I don't know what I'm looking for."

Allan grabbed her hand and held it in his. "A girl, fourteen years old, brown hair?" he asked.

She looked at him startled. "Yes. Exactly. How do you know?"

"I heard you talk to some people over there. I'm afraid I haven't seen her. What did the man look like? The man she is with?"

The woman sighed again. "I don't know. That's the problem. Look it's a little complicated. I just know that she is in danger and I'm afraid she might have gone with him, maybe even voluntarily. He might have told her something to make her go with him."

Allan licked his lips while staring at the woman's soft skin on her neck. He fought hard to restrain himself. His hands were shaking as he imagined strangling her.

"Anyway," she said. "Here is my card in case you see something or hear anything or remember something that might help me. I will have to keep looking."

The woman handed him her business card. He studied it for a few seconds. "I'll be in touch ... Rebekka Franck," he said, then walked to the side of the car and opened the door to the driver's seat. He paused for just an instant. Part of him wanted her to look inside of the car and see the girl in the back seat. That would give him an excuse to grab her and drag her with him as well. He took in a deep breath and breathed her scent, as the woman turned her back to him and began to walk away.

"You were lucky this time around, Rebekka Franck," Allan said and started the car. Before he backed out he looked in the rear view mirror and looked at Camilla still lying unconscious on the backseat. Then he smiled to his own reflection. "Hi, I'm Allan, wanna play?" he said and stepped on the gas pedal.

19

AMALIE HEARD SOMETHING in the darkness and opened her eyes. She had been sleeping, exhausted after screaming and banging. Now she was yet again awake slowly realizing that her nightmare hadn't ended. She gasped and touched the roof of her box once again. It was still there. She sighed, desperately preparing herself for whatever was in store for her, when suddenly there was another sound. A new sound. It didn't come from her or from inside of her box, it came from outside, out in the room.

Afraid that it might be her captor coming to hurt her, she kept quiet to make sure it wasn't him. The sound was still there. It sounded like a moaning. Slowly it became stronger, then grunts and groans. Amalie listened carefully. She had gotten to know the sounds of the cellar very well in her hours of darkness, but this was certainly new. This was definitely one she hadn't heard before. The moaning came from a person. Someone else was in the room!

Amalie gasped and tried to look, but her eyes couldn't see much through the darkness. The only light that came into the cellar where she was kept, came from under the door where she had seen the stairs end. It was dim, but at least it was something.

Amalie blinked her eyes trying to figure out where the noise was coming from. The grunts became louder, and then there was a thump, like the person hit their head, then the familiar sound of someone patting, examining something frantically, and not finding what they were looking for, while slowly realizing that there might not be an escape. The grunting became louder and now Amalie heard fists hammering. It sounded just like when she had banged her fists against the plastic of her own cage. She exhaled deeply knowing exactly what the person was going through. A few seconds later the inevitable came. The person started screaming.

"HELP!"

Then a pause and more hitting, punching on the plastic.

"What is this? Hey, where am I? Hallo?"

That was when something got really stirred up inside of Amalie. She felt tears piling up behind her eyes. She knew that voice and even if she was happy to hear a familiar voice, it also filled her with tremendous waves of angst and sadness.

"Camilla?" she said and stared in the direction of the sounds. All she could see was the outline of a box similar to hers.

The other person stopped hitting the plastic.

"Is that you, Camilla?" she said again.

"Amalie?" she replied, her voice subdued by the box. She was sobbing as she spoke. "Where are we?"

"I don't know," Amalie replied with a thick voice. "I've tried to figure it out for a long time now." Amalie sniveled and put her palm on the plastic. She couldn't see Camilla, but liked hearing her voice even if it meant that she too now was a captive.

Prologue

"How did you get here?" she asked.

Camilla went quiet. "I don't know," she cried. "There was this guy. He was really nice, he ... he ... he had your phone. I recognized the cover, so I followed him to ask him how he got it. I had been looking for you for days. He told me he had found it somewhere ... then he ... then he put something over my mouth and nose, something that smelled horrible ... so horribly sweet ... and I guess I fainted after that. I have a terrible headache right now."

Amalie couldn't hold in her tears any longer. She put her palm on the plastic box's side and silently let it all out. She didn't want Camilla to see her losing it, so she kept it to herself.

"At least I found you," Camilla said. "It drove me crazy not knowing what happened to you or where you were. Have you been here all the time?"

Amalie wasn't ready to talk. Tears were still rolling across her face. She felt so lost. If Camilla was here, then she couldn't have told the police or Amalie's parents what had happened. That meant they weren't looking for her, they weren't on the verge of finding her. Now with Camilla being here, instead of on the outside, then no one would know where to begin looking. For all they cared Camilla and Amalie had gone sailing and once they didn't come back they would begin the search for them. But who would know that they had even been at the festival? Who would help track them down?

Amalie sulked and for the first time in her life, she gave in. She didn't hold it back any more.

20

I couldn't believe I lost her. I searched and looked and talked to everybody I could find. Once the concert was over, the parking lot at the festival turned into a conglomeration of people and cars moving. I knew I had to give up, I knew I had been defeated. I texted Sune and he came to find me. I was sitting on a bench at the parking lot with my head in my hands. I wasn't crying, but I was close. The frustration, the feeling of failing knocked me down.

"What's going on?" Sune asked and ran to me. He squatted in front of me, then grabbed my hand. "What happened?"

I looked into his soft eyes, then exhaled. "I lost her," I said. "I was this close to warning her, but I was too late. If it hadn't been for that man, maybe ... just maybe I would have found her."

"Whoa, hey, let's back up a little here," Sune said. He got up and sat next to me on the bench. "Try and tell me the story from the beginning."

I sighed deeply. "Okay. Where to start?"

"Well how about beginning where I left you? In the

press-room?"

I nodded. "Of course, sorry. Well after you left me, I wanted to finish my article."

"You never finished it? What have you been doing all this time?" He interrupted me.

"Let me talk," I said. "A phone started ringing in the room. At first I thought someone had just forgot it there, so I tried to continue my work, but then it hit me. Who has One Direction as a ringtone?"

"Someone who has a child that likes to play with your phone?"

"Or maybe a teenager! I got up and went to look at Camilla's phone that I had been charging for her and realized it was her phone that was ringing. When I looked at the display it said 'Amalie.'"

"So naturally you picked it up, I get it. But it wasn't her, was it?" Sune asked while putting his arm around my shoulder.

"No. It was some guy. Some creepy guy. Worst of all I told him where to find Camilla. I thought he was Amalie, it was before he spoke ... it's complicated. But anyway I had a feeling he wanted to find Camilla so I tried to warn her. But I was too late. Once I arrived at the tent, she wasn't there. I spoke to a couple of boys who said she had left with some guy. Then I figured he had taken her out of the festival somehow, and I ran here. But now with all the people crowding the place, I have no chance of spotting her." I gesticulated resignedly. "She's gone!"

"Well we're still here," Sune said. "We'll tell everything to the police."

"I thought about that, but ..." I looked up and met Sune's eyes. He tried to smile to make me feel better.

"But what?" he asked.

"I think I just realized something," I said and sat upright.

"What?"

"The girl. The first girl, the friend who disappeared." I found the poster in the pocket and unfolded it. I showed him the picture. "Why haven't I thought about this before?"

"Thought about what?" Sune said confused. "Please fill me in."

"Amalie. Her name is Amalie. Camilla told me she couldn't go to the police because the media would be all over the story in a matter of seconds."

"You know who she is?"

"Yes. Look at the picture. Imagine her five or six years younger. That's how many years it's been since the public last saw her face. After that her parents sent her to attend a school in Switzerland. I'm quite puzzled to know how she is in a place like this?"

"Could you please just tell me who she is?"

I looked at Sune. "She's the princess," I said. "Princess Amalie of Merchenburg. She is the daughter of His Royal Highness Prince Christopher, the younger brother to our queen who married the German countess Alexis of Merchenburg who later was given the title of princess from the queen. I don't know the entire story or the right titles, but I believe Amalie is an heir to the throne in case all the queen's children and her own father are killed or choose to abdicate. That's why Camilla couldn't tell me Amalie's last name. Simply because she doesn't have any! Royalties don't have a last name."

Sune looked like he had seen a ghost. "Wow," he said. "That's some story."

"You got that right," I said and rubbed my head. Thoughts were flickering in my mind. I couldn't keep them still. I realized I had no idea what to do next.

21

Allan couldn't sleep. He was too excited. In fact he had been so excited when he came home that he had thrown himself at the sleeping Sebastian and fucked him senseless without him even waking up. All in all it had been a perfect night. But still he couldn't sleep. The thrill of knowing what waited him in the cellar of his house kept him wide awake. So after trying to fall asleep for two hours, he decided to get up instead.

He threw on a silk bathrobe then walked downstairs. He found his iPad and sat with it in his lap.

Got another rat in the box, he wrote. Then he waited, hoping that there was someone else awake at this hour. No more than a minute later Michael Cogliantry answered:

Oh how I envy you. Tell me about her.

Allan smiled to himself. This was exactly what he was looking for. To be able to brag. *She is fine. You have no idea. Not as exclusive as the first, though, but perfect for my purpose.*

What is your purpose? What are you going to do to them? Cogliantry asked.

Allan chuckled. He knew how hard it could be to have to

stay away, to keep your path clean in order to not get caught. He had done it once a couple of years ago after killing a girl too close to the boarding school and the police came to investigate all the students. He, of course had a perfect alibi and knew he was the one they suspected the least with his charming and endearing person, but he knew he had to lay low for at least a year in order to be safe. It was the hardest thing he ever had to do. His next victim had been a Polish prostitute he picked up in the street outside a small Polish town. Driven by his cravings for the kill that he couldn't withstand any longer he had taken the car in the middle of the night, left the boarding school and driven all the way into Poland, where he had picked up the first girl he met. She was ugly as hell and he turned her head away while fucking her, then he beat her and in the end strangled her and left her in a ditch somewhere. It was the most boring kill he had made, but it had been necessary. He needed his fix in order to stay sane. That was just the way it was.

I'm not telling you yet. But I will post pictures later, once it all begins, Allan wrote. He found a cigarette in a drawer and lit it. He didn't usually smoke, but every now and then when the urge got too overwhelming, when he felt himself agitated and wanted to kill, he would sometimes manage to calm himself down with a cigarette. He needed to stay calm now. It was tickling in his fingers, he wanted to go down there and torture those two girls, just look into their eyes while he killed them. But no. That was not the way. That was not the plan. He needed to do this right and not destroy it by giving in to his desires and cravings just yet. This was supposed to be perfect. A true masterpiece.

Ah, come on. Throw me a bone here. I'm starving. Can't you reveal just a little bit. Just something?

Allan laughed out loud at the desperation in Cogliantry's

words. He would need to kill soon or he would definitely lose it. Allan recognized the signs. He remembered how he used to walk the corridors of the dormitory at night, fantasizing about his next kill, planning it, imagining it down to the smallest detail. And Princess Amalie often played a leading role in his fantasies. No, he had to restrain himself from acting too fast. This was a process and it was easily destroyed by moving too fast.

Come on, Cogliantry wrote again. *Maybe just some details about the girls. Do they smell good? Is their skin soft like silk against your lips? Have you tasted them yet? Licked them? Oh my god, I'm getting a boner on. You're torturing me here. Give me something.*

Allan laughed again. He listened to the muffled voices of his girls in the cellar. Let them talk a little, he said. Maybe they would even be able to encourage each other a little, give each other new hope. Oh he wished they would. That would make it even more gruesome when he did as he had planned. A victim with no hope was boring. One with hope would fight for her life. She would be feisty and resist. Just the way he liked it best.

He killed the cigarette in a half empty wineglass from earlier. He exhaled and let the smoke out. So Cogliantry wanted him to give him something, huh? Well he could give the man a little something to think about, if he craved it that much. Let him get off so he could sleep peacefully tonight.

Allan stretched his fingers, then he wrote:

I'm preparing a royal meal.

22

We tried to go to the police. I showed them the poster and told them I believed it was Princess Amalie of Merchenburg and that she had been kidnapped by some man and that her friend had been taken too. As the words left my lips I knew how insane they sounded. The police officer - one of two on duty in the middle of the night looked at me like he thought I was drunk, which he probably did. How else would I come up with such a story?

He smiled friendly and looked at the poster, then at me. "Well, I don't really know what to say to all that," he said. "I mean has someone filed a missing person's report? You say the girls are both fourteen, have their parents been informed? Are they searching for them?"

I sighed annoyed, knowing he would never take us seriously. I could tell by the tone of his voice. "No, they are not. Because their parents don't know that they have gone missing yet. The girls were at the festival when they were taken."

The officer tilted his head and smiled. "Princess Amalie of Merchenburg at Roskilde Festival? Well that's news to me.

Don't you think we would have heard about it somehow if she were to attend? Don't you think at least the paparazzi would be lurking everywhere? Don't you think the papers would be writing about it? I really think they would."

"You're not going to take this seriously, are you?" I asked.

The officer shook his head slowly. "I don't think so."

"Let's go," Sune said. "We're not getting anywhere here."

I left my card with him and then we left the police station. Sune drove the car downtown. We decided to spend the night at a hotel. I needed to get away from the festival in order to think. Jens-Ole kept calling me for the article and I promised to finish it and send it before I went to bed. He told me he left room for it and could manage to put it in anyway, but without reading it first, so *just don't make any mistakes*.

"What was that you told me about some guy being beaten?" Sune asked as he drove across town. We passed the old cathedral and I looked at the clock in the car. It was two a.m. I didn't feel like sleeping, I was tired, exhausted, but knew I wouldn't be able to close an eye. I stared out the window into the bright summer night.

"I don't know who he was. I found him when I was running out of the tent while looking for Camilla. He was lying behind the tent, badly bruised. I helped him get to the hospital."

"Hmm," Sune said and turned the car around a corner.

"What?"

"I don't know. It's just ... well don't you think it's a little too coincidental?" he said and drove into the parking lot in front of Hotel Scandic. He stopped the engine. I looked at him.

"You think it might be the same guy? Why would he beat someone up right before he went after Camilla? Isn't that a little too risky?"

Sune shrugged and pulled out the key of the ignition. "It might be. But you have to admit it is a little strange, right?"

I opened the door and got out of the car. Sune went in the back and took out our backpacks. I stared at the hotel in front of me. I would rather go back home, I thought. Back to Karrebaeksminde, to Dad and ... well Julie was still in Aarhus, so she wouldn't be there. Oh my god how I missed her at that instant. I knew she was fine with Peter. I had spoken with her earlier the same day and she had been thrilled. Peter was spoiling her by taking her to the Tivoli, shopping and eating at nice restaurants. With Peter money had never been an object. I was happy that she was enjoying herself, but slightly worried that she would get too used to living a life where money wasn't a problem, and she got everything she wanted. I couldn't give her that. But Peter could. He came from a rich family that went way back.

Sune carried our backpacks into the lobby and we received the key. A few minutes later we both threw our heavy bodies on the soft bed. Sune leaned over and kissed me gently. I wasn't quite in the mood for anything, so I pulled away after our lips had departed.

"I need to write this article, remember?" I whispered, then leaned over and kissed his forehead.

He looked disappointed while I opened the laptop and found the article. I wrote a sentence, then deleted it again. Then I wrote another one that I immediately deleted.

I sighed and looked at Sune. He had undressed and was under the covers. His eyes were closed but he wasn't sleeping. I could tell by the way he breathed.

"Are you awake?" I asked.

"No," he said.

"I have an idea."

"Mmm."

"It might get us in trouble."

"Mmm."

"Should I do it?"

"Mmm."

"You're right," I said and opened a blank page. "It never stopped me before."

23

"How long do you think he intends to keep us down here?" Camilla asked. Amalie had been crying now for a long time, and she had waited for her to be able to talk. Camilla wasn't going to give up that easy. She was ready to fight for her life. And for Amalie's.

"I don't know," Amalie said.

"I'll get us out of here," Camilla said.

"How? Did you tell my dad what happened?" Amalie asked.

Camilla sighed. "No," she said quietly realizing that it would after all have been the smartest thing to do.

"Why?" Amalie cried. "Why didn't you call home and tell anyone I was missing?"

Camilla exhaled deeply. "I was afraid you'd be angry at me if your dad had found out that you had lied to him. I didn't know if you were just drunk somewhere or doing drugs with some guy. Maybe you intended to just show up later. I was scared, okay?"

Amalie sighed deeply. "Well that was stupid. If you'd called home and talked to someone there they would have told my father and he would have found me by now. And you would never be here. At least you could have helped me when you were still on the outside. In here you're no help."

"I know. I'm sorry," Camilla whispered.

They both went quiet. Camilla wondered where they were. She hit the plastic once again trying to break it, but it didn't even move.

"Don't bother," Amalie said. "You're in a box, it's impossible to get out of it. Believe me I've tried. I have kicked, banged and screamed. No one will hear you, except the creepy guy who brought you here. I've seen him come down here once to get a bottle of wine. That's all I have seen. But I recognized him from the night he knocked me down with his flashlight. I have no idea what he wants from me ... or us. I'm hoping he wants money. My father will give him what he wants, then destroy him after we have been released."

Camilla inhaled sharply. "I hope you're right. I just don't get what he wants from me? Why has he taken me as well? And what's with these boxes?" she said and tried to push the plastic open with all her strength, but it was no use.

"I don't know the answer to any of that. I've been here in complete darkness for what feels like days. Only once has he turned on the light long enough for me to see the box. It's made from some sort of see through plastic. Impossible to break. Air comes in from a tube in the corner. I don't know how long this tube is, but at least it gives us air. I tried to stick my hand in it and feel it, but can't get it far enough in it. Maybe you could try. You're skinnier. Your hand is smaller."

Camilla felt around the box and found a small round hole in the corner. She stuck her hand inside of it as far as she could, but never reached the end.

"I'm sorry," she said. "I can't reach the end of it."

"I thought so," Amalie said.

Camilla took in a couple of deep breaths to calm herself down. It suddenly felt like the box was getting tighter, like it was closing in on her body. She started to sweat and kept moving around as much as she could to not feel trapped.

"It gets kind of claustrophobic after a while," Amalie said. "Just try your best to not panic. Move a little now and then to prevent it from hurting. It helps me to think about something nice. Like the open ocean, or my favorite horse Pompadour. It makes it less unbearable. Find something that makes you smile then keep thinking about it. Make it your happy place while we wait."

Camilla closed her eyes and tried to find something that would make her happy. She could only think about one thing. The salty kiss from Amalie's lips. Then she went even further and thought about her naked body against hers. The scent she had secretly smelled on her skin so often, the feeling of her soft breasts against hers. She could never tell her friend that, but she knew it was enough to keep her sane through whatever was in store for her.

"What do you think he wants to do with us?" Camilla asked once the fantasy had managed to calm her down once again and given her new hope.

"I don't know. But I have a feeling we're about to find out soon."

24

As expected I didn't sleep at all that night. I kept wondering about Camilla and why the kidnapper came back for her. He had taken Amalie, the royal princess and had to have a reason for picking her. It couldn't just be a coincidence, could it? It had to be deliberate. But why Camilla? Because she had seen him? But how could she? Amalie had left Camilla to go to the restrooms when she disappeared. If Camilla had seen the guy, she would definitely have told me. She would have described him to me and she would have known that something bad happened to Amalie. She wouldn't have expected her to show up at the festival or to maybe have gone with someone. Camilla would have gone to their parents and the police if she had known that something bad had happened to Amalie. So that wasn't it. Maybe it was just to keep her quiet. She was after all the only one who knew Amalie had been at the festival. The rest, especially her parents thought she was somewhere else, Camilla had told me. So maybe it was part of removing his tracks. With Camilla also gone they wouldn't know anything about Amalie's whereabouts on the day she disappeared. There was no one to tell where to look. In that way it would take a long time for the police to track him down. By then he would be gone and maybe Princess Amalie would be too.

So what did he want this kidnapper? Was he keeping Amalie alive somewhere? Was he going to blackmail the royal family? Was he demanding some ransom? Maybe they already knew about this. Maybe the kidnapper had already contacted the royal family and given his demands? They would most certainly keep that a secret from the public. No doubt about that. Maybe they were even taking care of it as I was lying there in my bed debating with myself? The thought made me feel calmer and I felt my eyelids slowly become heavier.

I might only have slept for ten minutes or so, when the tunes of One Direction woke me up with a start. I jumped out of the bed and ran towards the phone. I had put it in the charger overnight. The display said Amalie.

With pounding heart and sweaty hands I answered it. "Hello?" I said.

"Well hello there, Rebekka Franck," the voice from earlier said.

Every cell in my entire body froze to ice. I had to calm my breathing to not sound too agitated. "Who is this?" I asked.

"You know who this is," the voice hissed. "Don't patronize me."

"I'm sorry. I didn't mean to," I said afraid that he would hang up. "Why are you calling? What do you want from me?"

The voice chuckled. Then he made a smacking sound with his lips. "I can't stop thinking about you," he whispered.

"How do you know me? How do you know my name?"

"Again with the condescending tone. It's annoying, my dear."

I sighed annoyed. He was beginning to really piss me off. "Where are the girls?"

"Why do you care?" he said hissing.

"I care about them. I care that nothing happens to them," I said. Sune was beginning to wake up. He groaned and turned. Then he opened his eyes. I signaled that he should be quiet.

"Well isn't that nice," the voice said. "Maybe I will let you see them again. Maybe you'd like to pay them a visit."

"I would like to see them," I said feeling my heart drop. He hadn't made some deal with the family and I got the feeling that he wasn't about to either. That wasn't his plan. Money wasn't his goal. It was something else. Something a hell of a lot more scary.

The voice laughed hoarsely. "Be careful what you wish for," he said.

"Are the girls okay? Are they alright?" I asked. But it was too late. He had hung up. Angrily I pushed the screen and called him back. No one answered. I threw the phone on the bed. Sune looked at me, then jumped out of the bed.

"Who was that? Was it him again?"

I nodded, then let the tears roll across my cheek. "He still has the girls. He even knows my name. How does he know my name, Sune? How?"

Sune put his arms around me and hugged me. "I don't know. Maybe he's just really smart."

I looked out the window. It was almost morning now. I sniffed and hugged Sune again. Then I got up and found some clean clothes in my backpack. I put it on the bed. "We better get dressed," I said. "It's going to be a busy day."

Sune stretched himself. "Isn't it a little early? We worked till late last night. It's Sunday. We're done with this assignment, the festival is over."

I found a pair of his clean underwear and threw them at him.

"The festival might be over, but our work has just begun."

Sune grabbed the pants and held them in his hand. "Why do I feel like there's something you're not telling me?"

"Because there is," I said and went into the bathroom to turn on the shower. When I came out to get my shampoo Sune stared at me.

"There is? Do you mind telling me, then?"

"See for yourself," I said and looked at my laptop that was open on the table in the corner.

"What's this?" He looked at the screen.

"My article in today's paper."

Sune scanned it quickly, then stared back at me with wide open eyes. "Have you gone completely mad?"

I shrugged. "I might. I don't know how a person can actually tell if they have in fact gone mad or not."

"But ... but ...you wrote an article about Princess Amalie of Merchenburg and her friend being abducted during this year's festival? Are you crazy?"

"I guess. I thought it was the only way I could get the message out to people. Jens-Ole said that he wouldn't be able to read my article since it was finished so late. I guess he trusted me. Don't think he'll make that mistake again."

Sune shook his head. "You have finally completely lost it. Do you have any idea what kind of media circus this is going to create?"

"I have a feeling, yes. But I thought it was worth a shot."

"But you have no documentation. No police statement, nothing. You risk getting fired over this."

"I know. I wrote it as a personal story. I wrote about how I met Camilla and what she told me. Then I wrote that she had disappeared last night. I don't assume anything, I just tell them what happened and then I used the photo from the poster. I'm hoping to wake up the parents and get them to react somehow. And I'm hoping to wake up the population to get them to start looking for the two girls. Maybe someone saw something? If a small hint leads to their rescue, then I'm perfectly willing to sacrifice my job and career."

Sune smiled at me. "Now that's what I love about you," he said. Then he walked over to me and grabbed me by the waist. He kissed me gently, then demandingly. His hands were on my breasts when my phone rang. Then we laughed.

"And so it begins," Sune said. "Don't answer this now. Wait till you are done in the bathroom. If it's important they'll call again. You better get in that shower now while you still have the time. In about half an hour they will be all over you like vultures."

"I know," I said and kissed him one last time before I went back into the bathroom. When I got out Sune was sitting by the computer.

"Have you seen this?" he asked.

"I haven't seen the paper yet, if that's what you're asking." I took off the towel wrapped around my hair, then found my brush.

"It's not in the papers yet. It's all over the news agencies and the online papers."

"About Princess Amalie? That was fast." I walked closer expecting to see my story on the screen. Instead it was something completely different.

"Someone stole the remains of Erik Klipping from Viborg Cathedral. They found his grave under the altar empty this morning. They took the coffin and everything. Apparently removed the altar somehow, then dug themselves through the floor.

I dropped the brush on the bed and stormed to him. "Erik

Klipping? As in the King Erik Klipping? The king who was murdered in Finnerup Lade in 1286?"

"The one and only."

25

Allan had a great Sunday morning. He enjoyed the morning coffee and reading the paper next to Sebastian, before he sent him on his way with a smile, a kiss and a "see you tonight."

Sebastian had promised to visit his parents all day and take part of the usual Sunday lunch where he would sit and pretend not to be gay in front of the entire family even if they all knew that he was. It was a charade that Allan was very pleased with not having to take part of. Besides he had so much more to do this Sunday that Sebastian didn't need to know about.

Once he closed the door Allan ran upstairs and got dressed. He looked forward to finally being alone with the girls. And now it was time to have some fun.

He had been plotting his next move all night. It wasn't part of his original plan, but he was entitled to some fun on his own, wasn't he? Allan thought so.

As he ran downstairs to get ready, he kept thinking about that woman, Rebekka Franck. Ever since she approached him in the parking lot, he hadn't been able to get her out of his head. She was so striking. A perfect specimen. He just had to have her somehow. He had to fit her in. But how? How could he make her a part of all this? Maybe she could play a role somehow? Oh how he loved his twisted little games, he enjoyed plotting them as much as he enjoyed executing them. Well almost.

He walked to the garage and pulled out a tall jar covered with a red dishcloth. He felt the chill of excitement as he brought it with him to the kitchen. In the cabinet he also found the chloroform for later. Then he took the jar and the chloroform and walked towards the door leading to the basement.

He heard them move once he opened the door. Not that they could move much in those small boxes. He lit the light and looked at the fear filled eyes staring back at him from behind the plastic. Then he smiled.

"Good morning, ladies."

Both girls started yelling and hitting the sides of the boxes, while Allan calmly put the jar and the bottle of chloroform on the table next to them.

"Let us out of here, you sick bastard," Princess Amalie said.

He approached and looked at her inside of her box. "Tsk. Tsk. Now is that a way to talk for a young royal lady like yourself?" He said.

She hit her hand hard into the plastic while grunting. She seemed feeble, weak from starvation and thirst. That was good. Once he began what he had prepared for her, she would long to feel like that again.

Camilla grunted and started hitting the box with her fist.

"Don't bother. You'll only wear your pretty little self out," Allan said to her while taking down the body hanging on the hook. Camilla gasped when she realized what it was. Allan threw the body in the corner of the room, and then covered it with a black plastic bag. Then he walked to Camilla's box and knocked on it. "It's armored plastic. A bullet won't even be able to go through it. Cost me a lot of money to have it made, but it was well worth it."

"What do you want from us? Why are you keeping us in here?" Amalie yelled.

Allan turned his head like an owl and smiled. "Because I can," he said.

"Please," Camilla pleaded. It was pure music to Allan's ears. How he loved and craved the sound of a pleading victim. How he dreamt about it at night.

"Please let us go. We'll never tell anybody who you are or what you look like. We'll do anything you want us to."

Allan lit up and grinned. He liked the sound of that. "Well I don't need to set you free to get you two to do exactly what I want," he said. "All I want you to do, or rather all I want to do to you, is right in here. There is no need to get you out of those boxes."

Then he giggled and picked the jar up from the table. Like a magician he removed the dishcloth while exclaiming "Ta-da!"

Allan grinned as he watched the girl's eyes become big and wide. Then he closed his and enjoyed the sound of what came next. The sound of both of them screaming for their lives.

26

"I HAD TO do it, I'm not going to be sorry for it," I said into the phone. "I didn't want to leave this town and the two girls without at least letting the world know what happened to them."

I held the phone far from my ear while Jens-Ole yelled in the other end. "No documentation ... whatsoever! No police statement, no nothing. Now I have to explain to the entire world ... explain what to them? I don't even know! What the hell is going on?"

"Those girls were kidnapped. I'm positive. I had no way of finding their parents since I didn't know Camilla's last name and I don't believe I would be given permission to talk to the royal family, being stark raving mad as the entire world thinks I am. This is my way of helping the girls, I just pray that some good will come out of it. That's it. You can fire me if you want to."

Jens-Ole grunted a couple of times in the other end. "You know I'm not going to fire the damn best reporter I have," he said. "I've been called upstairs to explain myself to the big bosses later today. I'll fight for you, but can't promise you anything."

I smiled and looked at Sune. He was sitting next to his backpack with his phone in his hand waiting for me to be done so we could drive home. He looked like a little boy waiting for his mother.

"I can't ask for anything more," I said.

"Hmf." Jens-Ole went quiet. I was about to say goodbye, when he spoke: "But it is a damn good story, if it turns out to be true," he growled. "Is it true?"

"Yes. The kidnapper called me last night. I think he wanted to brag or something. He said he had the girls."

Jens-Ole inhaled sharply in the phone. He was thinking hard, I could tell. "You should try and contact the police again. Tell them he called. Yes, do that, then drive back home. We might need to send you back to Roskilde again soon if there's a development in the case."

"Does that mean we're on the case?"

Jens-Ole grunted again. "It's all yours. Make me proud."

Then he hung up. I looked at Sune. "Sounds like your plan worked," he said. "It was what you wanted, wasn't it?"

"I had hoped for it."

"It's all over the news agencies," he said and handed me his phone. I scrolled through the news bulletins and found several related stories under *Breaking*. Apparently they had bought the story after all. They were all quoting *Zeeland Times* for the story since they didn't want to get their hands dirty in case it turned out it wasn't true after all, but the story was too good to ignore. This was good, I thought. The best development I could think of. Now the police had to take it seriously and the parents would be informed. There really wasn't much more I could have hoped for. Pictures of the girls would soon be all over the medias and the public would be talking about it, looking everywhere for the girls.

"So we're going back now?"

I bit my lip. "I guess we have to. Julie is coming home tomorrow from Aarhus. She has camp next week, Tobias too, right? That riding camp?"

Sune nodded. I only paid the nanny for four days. I can't afford anymore."

"Okay. Let's go home, then." I grabbed my backpack and swung it across my shoulder. "We need to go past the police station first. I have to tell them about the call last night."

This time we were taken a lot more seriously when we walked into Roskilde police station. An officer showed us into a room and soon another officer joined us with a stack of papers in his hands. He greeted us and told us his name was Richard Brandenburg. He was dressed as a civilian and told us he was with the NEC, the National Investigation Center. He was very pleasant to talk to. He lifted his fairly bushy eyebrows as he pulled out my article from the stack of papers and looked at me. "We have contacted the parents," he said. "Just as you explained in the article, they didn't know that the girls were at the festival and they were very surprised at all this, especially since they read about it in their morning paper."

"Well, that was unfortunate," I said. "But I felt it was necessary since I had no idea how else to contact them."

The officer nodded. "I get it. I think it was great you did it. The parents have since contacted the captain on the boat they were supposed to be on and confirmed that they were not there and no one has any idea as to where they can be. If you hadn't written the article no one would have discovered their disappearance for several days and that could be fatal in a case like this where time is of the essence. It has sure awoken some people up in here. This morning has been a true inferno at the station. Not something they are used to. They have an entire team of three people just to handle the press. It's quite the circus. But as long as it helps the girls, right?"

"Right."

"Now. I know you have written everything in your article, is there anything else we should know? Anything about the girls or maybe something you saw while looking for them? Anything would be a huge help right now."

He leaned back and poured a cup of coffee from a thermos next to us. "Anyone?" he asked and pointed at some empty cups. We both shook our heads. We just had breakfast at the hotel. Officer Brandenburg put sugar in his cup and stirred it with the spoon.

"There is something," I said. "I think I might have spoken to the kidnapper."

The officer almost choked on the coffee. "You spoke with him?" he exclaimed. "How? When?"

"He called me. Well actually he called Camilla. See I have Camilla's phone, she gave it to me, so I could charge it for her in the press area where we have access to electricity since we need it for our phones and laptops. You can't get electricity on the campground of the festival. So as I was charging it, it rang. Since the display said Amalie, I thought I'd pick it up in case she was looking for her friend. That's when I spoke to him. He was using Amalie's phone to get to Camilla. That's how I knew that he was coming for her, but I was too late. I tried to run to warn her and get her out of there, but she was gone when I arrived."

The officer nodded as he wrote down on his pad. "Yes, yes, good. Continue, please."

I felt Sune's hand in mine under the table. He knew how bad I felt for not being able to save Camilla, and for telling the kidnapper exactly where she was.

"Then last night he called again," I said.

The officer looked up and our eyes locked for a second. His were very serious. "What did he want?"

"He said he couldn't stop thinking about me, that I could come and see the girls if I wanted to. Something like that."

"So he told you that he has the girls?"

"Yes. And I believe that they're still alive. He spoke about them as if they were."

Officer Brandenburg nodded and wrote on his pad. "Okay, that's good, yes," he mumbled. "Anything else?"

"He knew my name," I said.

The officer lifted his head and stared at me again. It scared me slightly.

"Do you think she should worry?" Sune asked.

The officer stared at him. He didn't answer. "We don't know much about this guy yet," he said. "But I would advise the both of you to be careful. We can provide police-protection if that's what you want?"

I shook my head.

"My guess is he's just teasing you, you know playing with you," the officer continued.

"Why?" Sune asked. "Why would he want to tease Rebekka?"

The officer sighed. "Well maybe he gets a kick out of it. If he knows your name, then he most likely also knows that you're a journalist. Maybe he wants to be famous, to have his name in the paper. It's all a lot of guessing at this point in the investigation. Right now we're focusing on finding these two girls alive and then taking care of the press, naturally. The story of the abducted princess will go around the world in a matter of hours."

"Do you think that's what he wants?" I asked. "Could that be why he chose Princess Amalie?"

"That is very likely the motive," Officer Brandenburg said. "That or money."

27

Camilla was screaming. As soon as the man revealed what was in the jar, she began screaming and she couldn't stop. She pleaded, she begged.

"Please don't, please don't hurt us," she screamed. But nothing seemed to help. It was as if the man enjoyed listening to them scream and cry for help. It was like he enjoyed it, fed from their fear.

In the jar in his hand the Tarantula was crawling up the sides. Camilla looked at it and began hyperventilating as the man walked closer to their boxes. He stood between them, then pointed at Amalie.

"No, please, no," she pleaded.

The man smiled viciously, then turned and pointed at Camilla. She shook her head fast.

"No. No," she said. Then she cried.

The man laughed. "Now, who will it be?" he asked. He turned and pointed at Amalie. Then he started counting: "Eeny, meeny, miny, moe ... Catch a tiger by the toe. If *she* hollers, let *her* go ... Eeny, meeny, miny, moe."

Saying his last word his finger landed on Camilla's box.

She whimpered and whined. Her jaw was shivering in fear. "*Pleeease*," she pleaded.

The man looked at Camilla. "You won!" He said. "Lucky you!" His eyes were shining as he looked at her inside of the box, smiling like a child on Christmas day. Camilla was hyperventilating. She focused on keeping calm as the man moved closer to her box. She saw him approach the tube that she now realized was closed with a lid that was screwed on and could only be opened from the outside. The lid had several air-holes in it. The man took a screwdriver and began opening it slowly, one screw at a time. Camilla was whimpering while staring at the Tarantula in the jar. It was moving up the sides now. She shivered in fear. Camilla had always been terrified of spiders and this one was bigger than any she had ever seen.

Once the lid was off he picked up the jar, then took off the lid and helped the spider into the tube. Then he closed the lid.

Camilla stared at the Tarantula in the tube, while sobbing and trembling. She watched it come closer, slowly approaching the end of the tube. With its long hairy legs it crawled along the sides and into the box. It was above Camilla's head now, sitting on the plastic, so close Camilla could feel the hair from its back tickle her skin. She was breathing heavily, while Amalie was screaming from across the room.

"Stop it! Stop it!" she yelled. "My dad will pay anything. I'll do anything. Just get it ooout!!"

Camilla stared at the huge spider as it crawled across the ceiling and came closer to her hair. She could barely see it anymore but suddenly felt it in her hair. Then she screamed again.

"Please stop this, *pleeeeeease*. What do you want from me?!"

The man was dancing around the box, watching the show while clapping his hands and licking his lips. "Careful not to scare it with your screaming," he said sounding like he wanted her to scream even louder. "It might bite you in fear," he hissed. "We can't have that now, can we?"

The Tarantula was in Camilla's hair now, she felt its legs moving across her scalp. She closed her eyes and tried to find her happy place. Whimpering, moaning to keep from screaming she imagined being with Amalie, kissing her, swimming with her in the ocean, laughing and sharing their thoughts and worries. She imagined Amalie standing naked in front of her, she imagined touching her soft breasts. She imagined their bodies close together, the warmth, the pleasure. While her body was shaking and shivering with fear Camilla left the box for a moment, left the Tarantula, left the strange man with the blond hair and evil eyes standing outside the box, cheering for the spider. She hardly felt it in her hair anymore, and when it moved closer to her face, she remained calm when she felt the legs wandering on her nose. She breathed heavily, concentrating on not panicking and that was when it happened. Apparently it aggravated the man that she had stopped screaming. He kept cheering the spider on and soon he was the one banging on the side of the box, telling her to open her eyes, telling her what the spider was doing and that it would soon be biting her, then describing just how dangerous its bite was.

"It'll feel like a bee sting, but soon you'll know it's much more dangerous. You'll feel like you are suffocating, like you can't breathe as the throat swells. Your heart will begin to race and you'll begin to swell all over your body. Maybe your heart will finally give up or .. uh .. even better. Maybe you'll just slowly suffocate. Painfully having more and more difficulty breathing, then cutting off the oxygen to the brain and slowly die. That sounds like fun, now doesn't it?" he said giggling.

Camilla didn't answer. She didn't even open her eyes to look at him. She didn't want to give him the pleasure of seeing the fear in her eyes. Instead she stayed in her happy place. She stayed where she really wanted to be. She stayed with Amalie.

It didn't take long before the man became bored. Camilla thought she had won a small victory. But the joy didn't last long. A few seconds later the man disappeared up the stairs, turned off the light and shut the door.

After that Camilla opened her eyes wide and didn't close them again for many hours.

28

Officer Brandenburg told us we were free to go back to Karrebaeksminde. He would be in touch if they needed anything else from us. I gave him Camilla's phone for their investigation. It felt good to get rid of it, I thought. I really didn't want to have to pick it up once again and hear his creepy voice.

I knew I had done what I could for the two girls, as we left Roskilde and drove towards Karrebaeksminde. Still, I couldn't help but feel guilty somehow. Guilty for leaving them like this, for abandoning them and putting their lives in the hands of that strange man on the phone. I didn't like it one bit. There was something about him that was extremely frightening. I sighed and looked out the window. I asked Sune to drive since I was too upset by the whole thing and I needed to rest, and think. I had bought a chocolate cake for us to share on the way, but so far I had eaten the most of it myself.

"Are you okay?" Sune asked as we reached the main road.

I stared at the scenery. It was no more than an hour drive away, but it was through countryside and I loved watching the hills and blooming yellow canola fields. "I'm fine," I said without looking at him. "I'm looking forward to getting back and especially seeing Julie again. I've missed her."

I felt Sune's hand on my thigh. "Me too," he said. "I've missed Tobias a lot."

I scoffed. "It didn't become quite the trip we had hoped for," I said.

Sune chuckled. "It never does with you."

I turned and looked at him. He was smiling at me. "So are you ready to try again once we get back?" he asked.

I turned my head and looked outside again. Sune kept talking about making another child, one of our own. I had told him I wanted it too, and we tried for a couple of months, but nothing had happened. I was beginning to see it as a sign that it maybe wasn't quite meant to be. I couldn't figure what I really wanted.

"I don't know, Sune," I said.

He removed his hand from my thigh. "Why? What are you saying?"

I sighed. I wasn't in the mood to discuss this right now. "Nothing," I said. "I didn't mean anything. I'm just tired."

"So you are ready to try again once we come back?"

I looked at him and saw the desperation in his eyes. He wanted this child so bad. I guess I did too, I just didn't care for all the disappointments. I wasn't sure it was worth it. I was afraid it was going to come between us. Seeing his face every month when I took the test, was a little more than I could take. I was beginning to feel like some kind of a breeding animal that didn't live up to its owner's expectations. It wasn't great.

"Let's wait and see, okay?"

Sune growled. The road took a turn. After a few seconds

he spoke again. "I don't think I like the way this is going," he said. "I thought we agreed on this?"

"We did. It's not like I don't want to have a baby with you. I would really love to. Believe me, Sune."

"Then what is it? Why are you all of a sudden reluctant?" he asked.

I exhaled. "It's just that ..."

"What? Just tell me goddammit," he said and hit his palm in the steering wheel.

"I miss being with you without it being about making a baby. I miss just being close and making love, not speculating if we are doing it in the proper position where I'm most likely to conceive. Maybe it's just not ... You know meant to be."

Sune snorted angrily. He shook his head a lot and grunted. "That's ... well that's just bogus if you ask me." Sune sniffed. Then he sighed. "Of course it's meant to be. We just need to work at it a little more, a little longer."

"See that's the problem," I said. "It's become work. We never have sex just for fun. I really think it's something we should talk about.""

Sune was biting his lip. We passed a sign letting us know we were entering Karrebaeksminde. For minutes we didn't speak. I could tell he was furious. He parked the car in the street in front of the apartment.

"You know what? I'm tired of talking," he said. "Maybe you should sleep at your dad's tonight," he said. "I'll take you there."

29

Allan felt frustrated. He was walking around in his open kitchen mumbling, spitting and hissing. "Little bitches," he hissed while biting his nails frantically. Then he kicked the extremely expensive garbage can that the Danish company Vipp had the lead singer of U2, Bono design for them, the same garbage can that Sebastian had convinced Allan to buy at a charity event in New York. "To help the poor children," he had stated. Allan didn't care about any poor children or about this stupid can that he was now kicking so hard it fell to the ground and was severely dented.

He grunted and hissed as he kicked it again and again until all his furor was finally out and he could calm himself down. The little bitch had ruined his game, he thought and slicked his hair back. She had completely destroyed the fun. Now he had left her down there with the spider in her box in complete darkness. She deserved it, the little whore. Now she could stay down there a couple of hours with the Tarantula. Allan wasn't afraid it would actually bite her, since the poisonous venom had been removed from it, but he wanted her to think it would. He wanted her to suffer, to squirm in fear and anxiety inside that tight box. Most of all he wanted to watch her as she did. He wanted to look into her eyes and enjoy the music from her screaming. But she had destroyed that pleasure for him by lying still, by keeping her cool and closing her eyes. The little bitch.

Allan stared out on the ocean. It was calm and quiet. So should he be. It was important not to lose it now. After all, the little game with the spider had nothing to do with his plan. Nothing was ruined yet. And nothing would be. Maybe he should just stick to the plan instead. It was after all going to give him more pleasure than anything he had done before. It by far excelled any of all the cruelty he had displayed. It was his *magnum opus*, a work of genius.

Now he would let her suffer a few hours longer, then the real plan would begin. Allan massaged his neck. He felt sore. *All the stress*, he thought. It was important he didn't let it get to him. He found a couple of painkillers in the cabinet and swallowed them. Washed them down with a shot of whiskey. That usually did the trick. Then he walked into the garage and stood in front of a large object covered with a white sheet. He hit the light switch and smiled comfortably with a deep sigh. No reason to get all worked up over some stupid game that hadn't succeeded like he wanted it to. Not when he had something much, much better in store for them. Something that would definitely get the little hairs on their backs raised in fear. A wave of pleasure rushed in over his body at the very thought of what was going to happen. A wave of almost orgasmic proportions.

He bent down and grabbed the entire package including the sheet, and then carried it inside the kitchen. He put it on the kitchen table, then pulled off the sheet. He touched the metal gently, caressing its sides. It had traveled a long way to get to him. He had ordered it online and then kept it in the garage for months waiting to be used. Now finally it was time. He plugged it in and saw that it worked, then began preparing it for use.

A couple of hours later it was ready and so was he. He opened the door to the basement, then picked the instrument up and walked down the stairs, careful not to trip. When the light turned on, he heard the girls moan. Allan put the instrument on the table, then looked at Camilla. She had finally opened her eyes and was staring directly at the Tarantula that was sitting on her face now as if it was looking back at her. None of them were moving.

Allan smiled relieved. It had worked after all. The look in her eyes was priceless. He knocked on the box. The Tarantula moved a little. Camilla didn't. She was panting, whining. Her body shivering. Allan waved. "Having fun, are we?" he asked.

"You bastard," Amalie yelled from her box. "Get the spider out now. Leave her alone."

"Tsk, tsk. Don't be jealous now," Allan said. "You'll get something fun too." Then he giggled and Amalie's eyes landed on the instrument on the table. She gasped. Allan clapped excitedly. Then he picked up the chloroform that he had placed on the table earlier. He walked to Amalie's box and stood in front of the tube. Then he opened the bottle and started pouring the chloroform into the tube through the air holes.

"Just a few drops," he said giggling. "Careful not to use too much."

"What are you doing? You bastard!" Amalie screamed. "You're crazy!"

Allan laughed out loud. "We all go a little mad sometimes," he said, quoting one of his all time favorite classic movie villains, Norman Bates in *Psycho*.

30

I was startled to put it mildly. Sune dropped me off at my dad's without a word to me. All he said was: "See you tomorrow." And then he was gone.

I couldn't believe him. Was it really so bad that we couldn't even talk about it? Was this about to be so bad it could end up coming between us? Destroying us? I picked up my backpack truly hoping it wasn't going to. I rang the doorbell at my dad's house and stepped in.

"Dad?" I yelled. "It's me."

"Rebekka?" His voice came from upstairs.

"Yup. I'm back from Roskilde." I put my backpack on the floor then looked around. The place was a mess. Nothing like it used to be. Dad came down the stairs. He looked tired, worn out.

"How are you, Dad?" I asked after we had hugged.

He leaned heavily on his cane. "So damn tired lately. I don't know what's going on with me. It's like I can hardly get out of bed. I'm sorry for the mess."

"It's okay. Let me help you clean the place up a little," I said.

"You're an angel. I'm so happy to see you. How was Roskilde?"

I found a plastic bag in the cupboard and began cleaning. "It was okay, I guess. We got mixed up in a big story that I am going to follow up upon in the coming days. Kind of got to me a little, I guess. Two young girls kidnapped."

"I heard about that on my radio just now," he said. "The young Princess, huh? Sounds like a terrible story."

I sighed and looked at him. I didn't want to bother him too much or have him worry about me, so I decided not to go into too many details. "It is," I said. "But the police are on it, they will find them eventually."

"Let's hope so," he said. "Or maybe you and Sune will."

"Very funny."

"Speaking of the devil," Dad said and looked at my backpack then at me. He had that worried look in his eyes. "Where is he?"

"We had a fight," I said and found a sponge and started scrubbing the kitchen table.

"A bad one, huh?"

"I guess. I don't know. Maybe we just need some time apart."

Dad pulled out a chair and sat down. Then he pulled out another one and pointed at it. "Sit," he said.

I obeyed with a deep sigh.

"Now I want you to tell me everything," he said.

"Really, Dad? Do you really want to hear about our silly argument?"

"I really do. You have to remember that you and Julie are about the only part of the real world outside this house that I get. You're the closest I get to actually having a life, plus I don't watch soap operas so your life is all the excitement I get."

I chuckled. Dad always had a way of making me feel like he was the one needing me when it was in fact the other way round. I patted his hand with a sigh. "Let me at least make us some coffee first," I said and got up.

I didn't get to do much cleaning that day. Dad and I talked for hours instead. It had been many months since we had last talked like this. And since I had last inhaled that much coffee. By the time we were done my mouth was dry and my stomach very upset with me. I looked in the cupboards and found some pastries that we shared with a soda.

"I can't tell you I don't understand him," Dad said while I poured orange soda in two cups.

"I know," I said. "I did tell him I wanted to have a baby, and I really do, but ..."

"But what?"

I exhaled, then took another bite of the pastry. "But I don't want to fight this much for it. I'm too old for that. I'm nearly forty."

Dad shrugged, then grabbed another pastry and ate it. It left a white moustache of sugar on his upper lip. "So you want the baby, you just don't want the work. You don't want to fight for it. Is that it?"

"I guess. I just thought that this would be a time in my life when I enjoyed my child, when I was done with babies and diapers and stuff. I thought this was the time to build up my career and maybe drink some red wine and go out to dinners and so on. Julie is finally so big that she can do most things on her own. I feel like I have finally gotten my life back and now I'm going to ruin it by having another child." I paused and looked at Dad. "What?" I said. "I'm just being honest. I know it sounds selfish, but that's how I feel, okay?"

Prologue

"So what you're saying is you don't want to have another child after all."

"No, that's not it. If I get pregnant tomorrow, then fine, I'll be thrilled. I just think that we can be just as happy without it. Our happiness doesn't depend on us having a child. That's why I don't think it's necessary to make it all about the baby, to make our lives - and our sex life - all about having a baby. I want to have fun while having sex."

"A little more than I needed to hear, thanks." Dad shook his head and drank his soda.

"Well you asked," I said.

Dad put his hand on top of mine. "It's not an easy one, sweetie," he said. "You'll have to figure it out among yourselves. And soon before anyone younger than you gets hurt."

"I know. Julie has gotten pretty attached to Sune and Tobias."

"You'll have to make your decision soon. You and Sune have to talk this through properly and figure out if you can stay together without any of you getting bitter for not getting his or her way."

I sighed. "I know you're right."

The doorbell rang and I got up. Dad looked at me. "It's probably Julie. I texted her and told her where I was. We're staying here tonight, if that's okay with you?"

Dad looked confused. Then he smiled. "You're always welcome. You know that."

I kissed his forehead then ran towards the door.

31

Amalie felt horrible when she woke up. Her head was aching like crazy and she couldn't move her hands. Something was very wrong, she thought, still half asleep. Her body, her head, it all felt so very wrong. Slowly she regained consciousness and suddenly she opened her eyes. When she did she tried to scream, but she couldn't. She breathed heavily, almost panicking as she realized something was in her mouth, something was in her throat, something big. She moaned in fear and tried to see what it was. Then she tried to scream again, but only a muffled sound came out of her mouth. What was this? What had he done to her? She tried to move her arms, but they were tied up on her back with duck-tape. She groaned and moaned trying to get free from this thing going into her mouth and throat, this big metal pipe of some sort, which was attached to her head with duct tape around the back of her head. She tried to turn her head, but she was stuck. She looked up and realized the pipe in her throat was attached to the box's tube creating one long tube going directly into her throat. She tried to bite down, but she couldn't. Her jaws hurt badly from being stuck in the same position.

A face appeared outside of the box. His face, her captor's evil eyes stared back at her. Then he knocked with a giggle.

"Oh good, you're awake. I was waiting for you to open your eyes. Wouldn't want you to miss out on all the fun, now would we?"

All Amalie could do was groan and growl in anger. She tried hard to speak, to yell at him, but with very little success.

The man laughed then started mumbling to himself. Like he was trying to remember what he was to do next. Amalie tried to turn her head just enough to be able to see Camilla. She was still in her box staring at the spider, it had moved down towards her feet now. Their eyes met shortly. Her look wasn't comforting nor did it fill Amalie with hope. The fear and anxiety seemed to have won. Camilla put her hand on the side of the box and Amalie saw a tear escape her eye. Amalie fought hard not to panic. She felt dizzy from the lack of air and had to focus on breathing through her nose.

The man walked around still while mumbling to himself and counting on his fingers. "Now a goose gets four pounds a day ... so with her body size she'll need what? Ten times as much? Not in the beginning of course, it'll kill her too fast. She'll need to go to the bathroom too. The boxes are beginning to smell of urine from both of them. I'd better write this down. Need to clean boxes soon ..."

Amalie tried to follow him with her eyes as he walked to the table and wrote on a piece of paper. He seemed to be calculating something, then he returned. His face appeared outside the box once again. He was grinning.

"You know what?" he said. "I'll figure it out as we go along. I think we should just get started. Don't you? You hungry?"

Amalie grunted and tried to nod. She was extremely

hungry. She hadn't eaten for days. She was dehydrated and starved.

"I thought so," the man said. "I bet Camilla is thirsty too, am I right?" he said and turned to look at Camilla. She nodded cautiously.

"Well I haven't been very nice to my guests, have I? I'll get you something right away," he said and went to Camilla's box. He screwed off the lid to the tube. He went to the corner of the room and came back with a hose that he lowered into the tube. Then he went to the wall and turned on the faucet. Amalie watched as Camilla opened her mouth to receive the long-awaited water and as he turned it on, she drank the fresh water as it sprayed all over her face. Camilla was moaning and grunting while drinking greedily, but soon she had enough and stopped letting the water in her mouth. It was coming in too fast. Soon the water began to rise inside of the box and her clothes were soaking wet. Camilla began to ask him to stop the water, but instead he turned it up and more water gushed inside of her box. Amalie grunted and cried, trying to scream as Camilla's box slowly was filled halfway with water. Camilla screamed and yelled. The spider ran for its life inside the box, climbing high above the water, getting to the ceiling and as the water kept rising, it found the hole to the tube and by crawling on top of the hose, managed to find safety in the tube.

Camilla was sputtering and making gargling sounds as the water reached her ears and cheeks. She was just barely holding her nose above the surface by lifting her body up on her elbows and putting it up against the hole leading into the tube. The man finally turned off the water. He walked closer, still grinning, and then he pulled out the hose and helped the Tarantula get out. It crawled on his hand; he put it carefully back into the jar and put the lid on.

Prologue

Camilla was grunting, gasping for breath barely managing to keep her face above the water as the man looked at her through the tube.

"I guess you're gonna stay up late tonight. Better not fall asleep huh?" he laughed and put the lid back on the tube and sealed it by putting screws back in with a screwdriver.

Then he turned on his heel and looked at Amalie.

"Now where were we?" he said, rubbing his hands together. "Oh yeah. You were hungry."

32

I FELT MY heart drop as I opened the door. Outside I saw Julie and her dad. She was in his arms, wrapped around him like she never wanted to let go again. Peter smiled.

"Wow," he said.

"What?" I asked.

He shook his head. "Nothing. You just ... well you look really great."

I stared surprised at him, then touched my unruly hair. I wasn't even wearing make-up. "No I don't," I said. "I've hardly slept all night and I'm exhausted after a couple of really hard days, so I ..."

Peter put Julie down. "Well I'm sorry if I think you look wonderful," he said and looked at Julie's face. "I'm sorry sweetie pie, but it's time to say goodbye now. But I'll see you again soon, right?"

Julie wept and whined slightly. "But that's gonna take forever, Dad. I'm gonna miss you. Can't you stay a little?" They both looked at me with pleading eyes.

"I'm sure Peter has somewhere to be, somewhere important," I said and looked at him wanting him to help me out.

Prologue

But he didn't. Instead he shook his head. "No I don't. I really don't."

"Don't you have work tomorrow? Don't you need to be back in Aarhus early enough to be able to get up tomorrow?"

"Actually I don't. I don't have anything all summer. I was looking forward to spending some time with Julie, actually. I wanted to talk to you about it, since you work all through the summer."

"Yes, but she has that camp, the riding camp the next two weeks," I said. Then I shook my head. "We'll figure something out."

"Does that mean that Dad stays for dinner?" Julie asked with joy.

I shook my head. "No. No. That wasn't what I meant."

They both looked at me with big eyes. "Pleeease?"

I gesticulated resignedly. "Okay," I said. "Stay for dinner. I'm sure Dad won't mind."

"The old man always liked me," Peter said smiling.

Julie ran to me and gave me one of her warm hugs. I closed my eyes realizing how much I had missed her.

"So how was Aarhus?" I asked when we had walked inside. "The old house still standing?" Peter put Julie's backpack on the floor next to mine. He stared at mine for a few seconds.

"We didn't go to our old house," Julie said. "We went to Daddy's castle in the country. But we did go into Aarhus almost every day; we drove in Daddy's car. Did I tell you we went to Tivoli Friheden? We went to the beach one day too. You know close to where we used to live. Daddy said the old house had too many bad memories, so he put it up for sale."

I looked at him startled. "Really? Daddy has a castle?" I asked.

Peter chuckled. "No. It's just the old family estate outside of Aarhus by Lake Brabrand. You remember that, don't you? It's been in the family for generations."

"Dragonsholm?" I asked.

"Yes, that's it," Julie answered. "It was really fun. Lots of spooky places, Mommy. Great place to play hide and seek. You should go there, Mommy. It's huuuge." Julie gestured widely as she spoke.

I nodded. "Well that sounds like a fun place to be," I said as we walked into the kitchen. Julie ran to my dad and hugged him tightly. He enjoyed that and grunted contently. Julie saw the pastries on the table and grabbed one.

"Dragonsholm, huh?" I said and looked at Peter. "I thought you never wanted to go there again after that dispute with your brother."

"Well things change. People change. Plus he moved to Spain with his family, so he hardly uses it anymore. I thought I might take advantage of that. I've been going there a lot lately. When the old house reminds me a little too much of all the bad things that happened there, you know. I feel like I'm stuck there sometimes, like the walls keep reminding me of how bad a person I've been. My shrink says it's normal. She's the one who told me to try and sell it. You know, start over. It would give you a little extra cash too, maybe get a place of your own down here," he said. "I thought it was in both of our interests."

I poured coffee in two cups, then gave Peter one. "I guess so," I said pensively.

"You think it's a bad idea?"

"No. I think it's a great idea, Peter. It's time for all of us to move on. Put it all behind us, you know. But it's just so definitive, right? Like we're selling our past together. We both loved that house, remember?"

"I know," Peter said while sipping his coffee. Then he

chuckled. "We did have some great times in that house. It's hard to give all that up, but it's time, Rebekka."

"I know," I said. "I know. It just takes a little time getting used to. I want to let go of all the bad things, but the good things I want to remember."

Peter nodded. "Then let's do that. Let's just remember the good things."

I looked at him and our eyes locked. For a second I felt something, a sentiment I hadn't felt in years. His eyes smiled gently like they used to. There was something in those eyes that reminded me why I had fallen in love with him in the first place. Then I averted my eyes and looked at Julie. "So you and Daddy had a lot of fun, huh?" Julie had captured my phone and was playing some game on it, not paying attention to anyone else anymore. "Well I'm glad you had such a wonderful time together," I said and looked at Peter again.

"And how was your trip?" he asked.

I sighed deeply and rolled my eyes. "Well that's a long story," I said. "But it was ... how do I say it ... eventful."

"Isn't your life always eventful?"

"It tends to be," I said finishing my coffee.

"I can't help noticing that you came here alone? And you brought your backpack? Are you staying here tonight?" Peter said and sipped his coffee.

"That's none of your business and you know it," I said.

Peter shrugged. "Do I detect trouble in paradise?"

I shook my head. "It's nothing. Just a small bump in the road."

"If you say so."

"That is exactly what I'm saying." I looked at my watch. "Now if you'll excuse me, then I have to go do some grocery shopping if we're to have any dinner tonight."

Peter grabbed my hand as I stood up from the chair. His

touch stirred something in me, something I didn't want to be stirred up.

"Let me treat you to a dinner tonight," he said. "I'll take you all out. What do you say to Italian? I know it's your favorite."

Julie shrieked with joy. "Say yes, Mom. Say yes, say yes! I want pizza, I want pizza!"

I sighed. It had been months since we had been able to afford to eat at a restaurant. Ever since I had moved out of Dad's place and started paying half of the rent for Sune's apartment I had been a little short. Plus I was trying to pay off my credit card debt, so money had been very tight lately. Peter always had enough money, coming from an extremely rich family and he always had a way of sweeping in with his wallet and saving the day for both me and Julie. I wasn't in the mood to cook anyway - or grocery shop - so eating out was exactly what I needed right now.

"Please, Mom?"

I sighed resignedly. "Okay then. But I'm not driving. I want wine with my dinner."

Peter smiled widely. "It's a deal."

33

Allan felt good. He was actually happy and ... well *almost* content with himself. Everything was going according to plan. While she was sedated he managed to tie Princess Amalie to the pipe, stuff it into the esophagus and put her back in the box without any problems. The hard part was over, he thought as he prepared the liquid that was a mixture made from grain and fat. He had bought it all over the Internet. Everything needed to produce the perfect foie gras, his favorite meal of all time. The pipe and pump arrived first and then the food.

Allan stared down into the huge can of thick, mushy yellow goose feed. He had several just like it in the garage. Not knowing exactly how much it was going to take for the Princess's liver to bloat up to ten times the normal size, he had probably bought way too much. But better safe than sorry, he thought.

He found a funnel and placed it in the open tube leading into Princess Amalie's box. Then he carried the big can with the yellow mush closer and began pouring it in. At first he needed to use a cup, since he couldn't carry the heavy can close enough to the tube to pour. But it suited the situation well, he thought, since the girl first had to get used to being force-fed. There was no reason to overdo it the first time. Allan had to be careful that she didn't die too early. That would ruin everything. So he took it easy on her on the first feeding. Four times a day they did it to the geese, so he was going to do the same. Only he would do it even more often than that. He would feed her with this fatty mush eight times a day until her liver was engorged enough for him to take it out and prepare it. It was risky, he knew that - thank you very much, since it had never been done to a human before and he had no idea how the human liver and body would react to ingesting this much fat. He had read about how some geese and ducks developed foot infections, kidney necrosis, spleen damage and tumor-like lumps in their throats, so he was aware that there might be severe side effects to the procedure. He was going to look out for that, since the Princess was one of a kind and it just wouldn't be the same doing it to someone else. The irony was that he knew the Princess herself had enjoyed eating foie gras most of her life and now she was going to end up on a plate just like those poor geese.

"What goes around, comes around," Allan said to himself as he shoveled the yellow mush into the funnel and watched as it slowly ran into the tube and into the pipe. Then he plugged in the pump. Princess Amalie gagged when the mush went through her throat and was pumped directly into her stomach. Allan heard how she tried to scream or speak, but the pipe and the mush forced her to stay calm while she was being fed. Allan tapped the side of the box and smiled at her.

"Tastes good, right?" he said. "I had it imported from France. Only the best for my Princess," he said grinning.

Amalie was grunting, gagging while the funnel slowly

emptied. Allan looked at it as the last bit disappeared from it. He counted to ten, letting Princess Amalie breathe for a few seconds thinking it was over now, then he lifted the can and emptied the rest into the funnel, filling it to the top so much than some of it flooded over the sides and landed on the floor.

Allan grunted, and then went to get a paper towel that he used to wipe it off the floor. Princess Amalie was moving, tossing her body from side to side, while grunting heavily as the next shipment of yellow mush reached her stomach. Allan watched her for awhile to make sure there was enough room in her stomach for all of it. He didn't want her to throw up and possibly choke. That would be catastrophic. He didn't know if it was even possible with the pipe in her throat, but maybe it was? Amalie was now gagging again and he realized that she was in fact about to throw up. He hurried to the funnel, and pulled it off. He put it on the table behind him and waited. He listened for a little while. Then he heard Amalie cough. Phew, she was alright, he thought. He had to be more careful. It could so easily go wrong. One little mistake and everything was ruined. He had to let her stomach get used to being fed this heavily, he had to let it expand slowly, not too fast, too fast would be disastrous. Oh, he thought and rubbed his fingers nervously against each other. Oh how he had to be careful.

Allan put his head against the plastic-box and looked at Amalie. She opened her eyes and looked back. He sighed relieved. She was exhausted, but he detected anger in her eyes as well. That was a good sign. No it was more than that. It was a great sign.

34

Peter helped me get Julie to bed once we returned from the restaurant. I was so full I could have rolled all the way home. And a little tipsy as well from all the wine I had enjoyed. My cheeks were warm and I felt really good. It was Julie's idea that we tuck her in together like we used to when she was younger. We were sitting on each side of her bed while holding her hands. Peter was reading *Pippi Longstocking goes to circus* out loud to her. I closed my eyes feeling like the room was spinning a little bit, while enjoying listening to Peter reading about the world's strongest girl that I myself had enjoyed reading as a child. Julie put her head on my shoulder and squeezed my hand tightly. I opened my eyes and looked at her while caressing her hair gently. She was so happy at this moment. I could tell by the way she was looking at us. Peter kept reading:

"I can go with you most anywhere," answered Pippi, "but whether I can go with you to the surkus or not I don't know, because I don't know what a surkus is. Does it hurt?"

Peter paused and laughed. Julie laughed too. "Silly Pippi," Julie said and shook her head. Peter looked at her with affection, then kissed her forehead and pulled her close. Then he lifted his head and looked at me.

"This is nice," he said. "This is really nice."

Our eyes locked for a long time. I bit my lip while trying hard to fight all those emotions from rising in me. I didn't want to feel anything for Peter again, not after what we had been through. But could I stop it? Had it ever stopped?

I shook my head feeling confused and tired. No, Peter had disappointed me so many times. Why should this be any different?

"It's time to sleep now," I said and kissed Julie on the forehead. "Your dad has to get back to Aarhus. It's a long drive." I got up and looked at them both. "You better say goodbye."

Peter shrugged. "I could stay," he said.

Julie shrieked with joy. "Could you Dad?"

He nodded. "I don't have anywhere I need to be tomorrow. It's not like I really want to get back to that empty house and be all alone again."

They both looked at me. "Could he stay, Mom?"

"I could stay at a hotel," he said. "Stay a couple of days and spend time with Julie. You need to go to work anyway, right?"

I shook my head. "It's just not a good time, she has camp. It starts tomorrow and lasts for two weeks."

"I'll take her there and pick her up. That way you don't have to, you can focus on your work and that big story you told us about at dinner."

"Please, Mom?"

I exhaled deeply. What kind of a mother would I be if I said no to that? I tried to find an excuse, I really did. I scrutinized my entire brain, but found nothing. Not one single reason to not say yes. Peter taking care of Julie would make my life easier and I did have this story that would definitely take most of my time the next couple of days, maybe even the entire week. My only problem with this solution was that I had no idea what to tell Sune. I enjoyed Peter's company this evening and feeling like a family again and giving Julie that back. Sune and I weren't doing very well and I was scared that this would drive us further apart.

"Okay, then. I could use your help and Julie loves to spend time with you. It is a great offer, really. But what about your business, don't you have to work?"

"All I need is an Internet connection and I'm up and running," Peter said. "I might as well take care of things from down here. I think it'll do me good to spend a couple of weeks away from it all, and close to my kiddo," he said and pretended to take her nose. Julie whined with joy.

"Okay," I said with a smile. "We'd love to have you around." I raised my finger. "But you're getting a hotel room."

Peter's smile froze a little, then he nodded. "Of course. That is the only right thing to do."

"And you young lady, you need to go to sleep now. Big day tomorrow."

I kissed her forehead and stroked her cheek. She smiled widely. "Goodnight," I said and went to the door.

"I love you, Mom. Thank you, thank you for letting Dad stay," Julie said.

"You're welcome," I said and closed the door.

Peter stared at me. "Thank you," he whispered.

"Don't make me regret it," I said and began walking towards the stairs. Peter grabbed my hand and pulled me back. He looked into my eyes, and then stroked my cheek gently the way he always used to do. He lifted my chin with his finger.

"I have missed you so much," he said. "You have no idea how much I've missed you."

I swallowed hard, then pulled back. "Well I'm just glad

you're better now and that Julie can have you in her life again."

"What about you?" He asked.

I shrugged. "What about me?"

"Are you happy to have me in your life again?"

I pulled further away. "Don't push it, Peter. One step at the time."

Peter sighed then bowed his head. "Of course," he said. "I know I've disappointed you, I know I've hurt you and that it takes time for you to trust me again. But I'm willing to fight for it, to have you be able to trust me again."

"That's all very good, Peter, but you're forgetting one thing."

"And that is?"

"I'm with someone else now."

35

Camilla was fighting to breathe. She had her body elevated on her elbows, but knew it wouldn't be long before they would cave in. They were hurting and shaking already. She took in a deep breath, and then let her body be covered by the water while her arms rested. Shortly she lifted herself up again, in order to take a breath. She gasped for air, filling her lungs, panting. Her arms began to shake again and she had to repeat the maneuver. She did so a couple of times, but soon she wasn't able to stay above the water for long. She tried to scream when she was above the surface, but didn't have much strength or enough air. She swallowed water, then coughed wildly. Meanwhile the man seemed to be occupied with Amalie. Camilla tried to catch his attention to her and to let him know she was about to drown in here, but he was preoccupied by what he was doing to Amalie. Camilla managed to keep her head above the water long enough to look at her. What was he doing over there? Amalie seemed to be tied to something, a pipe and he seemed to be force-feeding her through it with something. What was he doing? He seemed to be dancing around

Prologue

Amalie's box, then there was a light, like a flash. Was he taking pictures?

Camilla didn't understand what was going on, and she wasn't certain she wanted to. All she could think of was her own survival. She felt her mouth fill once again with water and coughed and spat it out. Then she took another deep breath before she let herself go under the water while resting her arms. She returned above the surface spitting and panting, gasping for air. She didn't know how much longer she could sustain this. Was that his plan? she thought with dread. Was she just supposed to drown in this box once she couldn't hold her head up any longer? She sobbed and moaned, feeling sorry for herself and for ending her life like this. Her parents were going to be devastated. She wanted so badly to see them again. She didn't blame them for anything. Yes they had been very absent in her life, but they had only done so to be able to give her a life in luxury, a life where she had everything she could ever want in life. Camilla used to blame them for not being present enough in her life, for letting their jobs be more important than her, than their family, but not anymore. Now all she could think of was to be able to once again be with them, to hug her mother like when she was only a child, before the money, before the luxury when her mother had time to hug and listen to her talk. She knew they could mend the broken pieces if only they tried. All she had to do was to forget all the anger towards them, all the resentment she felt in her heart for being left alone so many times, for them not showing up to watch her in her school play, or when she scored that goal in soccer. She saw that now. All she had to do was to let it go, let the bitterness go. She saw it clearly now. But it was too late. It was much too late. She was going to die here, in this awful box by the hands of this horrifying killer. Her arms were shaking heavily once again, hurting like hell too, and she had to let go. With a great sigh she fell back in the water without even taking a deep breath first. A few bubbles left her mouth and travelled towards the surface. She stared at them while getting ready to meet her creator. Bye Mom, bye Dad, she thought. I'm sorry I didn't get to say a proper goodbye. Everything around her seemed to go in slow motion now. Her arm floating in the water next to her head, her hair looking like waves. Pictures of the ones she had loved danced before her eyes in a bright light. Her parents were holding each other like they used to when Camilla was a child, they were happy again and waving at her. Then her grandmother showed up looking like she did before she died and finally she saw Amalie, blowing kisses at her while running at the beach. A song popped into her head. A song she and Amalie used to sing along to.

Seven devils all around you
Seven devils in my house
See they were there when I woke up this morning
I'll be dead before this day is done

She repeated the lyrics from Florence and the Machine in her head several times, while the water slowly swallowed her and she felt it enter her body, her nose, her mouth and finally her lungs.

Then it all went black.

36

Allan was getting ready. He found a new shirt and put it on in front of the mirror in his bedroom. He had chosen a light blue to make him look trustworthy. He read in a magazine once that women found a man in a light blue shirt more likable and reliable than any other color. And that was what he needed to signal. Most of his friends dressed in camouflage-green when going hunting, but Allan dressed in light blue.

He turned his torso in front of the mirror, then slicked his blond hair back with some wax. He nodded slowly while correcting the shirt and rolling up the sleeves. It was a warm night out. The right kind of night for hunting, he thought.

Sebastian had called earlier and said that he would be over later to spend the night. It would give Allan the alibi he needed in case anyone would ever think of suspecting him of anything. Though they never did. He was way too good and way too careful for that.

On the table his iPad lit up. A message on the chat. It was from Cogliantry.

Good luck tonight, it said. *Think of me as you grab her.*

I won't, Allan wrote. *I don't want to ruin the moment, lol.*

Point taken. At least I will be thinking about you. All night long. Imagining what you're doing to her, fantasying that it's me. Me who smells her skin, me who looks into her fear-filled eyes before I end her life. Me, who fucks her afterwards, chops her into little pieces and feeds them to the pigs.

You're sick, Allan wrote.

No, my friend. You're the sick one here. Posting any pictures soon?

Allan looked at his watch. He had to get going, but he really wanted to show his friends the pictures he had taken of his Princess.

Give me a sec.

I'll give you more than that if you promise me it's good. Boy are you gonna make my night if it's anything as good as your earlier works.

Oh, it's better. It's much better. Just wait and see.

Allan found his single-lens reflex camera and hooked it up to his Mac. He found the best ones, then uploaded them. As soon as he plugged in his iPad they were immediately transferred and now he could upload them to the secure chat. He smiled widely as he watched them again, then waited for the reaction. It took a few minutes and Allan was about to get impatient, when a new message popped up:

That, my friend, is a true masterpiece.

Allan chuckled satisfied. His fellow artist's opinions were more important than any opinion. He was his own worst critic and hard to please, so like many other artists he was constantly looking for encouraging words and acceptance of his art from others.

Allan logged off the chat. He was getting ready and had to get in the mood. There was no time for other stuff, he needed

Prologue

to focus. But there was something that seemed to be bothering him, he thought as he glanced at his reflection in the mirror once again. *She* was bothering him. Her. She had been on his mind ever since that night in the parking lot. He exhaled and straightened his back to make himself look taller. What was it with her? Why did he want her so bad? He kept fantasying about what he could do to her and how she was going to make him happy. He was getting too obsessed with her face, well with everything about her. If he wasn't careful it could end up destroying him. He risked losing his focus and maybe getting too careless. He could end up making a mistake if he wasn't careful. History was filled with people who let an obsession destroy their work. A passion for someone could end up devouring him. There was really only one way to get rid of an obsession like that.

He had to kill her.

Allan grabbed his car keys and ran downstairs. Luckily everything seemed to come together for him lately. A message in the chatroom earlier today had come as a blessing to him. It was almost like someone knew about his secret desire and wanted to bless him. It could hardly be just a coincidence, could it?

Just before he went outside he stopped by the door leading to the basement and listened. Not a sound from the girls. Good, he thought. They were definitely exhausted after a busy day. He chuckled as he was walked towards the main door, throwing his car-keys casually in the air and catching them again. It was good the girls got some sleep. They were about to have a busy day tomorrow again.

Allan locked the front door carefully, and then took two steps at a time down the stairs into the gravel where he jumped inside of his car. The Mercedes spun like a cat as he turned on the engine. He turned on the GPS in the car and plotted in the name of the town that had been chosen for tonight's hunt. Karrebaeksminde, it replied. One hundred point nine kilometers, one hour and seventeen minutes.

Allan smiled at his own reflection in the rearview mirror, then drove off.

37

"So what do you think of the story about Erik Klipping?" Peter asked.

We were sitting in my dad's yard drinking a glass of wine. I offered him one after Julie had fallen asleep and my dad had turned himself in. I don't know what it was or why I asked him to stay, but I guess I enjoyed being with Peter again. I enjoyed his company and that he seemed to be back to his own self again. I had been thinking about Camilla and Amalie all evening, unable to stop wondering where they could be and if they were alright. It upset me that I couldn't do anything to help them right now. But I had to trust the police were doing all they could to find them.

"I don't know," I answered. "Why would anyone want to steal the remains of a king buried more than seven hundred years ago? I don't get it. Is it worth anything?"

Peter shrugged then sipped some wine from his glass. "I guess it might be, but who would buy it?"

I chuckled trying to imagine a wealthy Saudi Arabian oil-sheik paying millions to have Erik Klipping's coffin in his mansion somewhere. Then Peter laughed. "The real question is why? Why would someone buy it?"

"Maybe someone who collects these kind of things," I said and put my glass on the table. It was a nice bright summer evening. I had put on a sweater since it had gotten a little chilly, but otherwise it was very nice sitting on Dad's patio furniture with Peter. "Like weird rich guys who collects national relics and treasures."

I thought for a second about Sune while looking at Peter. I knew he would be so hurt if he knew I was hanging out with my ex. But wasn't I allowed to do that every once in a while? I mean we used to be married. We used to have a family and hang out all the time. I missed him. Wasn't I allowed to do that? It was after all best for Julie that we remained friends. It was in her best interest.

The guilt was nagging me. I found an old packet of cigarettes in the pocket of my sweater and took one out. Peter stared at me. "I thought you'd quit."

"I did," I said and lit it.

Peter shook his head. "Well, at least share with me," he said and put his fingers in the air to signal that he wanted the cigarette. I hesitated, then smoked a little more before I handed it to him. He smiled and inhaled. Then he coughed.

"Too strong for you, huh?" I said laughing. Peter handed me the cigarette back. I took a couple of puffs, and then killed it with my shoe.

"No, just too long since I last smoked. Phew I remember why this was never for me," he said still coughing.

"You used to smoke."

"When I was younger. Before I met you, yes. Guess I'm getting too old."

I smiled. "You are kind of old. But heck so am I. Too old."

Prologue

Peter stopped coughing then looked at me. "Too old for what?" he asked.

I exhaled. "Too old to be having more children," I mumbled, then picked up my glass and drank my wine.

Peter burst into laughter. "Ha. You having more children? Where did that come from?"

I chuckled. "I know. It's kind of silly, right?"

Peter stopped laughing. "You're being serious? Do you really want more kids now? I thought you were happy with the way things were. With Julie and your job here and living the life you do now? Do you really want to start all over again with a baby?"

I inhaled sharply. "Tricky question. Not sure we should go there right now."

Peter nodded. "Ah, I see. He wants to have more children, you don't?"

"Well it's not that simple. It's a lot more complicated than that. I do want to have more children, or I did, but we have been trying for a long time now and nothing is happening. Now I feel like we're wearing each other out on this subject. It's grown too big, you know? Plus I'm not getting any younger as we wait for it to happen. I'll be thirty-nine in October."

"I know. You're getting up there with the rest of us," Peter said with a grin.

I slapped him amicably on the shoulder. "I'm not old. Not like you."

He grabbed my hand. "You'll never be as old as me. You'll always be young and absolutely gorgeous."

Peter pulled me closer to him till we were face to face. He closed his eyes with a sigh. "I've missed this," he whispered. Then he opened his eyes. My heart was beating fast. I wanted to run, I wanted to tell him to stop, to tell him to leave, but something inside of me refused to do it.

"I still love you, Rebekka. Things have changed. I have changed ..." In the middle of the sentence he leaned over and kissed me.

To my surprise I kissed him back.

38

He watched them from afar. From behind the neighbor's privet hedge. He had been lucky, Allan thought to himself. Lucky to have been able to find her this fast. He hadn't been able to locate her address from the yellow pages by using her phone-number from the business card, but he had been able to locate her father's address by typing in the last name and much to his surprise, he had found her there. There she was.

When he passed the house in his car for the first time, he saw her walk into the house with what he assumed was her family. Allan had been watching them through the windows with his binoculars for an hour or so before she to his great joy suddenly stepped out in the backyard with a bottle of wine and some guy Allan didn't care much for. There she was. So close to him again. Looking striking in her summer-dress and soft, tanned skin. Deep in a conversation with the guy, laughing, drinking wine and even smoking cigarettes.

Allan listened in on their conversation about the remains of the King Erik Klipping. He himself had been wondering about that story as well. It had taken all too much space in the media, taking space from the abduction of Princess Amalie and her friend, from his story, his masterpiece. Allan growled thinking about it. At this time of year the media normally had nothing to tell, so a story like his would fill everything, would be everywhere, but he hadn't counted on competition from a dead king. Allan got why they liked the story. There was some fascination about that specific person in the country's history, since he was assassinated, stabbed to death and the murder was never solved. But other than that, Allan couldn't see what the fuss was about. Who cared about some old dead king, when there were so many lives to take, so many living that could be killed in so many fascinating ways. Over the years Allan had done many killings, so many he no longer counted them, but to him the fascinating part wasn't why he killed them, but more how. The art of creating a horrific death for someone, and creating it to perfection was his passion.

With Princess Amalie it was slightly different than his earlier works. With her it was both. It was both the why and the how that was interesting. It was personal. She was chosen for a reason, but that was the first time for him, maybe not the last, since he had quite enjoyed himself so far. It gave the kill an extra touch to it, an extra thrill.

Normally it didn't matter who she was, as long as she served her purpose. And the girl Camilla? Well she was just there as a way of tormenting the Princess. Seeing her suffer was an extra plus, a bonus. He knew Camilla was one of the very few that the Princess actually cared about. He even knew they had shared a kiss once. He had seen it, when he was watching the Princess, preparing his plan for her death. She had pretended to not like it, but Allan knew she did. He knew she liked Camilla much more than she would care to admit. Allan shook his head while watching the man cough after smoking. All those deceits and lies, he mumbled to himself. Why couldn't they ever just tell the truth? Why had Amalie's parents pretended to be a family even after her mother left? he asked himself. Amalie's mother and father had pretended towards the world to be this happy couple. Whenever they went to anything official, whether it was the opening of a museum that they had to cut the red velvet cord, or if it was gala at the queen's castle, they went together, smiling at the cameras, waving at the people, pretending that everything was alright. But it wasn't. Allan knew it wasn't. The mother had moved to Spain and lived with another man. Why did they insist on deceiving the world like that? Why all the lies?

Allan growled and shook his head heavily in anger. He was so tired of all the lies! He clenched his fist while staring at the woman he desired so badly. He wanted to kill, he thought. He needed to kill tonight. The voices in his head wouldn't stop demanding, wouldn't stop yelling at him.

Kill, kill, kill.

He clenched his fist harder and harder. Soon his nails were penetrating the skin of his palm, but he hardly noticed. Not until he saw the man kiss the woman and he lifted his hand and realized he was bleeding. Blood was running down his arm from his hand and dripping on his new black shoes made from expensive Italian leather.

39

"I think you should leave," I whispered.

Peter's lips had just left mine and he was breathing heavily. I closed my eyes feeling the guilt and condemnation growing inside of me. What was I doing? "I need you to leave," I repeated.

"But, Rebekka ..."

"Peter. I'm serious here. I'm with someone, remember? I need time. I need space." I closed my eyes trying hard to fight my urge to just let go, to just give in to Peter.

"Rebekka," he moaned under his breath.

Then he kissed me again and held me tight. I didn't stop him. He looked me in my eyes as our lips parted. I felt helpless in his hands, powerless. He always had that affect on me. He held my head between his hands while looking into my eyes, like he was searching, scrutinizing my soul.

"Peter," I said. "This is not something we should be doing."

"But I want to. I want to be with you. I want to touch you, I want to be close to you. I want you so badly."

I grabbed his hands and removed them. "I know ... But it's just ... not ..." I didn't finish the sentence. Instead I leaned over and kissed him. His lips felt soft and gentle. I was greedy, demanding, longing to feel his touches. "Oh my god," I moaned while he kissed my neck. "This is so wrong. This is so, so wrong."

"I know," he moaned while kissing behind my ear. "But I can't stop."

"But ... but Peter, we have to."

"Shh," he said and put a finger over my lips. "Don't speak."

The wine made the yard spin while Peter was all over my body, touching, kissing. I was moaning, enjoying every little bit of it, pushing all the guilt far, far away, pushing thoughts about Sune, the two abducted girls, even Julie, far away. I closed my eyes and let him pull up my dress. Then he pulled off his shirt. I sighed at the sight. He was still so handsome, so well trained. I touched his muscles and pulled him close to me. His lips were everywhere on my body, then he lifted me up and put me up against the table. He entered me with a deep moan.

My head was still spinning when we were sitting on the table, smoking a cigarette afterwards. But now I was beginning to get a headache too. Peter smiled and kissed me on the lips. I felt my stomach twist. I hid my face in my hands. What had I done? How was I ever going to explain this to Sune? I had completely destroyed everything we had together, just for what? For pleasure? In order to get laid without thinking about babies and pregnancy? I inhaled and blew out smoke while looking at Peter. Or could it be something else? Was I not done with him? Was it possible for us to start over? Was that what I wanted?

I rubbed my forehead while giving the cigarette to Peter. He was still smiling happily. Of course this was exactly what he wanted. But did it mean I wanted to get back with him? It would be great for Julie, she loved Sune but she loved her daddy and being a family even more. But would it destroy her friendship with Tobias? Not being able to clearly see the consequences of all this I shook my head as the cigarette came back. I smoked. I felt so confused and that stupid yard wouldn't stand still. It kept spinning and I couldn't even think straight. Maybe I was just too drunk to make any decisions right now. Maybe it would all be better in the morning. Maybe I would be able to think clearer.

"You should go," I said to Peter. "I don't want Julie to find you here in the morning. Or my dad."

Peter looked disappointed.

"Peter, I need some space. I need to sober up and then I need time to think."

He nodded heavily. "Okay," he said and got up from the chair. "I'll leave you alone, then. I'll be back tomorrow to pick up Julie and drive her to camp."

Peter leaned over and kissed my forehead. I breathed his scent. I had missed it, I realized. I had missed him. "See you kiddo," he said and left.

As I watched him walk off, I lit another cigarette. "Last one before I quit again," I mumbled and blew out smoke. I stared at the light summer sky with its bluish light. It was almost impossible to see any stars. I lowered my eyes and looked into the neighbor's yard. I thought I spotted something in there and kept looking in that direction. I blinked my eyes a couple of times. What was that? Was someone standing behind the hedge? I felt a chill run down my spine. Had someone been watching us?

40

Allan watched the woman through his binoculars. He still had a boner on from watching them have sex on the patio-furniture. It had excited him in a strange way. And now the woman was looking right at him. He pulled out the knife in his pocket and felt the blade. Should he go with the knife? Or simply knock her down with his binoculars? He could go with the handkerchief and chloroform like last time if he didn't want to bruise that pretty face. It would be a shame to leave a mark.

What was she doing now? he thought. *Oh my god, she is coming over here.* This wasn't a part of his plan. But he was already far away from his original plan, which had been to ask her to help him find his daughter. He had prepared a story about how they had been walking in the neighborhood on their way home from the movies, when they had started a fight and she had been angry with him and run off. He was certain he had seen her run towards the woman's house, had she seen the girl? Being a mother herself, he knew she would fall for it. Plus he was wearing his expensive light blue shirt, and no one ever suspected someone this nicely dressed - and handsome - to have wrong intentions, was his experience.

Think fast, think fast, the voices yelled in his head. She was coming closer now. He had to do something. He looked at the empty street. He could run. That was always an option. He was a fast runner, she would never be able to catch up with him. He tilted his head still while staring at her. She was slowly walking closer and closer, with a curious look. Now it would be a shame to run now, wouldn't it? Her skin probably still smelled of him. Smelled of having sex with that other man. Allan would lick her body with his tongue, to get the taste. Oh the joy, he thought. So what if meant he deviated and took a chance. It was against the rules that the Master had set up for them. But Allan didn't care. He was not like the others in the group, he was better than them. He never got caught. He never left any traces behind. He didn't care about the Master and all his games anymore. He wanted the woman to himself. He wasn't going to share her.

Allan knew he risked bringing the Master's anger upon himself for messing it up, but he had to do this kill on his own.

The woman's face was now too close to be seen in the binoculars and Allan lowered them and looked directly at her.

"Hello?" she said. "Who is there?"

Allan of course didn't answer. He stared back at her and watched her come close. He remained motionless with the knife in one hand and the binoculars in the other, still undecided which one to use. He had never been in this uncontrollable situation before. Usually he had everything planned to the smallest detail. It was dangerous but it also made it so much more thrilling.

Like his first kill.

Prologue

The girl's name had been Isabella. She lived on a farm close to where he had been on vacation as a child. It was just after the arrival of the baby. The people Allan had considered to be his mother and father had just told him they were sending him away. Away to boarding school and he wasn't going to come back to them, not even on vacations. They would make arrangements for him to stay at the school and once he graduated he would be sent to a business school in Switzerland. They had enjoyed having him with them, they said, but it was time to move on. There was no more room for him at the castle in Moegeltoender. That was when Allan had thought about killing for the first time. He thought about killing the parents, he thought about strangling the baby with a pillow. So he ran out without anyone noticing him, found a young girl sitting by the lake with her feet in the water, playing with a frog she had caught in her hand. She had showed it to him with such joy in her eyes. Allan had taken it, then squeezed it till it exploded in his hands. The girl screamed, but Allan hadn't cared. He knew she could scream all she wanted to, but no one could hear her out there. That was the first time he had enjoyed the thrill of having the power over someone's life and death. Of being the one to choose whether a person should live or die.

He decided she needed to die.

With his bare hands he strangled her, then thrown her in the water. He stared at her while she floated lifeless in the surface, studied her, and studied the wondrous mystery of death. Once her body filled with water and she started to sink, Allan had run back feeling like everything was going to be alright after all.

Now for the first time in many years he thought about the little girl who had been his first prey as he stared into the eyes of the woman who was going to be his next.

"May I ask what you're doing out here?" the woman asked. Then she froze.

"Do I know you?"

Like he had done fifteen years ago, Allan smiled when he lifted his hand with the binoculars and slammed it hard into the woman's head and she landed on the grass, bleeding from the huge mark on the side of her head.

"I don't believe we've been properly introduced," he said and picked her up.

41

Amalie's throat was so sore. She felt so incredibly thirsty and was crying. Her body felt swollen, like it was about to explode. Like her internal organs were blown up, out of proportion, like there wasn't any more room for them inside of her body. Maybe she was just imagining it, but it felt like her liver was already engorged. Did it really happen this fast? Her stomach was hurting the most from being filled again and again. She wondered how many times her body would be able to sustain this treatment. And even more she wondered when the man would be back and continue the force-feeding.

She remembered seeing the man go upstairs and turn off the light as he left them. She tried to scream, but her body hadn't been able to cope with anymore. She had passed out for what she believed had to be hours. Ever since she had awoken to the horrific reality she had been sobbing in the darkness, trying to catch a glimpse of Camilla in the box next to her. The last she had seen of her was after the man had been done with feeding her and taking pictures. Amalie could still hear the gurgling and choking sounds coming from Camilla's box and she still had that eerie feeling that maybe her friend was dead. The man also heard it once it had started and turned to look at Camilla. Amalie had watched him while he was taking pictures of her as well. It had filled her with disgust, the way he watched Camilla drown in the water, the way he almost enjoyed himself while Amalie banged on the box, tried to scream with this infamous pipe down her throat. *She is dying*, she had tried to yell, but nothing but muffled sounds had emerged from her throat. Camilla is drowning, she thought while sobbing and crying quietly inside.

Camilla, my love.

Yes, she knew that Camilla was in love with her. Of course she did. They had been best friends for almost a decade, well almost all of their lives. Of course Amalie knew. And when Camilla had kissed her the first time at the party? Yes, she had enjoyed it. She had wanted her to do it for a long time. But as part of the royal family she also had a responsibility. She could never come out as a lesbian. Just like her mother and father never could be properly divorced without the Queen's acceptance, one they would never get. That was just the way things were once you were part of the royal family. They didn't get divorced and they certainly weren't gay.

Amalie sobbed. She wanted badly to wipe the tears from her face, but her hands were still tied behind her back so she wouldn't pull out the pipe. It tasted ghastly and the metal was hurting her tongue.

Will I ever get out of here alive? she thought sobbing. *And what about Camilla? Do I even want to live without her?*

Amalie tried again to see through the darkness of the room and see if Camilla was moving at all. The man had pulled out a small plug at the bottom of Camilla's box and let

Prologue

all the water out just before he left. But it was long after Camilla had stopped making the gurgling sounds and went quiet. The only sound worse than listening to her drown was the sound of silence. Was she alive? Was she dead? Amalie hadn't heard a sound since the man left them to go only god knows where. How long did he intend to keep them there? Why hadn't her father come for her yet? He always came. Couldn't he find her? Had he finally reached the limits to what his power could do?

She'll be back, Amalie. Don't worry. I'll make her come home. Those were the words he had used when Amalie had come into his office on that day her mother had left. She hadn't cried or in any way showed she was sad that her mother had left. She wanted to show him that. She wanted to make him proud. Yet he could tell by looking in her eyes. His words comforted her and assured her that he was right. He was going to get her back. If anyone could do that, it was her father. And he did. Amalie's mother did come back, right after Pedro had been attacked. She came back and stayed for a week. And that was when Amalie had heard them talk.

"If you want a puppet, you've got it," her mother said. "But I'll never be more to you than that. I won't talk to you, I won't make love to you. Not after what you did. Not after knowing that you ... that you had sex with that woman and ... No, never again. That poor kid. And what about Pedro? I'm only here because you forced me to, by threatening Pedro. Your people told him that I'd better come home, or they would destroy him. They showed him a picture of his daughter and set it on fire right in front of his face! Goddamit, Christopher. Being royalty you should learn to act like one. Better hope the Queen doesn't hear about all of this."

Amalie's mother had played the best card she had in her hand. The Queen. She was the only one who could reprimand the prince, she was the only one Amalie's father had ever been afraid of.

After that conversation Amalie's father had let her mother go for good, only having her promise that she would attend all official events and making sure no one in the kingdom ever knew that she didn't live at the castle anymore. Those were the terms and to those she agreed.

Amalie cried harder now while thinking about her mother and all the things she would like to say to her now, before ... well before it was too late. When suddenly she heard the sound of someone in the room with her. It was the sound of someone groaning.

42

"Good morning."

Allan opened his eyes slowly. Sebastian stood next to the bed with a tray in his hands. Among the cups and plates was a rose in a vase. Allan blinked, then sat up. Sebastian pulled the curtains apart and the sun was hurting Allan's eyes.

"What's going on?" he asked, his heart pounding.

"Breakfast in bed!" Sebastian chirped.

Allan stared at him. He felt a tick in his right eye and tried to suppress it, but couldn't stop it. "You made breakfast?" he asked shakily. "You didn't go down in the basement did you?"

"No, silly. You keep that door locked. Though I do from time to time wonder what you have down there, hidden from me." Sebastian smiled viciously. "I keep imagining it's a sex-swing and chains from the ceiling. But that's just my imagination. Or maybe wishful thinking, huh?" He laughed.

Sebastian stood naked in front of him and lifted the tray in the air so Allan could see everything. "I made you breakfast in bed. Thought it was about time I treated you for once.

You always make such wonderful meals for me. Let me give a little back. Plus I looked in your calendar and realized it's actually a very special day today." Sebastian put the tray in Allan's lap and then he leaned over and kissed his forehead. "Why didn't you tell me it was your birthday? I would have gotten you a present."

Allan thought of the presents he had gotten for himself. The three big ones in the basement. Then he lifted his head and looked at Sebastian while smiling widely. This was going to be the best birthday ever. He looked at the tray in his lap.

"I made pancakes, toasted bread, fruit and I even found your favorite food in the refrigerator," he said and pointed at a brown pâté on the plate.

Allan smiled again. "Foie gras," he said.

"*De canard*," Sebastian said in perfect French. "From duck. The best you can get. With mustard seeds and green onions in *jus de canard*. Enjoy."

Allan chuckled while picking up a knife and a piece of toast. Carefully he spread some of the foie gras on the bread. *The best you can get*, he repeated in his head and opened his mouth widely to take a bite. Not exactly the best, he thought as his teeth went through the smooth pâté and into the crunchy bread. He closed his eyes while chewing. It was good, admitted it was very, very good. Rich as it should be. But the one he was making was going to be better. Well it was going to be *royale*, he thought laughing to himself.

"So what do you want to do tonight?" Sebastian asked.

Allan froze. He opened his eyes. Sebastian was close to him, sitting on the edge of the bed, naked. Too close, Allan thought. All he could think of was how to get him out of the house today so he could get to work with all the fun he had planned for himself for this day.

"What do you mean?" Allan asked.

Sebastian shrugged. "We should celebrate, shouldn't we? Have a fabulous party, invite anyone who *is* somebody."

At first Allan didn't care much for the idea, but after a few seconds he changed his mind. It did sound kind of fun. Plus he would never be able to eat all the food he was going to prepare on his own. There was going to be enough for an entire army.

He smiled. "You know what? That sounds like a wonderful idea."

Sebastian clapped his hands eagerly.

"But on one condition," he said.

"And that is?"

"You let me cook the food."

Sebastian gesticulated widely. "Sounds perfect to me."

"And make sure you invite Prince Christopher and his beautiful wife. He is a close personal friend of yours, right?"

Sebastian looked at Allan. "He is. But you do know that their daughter has disappeared and that they think she has been kidnapped, right? I hardly think they'll have the time. Or would want to go to a party."

"Call him and tell him who the party is for. Tell him Allan 'the Greenlander' wants to see him. Tell him it's vital that he comes. He'll be here. He wouldn't dare not to."

"What do you mean? You make it sound almost like a threat?"

Allan burst into laughter. "Well I believe it is. He couldn't possibly afford to miss out on the social event of the year, now could he?"

43

"Caaaiila?" The sound coming out of Amalie's mouth wasn't anything like she intended it to be. It was muffled and didn't sound much like "Camilla." She tried to call out her name again. Maybe she would react to the sound of her voice even if it wasn't understandable. But nothing. No reaction, no movement from the box next to her.

Amalie narrowed her eyes while trying to see better. She could see the shape of her body, but she didn't seem to be moving. She called out again, sobbing from the pain in her throat.

She had almost given up hope, thinking she had imagined it the first time, when she heard the groaning again. She felt relief go through her body. Camilla was alive. She had to be. Amalie tried to move in her box. Her legs and arms were hurting. The smell in the box was becoming unbearable. Amalie's pants were wet and disgusting, since the man never let her go to the bathroom. The stench was horrible and made it even harder for Amalie to breathe. She gasped for air while looking at Camilla's box, wishing she had been honest with her from the beginning, from the first kiss.

Prologue

I love you, Camilla, she thought to herself. Those were the words she should have uttered a long time ago. *I love you so much it hurts.*

Then there was a groaning again, and what was that? Amalie tried to see clearer through the darkness, to better get a picture. Light came from under the door now and she heard voices from upstairs. Voices and loud music. The light made it easier for her to see. What was it? Could it be? Was it ... another box? Another box next to Camilla's?

Amalie fought hard to breathe. Had he caught another girl? Was it someone that she knew? Someone she loved? The agony was unbearable. Who was this bastard doing all this to her? And why? Why had he picked her of all people?

She tried again to speak, but with no luck. Still nothing but strange noises. Amalie whimpered again. The groaning must have come from the new person, she thought. Not Camilla. That meant Camilla could still be dead. Amalie didn't dare to finish the thought. There was no way she could live on without Camilla. But maybe that was the point of it all? To make her give up, to have her cave in? Was that the pleasure he enjoyed so much, this man, this beast, this monster?

Oh for the love of god, why can't he just end this now? Why did she have to suffer so badly before he killed her? Hadn't he had enough by now? Wasn't it sufficient to see her like this? Broken, defeated, destroyed? If he planned on killing all of them anyway, why not do it right away?

Someone was moving and moaning. Amalie guessed it was the newcomer since Camilla's body still didn't move. The waiting was the hard part, Amalie thought. Waiting for him to be back, waiting for him to torture her, anticipating the door opening at any moment and the lights turning on, knowing the anguish it would fill her with once she saw his face again. After that there was nothing but pain. No thoughts, no anxiety of what will come next. Eight times had he force-fed her the day before. Eight unbearable times had her stomach overflowed and she had almost choked on the disgusting mush that tasted like fat. It overwhelmed her with repulsion just thinking about it. The taste and his face. She loathed his face and especially his eyes. She tried hard to not think about him when he was gone, but every time she closed her eyes, he was there. He was looking at her with those strange eyes and a grin that scared her more than anything in this world. She was beginning to think he wasn't human. How could anyone be and do this to other people? And the way he moved, he was so incredibly fast. It was almost inhuman, she thought. It helped a little to think of him as some sort of extraterrestrial or paranormal being. If he wasn't human, then his actions somehow didn't seem quite so gruesome.

There was more groaning and now a mumbling that caused Amalie to raise her head even if it was almost impossible with the pipe holding her down. The reason for her reaction was simple. She recognized the sound of the mumbling voice.

It was Camilla's.

44

"The Prince is coming."

Sebastian looked at Allan with a wide smile. He was still holding the cell phone in his hand. Allan looked at the happy face next to him in the kitchen where they were trying to make a plan for the party. Then he smiled as well.

"You can thank me later," Sebastian said. "But apparently what you told me to say, worked. At first he declined, but as soon as I said those words ... well he growled slightly before he finally caved. I guess I had a little something to do with it as well."

"What do you mean?"

"Well, I have known the Prince a little more than 'just' personally. I have known him very, very privately for many years. Before I met you of course. He swings both ways, as we like to put it."

Allan stared at Sebastian. Not that he was surprised, he was more disgusted. With the both of them.

"Well you never asked me how I got to know him," Sebastian said. "He picked me up in a bar many years ago, when I was nothing but a young boy doing tricks for money. He does that from time to time, he does it secretively and disguised, at least he thinks so, but I recognized him right away and immediately thought I had struck gold. I was right. That's how I made my way up in this world. He helped me get to the right connections in the fashion industry. He even financed my education."

"Well you never told me that story," Allan said and stared at the shopping list on the kitchen table in front of him. He had to make it long to get Sebastian out of the house most of the day. He had to send him to different stores for specialties that were hard to find. That would buy him the time he needed to complete his work.

The music was playing loudly from the built-in speakers. Sebastian picked up Allan's keys from the table and walked towards the door leading to the basement. He went through the keys trying to find the right one.

"I'll get some bottles up from the basement."

Allan froze at the jangling sound of his keys and raised his head. He watched as Sebastian put one in the lock and his heart almost stopped as he realized it was the right one. Sebastian turned the key and the lock clicked.

"No!" Allan yelled.

Sebastian froze. He looked at him with surprise.

Allan moved fast. Like a whirlwind he was at the door and his hand on the handle. "No one goes into the basement," he said. "It's private. You know I like my privacy."

Sebastian stared into his eyes, then his face turned hurtful. He let go of the keys still in the lock and raised his hands. "Okay, then. If you insist on keeping me out of your life forever, then go ahead."

Allan sighed. A hurt Sebastian giving him a hard time wasn't exactly what he needed right now. He closed his eyes and locked the door again. *So close*, he thought. He had to be more careful. He really didn't want to have to hurt Sebastian. Even if he did annoy him immensely.

Allan put the keys in his pocket, then turned and looked at Sebastian. He turned his head away in a hurtful manner. Allan exhaled. Then he walked with fast steps towards Sebastian. He leaned over and tried to kiss him. Sebastian turned his head away again. Allan grabbed his hand.

"I'm sorry," he said. "I really am."

"What is down there that is so important that I'm not allowed to see it? Why do you keep me out of everything?"

Allan sighed. He knew he had to play his cards right. "I have a hard time committing to others, okay? I had a troubled childhood and I have trust issues."

"Is that why you never tell me anything about your past? 'Cause I know literally nothing about you, do you realize that? I've told you so much, but you never tell me anything."

"That is why I haven't let you in. It's still too hurtful. Give me time, okay?"

Sebastian sighed, then looked at Allan. "Okay, you silly buffoon," he said and mussed his hair.

Allan leaned over and kissed him as passionately as he knew how to. He placed the shopping list in Sebastian's hand. "Now would you help me get all this ready for tonight? We have a very busy day ahead of us."

Sebastian took the note and put neatly folded it in his wallet. "Okay. I guess we are in a kind of a hurry. Typical of us to be so spontaneous, huh? Doesn't it feel good? I love not conforming to the rules. You want to have a party? Throw a party!"

Allan smiled. "It sure does feel great."

Sebastian found his leather jacket and put it on. Then he kissed Allan again. As he walked past the door to the basement he stopped once again.

"So what do you hide down there anyway, bad boy?"

Allan shrugged. "Ah just the Princess that I'm about to kill soon and serve for the guests."

Sebastian burst into huge a laughter. "Ah you naughty boy. Always joking around, huh? Well if you won't tell me, then I'll just have to wait till you're ready, right?"

Allan nodded. "Right."

45

I woke when the light was turned on. I felt the worst I had in ages. My head was hurting badly and as I slowly regained consciousness I realized this wasn't just from bad wine, nor was it due to what I had done with Peter. My head was actually hurting.

Peter! I thought and opened my eyes. *What did we do?*

Then the strangest sight met me. It looked like a window in front of me. I reached out and touched it. Then I tried to sit up, but realized I couldn't. I touched the ceiling and then the sides again. My heart rate went skyrocketing as I felt the plastic surrounding me. What was this?

The panic rose in me as I felt the entire box surrounding me. Was I trapped somehow? What was this ... this thing? I grunted and tried to hit the plastic as hard as I could. Then I heard voices and turned my head. I gasped. Two boxes just like mine next to me. In them were two girls. I recognized both of them.

"Camilla?" I said and put my palm on the side. "Princess Amalie?"

"Rebekka Franck," Camilla replied. She looked terrible. She had become really thin and her eyes were so anxious.

"What's going on here?" I asked still feeling the sides, pressing them to see if I could get them to become loose or push them somehow. I stared at the princess. She seemed to be attached to something, a pipe of some sort. It went straight into her throat. She looked anxiously at me; she could make only muffled sounds.

Camilla was crying. "How?" she asked. "When did you get here?"

"I don't know," I said. "I remember being in the yard of my father's house when I saw someone ... a face behind the bush. I went to see who it could be. I stood face to face with him ... wait. I knew his face. He was looking at me. I had seen him before. I knew I had. In the parking lot at the festival, when I was looking for you, Camilla. When I thought I could still get to you before he did." I sighed and rubbed my head. "I was so close. I just didn't know it. He must have had you in the car. That's how he knew my name. He knew who I was when I spoke to him and asked if he had seen you. Oh, my god," I said. "I could have stopped him ... and then he was in the neighbor's yard looking at me. When I approached he hit me with something. The last thing I remember is the pain. Is he the one who put me inside of this thing? And you two? Have you been here all this time? What has he done to you? Amalie are you okay?"

Amalie looked at me, while tears rolled down her cheeks.

"Well at least you're both still alive," I said. "Now, how the hell do we get out of this thing?"

"You don't," Camilla said. "We've tried everything."

I began examining the sides. "If there's a way in, there's a way out."

"No," Camilla said. "There isn't. Plus he will be back in a

matter of seconds. He was just down here and turned on the light, then he went back upstairs. Don't upset him, don't make him angry. We never know what he'll do next."

Camilla was shivering as she spoke. My heart was pounding in my chest as I looked at Amalie and the things he had her attached to. What was it? Some kind of torture instrument? My heart dropped as I began imagining what he was up to, as I realized that soon it would be my turn. What kind of sick game did he have planned for me? Why had he even taken me? I had no relation to Camilla or Amalie. Was it merely to shut me up? To hide his tracks? Was he afraid I might have told the police about him, that I would be able to lead them to him? Well it was a little too late for that, since I already had talked to them. He couldn't prevent me from doing that. Could it be the article? It had to be. Maybe he wanted to prevent me from writing more about it, maybe he was afraid I knew too much and once I dove into the story properly, he would be exposed.

I heard steps approaching and a face appeared on top of the stairs. The man was smiling at us while grinning eerily. He wore a white apron and a chef's hat. In his hand he held a butcher's knife. Camilla and Amalie were both whimpering at the sight of him on the stairs. Camilla was shaking, her jaws trembling visibly. His voice cut through the room and evoked shrieks of fear from Amalie's throat.

"Good morning ladies."

46

"THERE HAS BEEN a slight change of plans," Allan said while opening a bottle of wine and pouring himself a glass.

Yes it was still morning, but it was after all his birthday and a day to celebrate. A good chef needed a glass of wine on his side. That was just the way it was. He drank from the glass with his eyes closed. He sloshed it in his mouth for a while to really taste it. Just like the French did it. Just like he had studied the prince do it through his childhood at the castle.

"Don't worry. The changes are only for the better," he continued once the wine was swallowed. "But it does mean that we are in a hurry now."

He picked up the cookbook on his table and began flipping the pages. "We're having a party tonight," he said while finding the right pages. "And I was thinking about treating our guests to some real delicacies."

Allan rose and went to open another can of food for the Princess. He poured a big portion into the funnel and started the pump. Then he watched as the food was slowly forced

Prologue

into Amalie's stomach. She was whimpering and gagging, but down it went. It was a little premature to take her now. He had been planning to wait at least a week. He would have to keep it on all day to make the most of it. It didn't matter if it killed her, since she was going to die today anyway. Then he would cut out her liver and prepare it for the guests. He was thinking about serving her gastric entrails as well, since it would be stuffed by the time she died.

"You just hang in there, my Princess," he said and tapped at the side of the box. "It'll be over soon."

Then he went to look in his cookbook and sip the wine while feeling excitement spread in his entire body. This was perfect. He couldn't have imagined a better plan. Forcing the prince to eat the foie gras made from the liver of his own daughter. It was the completion of his masterpiece that he had been looking for. This was perfect. Finally Allan was happy. Happier than ever. For the first time since the day they had told him they couldn't have him at the castle anymore, he was actually happy again. He closed his eyes and took in a deep breath of satisfaction, but was disturbed by the constant banging on the box from the journalist woman. She hadn't been quiet ever since he walked in, but he wasn't going to let her ruin his moment with her screaming.

"Let me out! Let us out of here!" She went on and on, but Allan had become immune to the plead of his victims. On the contrary it had become his fix, it had become the thing he enjoyed the most. He walked towards the box with the woman in it, holding his book in his hand and the wine in the other. The pump force feeding Princess Amalie was humming quietly across the room, a humming that to him sounded like the sweetest music.

The woman was grunting and kicking the ceiling of the box, while screaming at him to let her out, to let them go.

Allan put the book and the wine down and listened to every word she said and like a conductor he put up his fingers and pretended to be directing an orchestra. The other girl Camilla was now joining the choir with her crying while the sounds coming from Princess Amalie was like an extra addition to the music, like drums or a violin joining in every now and then. It was beautiful, he thought. So perfect.

"You crazy lunatic!" the woman cried. "What do you want from us? Why are we being kept in here?"

Allan stopped conducting and opened his eyes. He stared at the woman then picked up the cook book and leaned over her box to better show her the pictures.

"See these pictures?" he asked. "Now let me explain. We all enjoy a great meal, don't we? Do you enjoy a good meal, Rebekka Franck? Are you *une gourmante*?"

The woman stopped screaming and stared back at him with distrust. She didn't answer. It annoyed him. He wanted them to obey him, to fear him enough to not dare to not answer when spoken to. Where were people's manners these days anyway? Allan had been taught strictly as a child. You always answer when spoken to.

"I take that as a yes," he said trying to not let her silence get to him. "We all love a good steak or a roasted chicken and it's no secret that the life of an animal headed for the slaughterhouse isn't all smiles and happy songs, right? And sometimes you run across a dish that requires that the animal to not only be brutally killed, but also tortured in what most people would consider a horrifying and diabolical way. Unfortunately for the animals those kinds of dishes often turn out to be among the most tasteful. In many ways we can thereby conclude that sometimes cruelty can be delicious."

"I don't understand," the woman said. "Are you fighting for animal rights or something? Is that what this is all about?"

Prologue

Allan couldn't help laughing. "That was a good one," he said. "No I'm not fighting for animals." He paused for effect.

"I'm fighting for cruelty."

This time the woman's silence gave Allan great pleasure. He flipped a page in the book and showed it to her. "Look at this picture. Come on, just look at it. I think that's going to be you in a couple of hours. Yes, I think that's the one I'll pick for you."

The woman tried to hide it, but Allan saw the fear in her eyes. She was fighting to keep the panic down.

"Looks good, right? Ikizukuri. A delightful Japanese dish. It literally means 'prepared while still alive.' It works like this. When you go into a Japanese restaurant you choose the fish that you would like to eat, then the chef will grab it out of the tank and start slicing it up while it still flops around on the cutting board. The really hard part is that the chef - that would be me - has to cut the fish - that being you - without killing it. It is served with its heart exposed and beating, trying to gasp for air while it's staring at you with pain filled eyes while slowly dying right there on the plate."

Allan paused and waited for his audience to react. Just looking into the woman's eyes was enough of applause to him. "The good part is that it doesn't demand much preparation time. I will just have to cut you open after the guests have arrived. So I'll probably do you last."

Allan grinned and turned in one movement to face Camilla. She whimpered when his eyes met hers. "And you, my dear. You'll be prepared like an *Ortolan*. Do you know, what an Ortolan is? Well of course you don't. You're not familiar with French cuisine and its delightful cruelty, are you? No, you weren't born into richness like Princess Amalie and I. You are a worker. Your parents worked their way up to be like us. And look where that got them, huh? Never having any time for their precious daughter. Well I bet they regret that now, don't they? Don't you think so, huh, Camilla? Huh?"

Allan hit the box aggressively wanting her to answer him, to fear his wrath. Camilla whimpered and nodded.

Allan relaxed with a deep breath. It wasn't time to lose it now. He had to stay calm or he risked ruining everything. "Well an Ortolan is a tiny bird. It's only about six inches long and weighs four ounces. It's olive green and yellow with a touch of ruby. The recipe is easy, actually. First you capture the bird in the wild," Allan said and looked at Camilla with a smile. "Well I've done that. Next is to stick it in a tight cage so it can't move and then drown it in a snifter of Armagnac." Allan studied her face and went close to the box. "Well I guess we'll need something a little bigger than a snifter, won't we? I have an idea. Why don't we use the box? We've seen it work before, haven't we, Camilla? I bet this time you won't last as long." He laughed while thinking about the barrel of Armagnac he had ordered from France waiting for him in the garage. It was the best money could buy. Expensive as hell, yes, but completely worth it.

Camilla shivered with fear inside her box. Allan squatted next to it and looked in. *Oh the delight*, he thought and tilted his head while studying her anxiety inside the box, breathing it, sucking it out of her, letting it fill him with both strength and passion.

47

I HAVE TO admit I was scared to death. This guy was so creepy and clearly insane that it frightened me badly. I was hurt from the blow to my head and in constant pain. It made it difficult to think. It felt like a dream, a surreal dream. It was so unbelievable. The strange man was showing me pictures of food and telling me he was going to kill me, kill all of us, in order to prepare a meal for some party? If it wasn't for the sincerity in his eyes when he spoke, I would have thought he was joking, that he was just trying to scare us. But he meant every word. I had no doubt after he spoke to me and went to talk to Camilla with the book in his hand. I tried to wrap my mind around this entire situation. The box, the basement, the man, the girls and the strange machine he had the Princess hooked up to. I felt awful for her, she was in obvious pain, struggling for her life in that box. And there wasn't a damn thing I could do.

This can't be, I thought and tried once again to open the lid. There had to be some way out, some opening. How did we get in here in the first place? I wondered. I felt the sides and the corners. Yes, there seemed to be an opening, if I squeezed my body and crumpled up by my feet, I could reach the end wall and soon I realized that was where the opening was. The end could open up and that was the way he had gotten us all in there. Slid us through. But even if I kicked it hard it wouldn't open. It was screwed on with four screws on each side. Maybe I could somehow work them from the inside? I couldn't see the back of them, so the screws didn't go all the way through. Maybe if I tried with my nails, I thought, maybe I could scratch the plastic enough to reach them from the other side. I sighed resignedly. Even if I did manage to work my way through, it would take too long.

I watched as the man walked towards Princess Amalie. He squatted next to her and looked inside, like she was a fish in a tank. The sounds coming from her box weren't nice, they were the sounds of someone suffocating, choking. It was the sound of someone dying.

"Stop this!" I yelled and kicked the box so hard it hurt my leg. The ceiling didn't move an inch. The man got up and looked at me.

"You're killing the poor girl, can't you see? She's choking!" I shouted.

The man tilted his head and approached me. "Well don't you know that's the entire point?" He said with a gentle voice.

"Why?" I cried. "Why is it so important to kill her? To kill all of us?"

The man smiled. "Ah, we're doing that now," he said. "We're doing the talk. The talk where I tell you all why I am killing you? Well we might as well get it done with." The man walked back to Princess Amalie's box. "Well, my dear, sweet Princess. You don't know me, but believe me I know you. I know your family, because I used to be part of it. See, my name is Allan Witt, but just like you I didn't used to have a last name. I used to be living in the castle in Moegeltoender like you do now. Actually I lived there until you were born. Until you changed everything."

Allan Witt. The name didn't ring a bell to me. If he was a part of the royal family, I would certainly know. "You used to live with the Prince? How come?" I asked trying to keep the conversation going, trying to buy us some time.

"I was born at the castle," he answered. "I lived there the first ten years of my life."

"Were you parents working for the Prince?"

Allan lifted his head, then shook it. "No."

"Then how come you lived there? Are you related to the royal family?"

Allan exhaled in an eccentric manner. He was quite the drama-queen I realized. Maybe I would be able to use that to my advantage, I thought.

"You could say I'm related. Very much indeed."

"How come no one has ever heard of you? Why have I never heard your name before?" I asked.

"Because I'm what they like to call a 'well-kept secret.' One that isn't supposed to slip out to the public."

"Why is that?" I asked.

Allan looked at me, then snorted. "You're making me lose valuable time," he said. He began to walk towards the stairs. Then he turned and looked at me again.

"You haven't heard about me, because I wasn't supposed to exist."

48

ALLAN RAN UP the stairs with grace and strength. Then he closed the door and walked towards the garage. He opened it with the remote, and walked towards the corner where he had the barrel covered by a large tarpaulin, one he used to have on his boat. He pulled it aside, then found a garden hose and swung it over his shoulder. He whistled as he bent down and lifted up the barrel and held it in his strong arms. Then he carried it back into the house, when suddenly the front door opened.

"Sebastian?" Allan said and looked at the door to the basement to make sure it was closed. It was, but it wasn't locked. He put the barrel down on the tile floor.

"Wow, that's a lot of Armagnac," Sebastian said while carrying in the bags and putting them on the counter.

"You're back early," Allan said.

Sebastian gesticulated resignedly. "Well, I had to come home with the first load before I went to the next store. We don't want any of these expensive delicacies to go bad, do we?"

Allan sighed relieved. For a moment he had been afraid

that Sebastian was already done. "Of course not," he said. "Let me help you put the things away."

Allan grabbed the first bag and began unpacking. "Someone's dressed for cooking, huh?" Sebastian said and looked at Allan's outfit. Allan took off the chef's hat and put it on the table. Sebastian went close and sniffed his breath. "Oh beginning the day with a Chianti, are we?"

Allan chuckled. "It is after all my birthday."

Sebastian clapped his cheek. It enraged him but he kept his calm. It was all about getting Sebastian out of here again. "Just don't get too drunk like at the last party we went to," he said.

Allan fantasized about grabbing Sebastian's throat and killing him right there. The very thought made him shiver with joy. Maybe he should kill him next. To finally get rid of him. He didn't need him anymore. Police would never suspect Allan of anything. Not the nicely dressed, handsome, meek gentleman. No he was safe. And if they did, he would just kill them as well. He was untouchable.

"Well I'll be off again, then," Sebastian said and kissed him on the lips.

The kiss left Allan numb. Sebastian waved with a loose wrist and started walking towards the main entrance, when he stopped.

"What's that sound?" he asked.

Allan froze. "What sound? I don't hear anything." Allan laughed nervously as Sebastian backed up and stood in front of the door leading to the basement. "It's in your head, you're just stressed out. Now get going, we're in a hurry," he said.

Sebastian turned and looked at him. "You've been in the basement this whole time, haven't you?" he asked. "The door isn't properly closed."

Allan looked up with wide eyes. Sebastian was right. In

his hurry Allan hadn't closed the door entirely. *Damn it*, he thought.

"Are you drinking wine in the basement?" Sebastian asked. "What are you doing down there while drinking your wine?" He put his hand on the door, then looked at Allan. "Can I peek in?"

Allan sighed. Then he nodded. "Go ahead."

"Are you sure?" Sebastian said with cheer. "I don't want to push you to show me, it has to come when you're ready."

Allan exhaled. "I guess I'm ready now. Go ahead."

"Yay!" Sebastian cheered. Then he pushed the door open with the palm of his hand. He took a step inside, while Allan grabbed the kitchen knife, polished it in the towel, then approached him slowly from behind.

Allan hesitated, waiting for his cue while he watched Sebastian's body freeze. He stood completely still for seconds. The only thing moving were his hands that were shaking like leaves on a tree.

Allan waited until the scream came before he lifted the knife.

49

I HEARD NOISES from behind the door and looked in the direction of the stairs where the man had disappeared through the door. I had tried to talk to Camilla while he was gone, but she had been struck with such terror, she was unreachable. She was lying in her box, trembling while mumbling the same sentences over and over again. It appeared to be some song.

Seven devils all around you
Seven devils in my house
See they were there when I woke up this morning
I'll be dead before this day is done

She kept repeating the last sentence over and over again and hardly noticed that the door opened. I did however hear it and looked in that direction as a new face showed itself. Relief overwhelmed me when I realized it wasn't Allan Witt, but another man instead, a man I had seen before, a man I knew from all the magazines and the paper's high society-pages. Sebastian Devalnier was his artist-name, known in the fashion industry as one of the most successful designers in all of Europe. Widely known to be a party-animal and gay. He stopped at the end of the stairs and I realized by his look that he had no idea what he had walked right into. At first I thought he was with the royal family since he was known to be seen socially with them, and maybe just maybe he was sent by Princess Amalie's father to find us, but as soon as he began whimpering and screaming, I knew he had walked in by coincidence not expecting to find us or this basement of terror.

Our eyes locked for just a second as I saw the horror in his eyes and a second later spotted Allan Witt behind him with a big knife lifted in the air, ready to stab him in the back.

That was when I screamed. "Behind you! Look behind you!"

Sebastian reacted much faster than I had expected and turned to face Allan Witt and the knife. With a quick movement, he grabbed Allan Witt's wrist and managed to stop the attack or at least postpone it. Allan Witt groaned and tried to pull his arm free. Sebastian kicked him hard in the stomach forcing Allan to bend over and gasp for air. Then Sebastian wrenched Allan's hand and managed to get the knife out of it. The knife landed on the floor.

"You're forgetting who you're dealing with," Sebastian said panting. "I used to live on the street. I used to beat up guys like you. I'm used to watching my back and I know how to react fast."

Then he lifted his knee and placed a perfect knock-out under Allan's chin. Allan was thrown backwards and landed hard on the floor. I couldn't see him anymore, but I could hear it when his head hit the floor and then I heard the moaning.

Feeling the hope rise in me I stared with great anxiousness at the two men as Allan now got up and threw himself at Sebastian. The two of them were fighting massively, beating, punching each other while panting and gasping for air. It seemed Sebastian was the strongest, he kept ending on top of Allan to my relief. But Allan was the smarter one. As he was down on the floor and Sebastian was punching him, he reached over and grabbed the knife from the floor. I didn't realize it before it was too late. He raised it in the air and with a fast movement plunged it into Sebastian's chest.

"NOOOO!!" I screamed as Sebastian's body fell backwards down the stairs, bumping each step on the way. He landed on the stone floor with the knife still in his chest. He was still alive but bleeding heavily as he tried to grab the knife and pull it out. The sound of it leaving his flesh made me sick as he pulled it out and looked at it, then turned his head and looked at Allan as if to one last time ask him *Why*?

Allan panted and ran down the stairs. Then he leaned over him and as life slowly oozed out of Sebastian, Allan closed his eyes and took in a deep breath.

"NO!" I screamed again as hope fled me and left me helpless.

Allan touched Sebastian's face with a wide smile. Then he grabbed him by the neck and pulled him across the floor leaving a trail of blood. He tied Sebastian's hands together with a rope, and then hung him up on a meat-hook dangling from the ceiling. I watched with fear how the blood ran from his body onto the stone-floor and made a puddle underneath.

50

Allan left the basement, went into the kitchen and began washing his hands. He rubbed them with soap and found a sponge to scrub all the blood off. The water in the sink soon turned red. Allan wiped his fingers in a towel, then looked at the clock on the oven. It was almost noon. Sebastian probably had invited the guests to come around seven, so he still had a lot of time. With one more body to get rid of, he had a lot of work to do. But with Sebastian out of the way he was less likely to be interrupted again.

Allan walked towards the barrel when suddenly his iPad on the table lit up. Allan looked at it. There was a new message in the chat. It was probably just from Cogliantry, Allan thought. He probably wanted to see more pictures. The man was always hungry for more. Allan didn't have time for this. But he still checked.

It wasn't Cogliantry this time, he was surprised to discover. It was *him*. The master himself. The man who called himself Thomas De Quincey. Allan read what it said a couple of times. It wasn't a pleasant message. He wasn't writing Allan to congratulate him on his great achievements.

No he was angry. Allan could tell by the tone of his message. It simply said:

Where is my package?

Allan sat down on the chaise lounge with the iPad on his lap. He had to answer this right away. This wasn't just anybody who was writing him these words. He thought about what to write before he answered:

In my basement. I'm preparing it for you.

A minute went by before the answer came. Allan tapped nervously with his fingers on his thighs.

You have two things now that belong to me. I want them, tonight.

Allan took in a deep breath to calm his growing anger. He had other plans for those packages. He was sick and tired of this man telling him what to do and when to do it. This was his mission, his masterpiece and no one was going to destroy it.

I'll bring them both to you tomorrow. Wrapped and everything.

A few minutes went by without an answer. As he waited Allan feared he would incur the Master's wrath. No one messed with Thomas De Quincey. He was after all the one who had started it all, he was the one who had brought them all together. But Allan didn't answer to anyone. Those were his killings, Thomas De Quincey could get the leftovers. *Yes*, Allan thought to himself. *Leftovers had to be good enough.* If he wanted to kill them so badly himself then he should have captured them. Why didn't he just do it himself? Allan had been the one offering one of the packages to him. As a gift, a contribution if you like. Why was he now acting like he was entitled to it? What if Allan had changed his mind? What if Allan didn't care about all of that anymore and just wanted out? Wanted to go back to kill for his own sake? For his own pleasure and not to satisfy the Master? Allan could be his own Master. He was after all the best at what they did. He had killed many more than any of them. Why should he answer to any of them? They should be the ones worshipping him. No, he definitely wanted out. He wanted to be on his own.

Allan had already planned it all. After this, he would be gone. He would be out of here and the Master wouldn't know where to look for him. He had a private jet ready in the airport that was ready to take him to Monaco where he had secretly bought a house. Allan had made a lot of money the last years mostly buying stocks on insider knowledge and he would be able to live of it for the rest of his life. Plus the prince still paid him a huge amount every year to keep quiet about his existence. He was unstoppable and even Thomas De Quincey was about to discover that. Hell, if he came to punish him Allan would just have to kill him as well.

I want them tonight, Thomas de Quincey wrote. *Alive.*

I'll deliver them tomorrow. Dead. Take it or leave it.

Then I'll just have to come and get them myself, Thomas De Quincey wrote.

Allan froze when he saw that the Master had left the chat room. There was no way back now, he thought. The Master was coming, so he'd better be prepared.

51

I was still staring at the lifeless body of Sebastian Devalnier hanging from the ceiling of the basement. I couldn't take my eyes off it; I couldn't get the pictures out of my head of how cold-bloodedly Allan Witt had murdered this man without so much as blinking. It actually seemed like he enjoyed stabbing the knife into his chest and took pleasure in watching him die. It scared me like nothing had ever frightened me before. It seemed he took delight in killing.

I knew I had to think fast. This was a man who wouldn't think twice before slaughtering all of us. He hadn't been joking or just trying to scare us by showing us those pictures and letting us know what he was intending to do with us. If I didn't do something soon, we were all going to end up like Sebastian Devalnier. But what? How?

For some strange reason I suddenly felt an urge to have a cigarette. I almost craved it. But I always did in stressful situations, I thought. This just wasn't the time to be thinking about that. That was when it hit me. Maybe it was the right time? I recalled having smoked with Peter in my father's backyard before we ... *oh my god, before we did the unforgivable.*

It was immediately after that I spotted the man behind the hedge. Did I still have my pack of cigarettes in the pocket of my sweater? I put my hand in and felt it. Yes. It was still there. I pulled the pack out and to my great joy I saw that the lighter was still in it. I pulled it out and lit it. Yep, it worked. I almost cried as I held it tight in my clenched fist. In some way this was going to help me.

I jumped as I heard steps on the stairs and the lighter went back in my pocket while I wondered how come Allan Witt hadn't found the package in my pocket? He was too dumb to not have searched me for my phone or a pocketknife. Could it be that he just hadn't found it? The pocket was kind of deep, the package almost empty and I hadn't thought about it myself or felt it was there until now. Had he just made a slip-up? Had he made a mistake?

I watched Allan Witt as he walked slowly down the stairs carrying a big barrel in his arms and a hose over his shoulders while imagining what I could do with the lighter. There weren't many options that didn't include hurting myself somehow.

Allan Witt put the barrel down next to Camilla's box, then unscrewed the lid to the tube leading into her. I watched as she crumbled and shockingly stared at the hose coming down in her box. Her body was trembling while she pleaded for him to not do this.

"Please, Mr. Please, don't do this. Not again. I beg you."

Allan Witt put the hose in the tube, then a funnel at the end of the hose. He lifted the barrel on his shoulders and began pouring. It was heavy, too heavy and suddenly it slipped from his hands and it spilled on the floor and on his apron and pants. As the barrel hit the stone floor it spurted out on the floor almost to where I was. Allan cursed, then picked the barrel up again and continued pouring. The brown liquid ran across the floor towards the dip in the floor next to my box where it blended with the blood from Sebastian's dead body.

My heart stopped as I watched Camilla panic when the brown liquid hit her from the hose. She lifted her hand and tried to stop it from flowing, tried to block the hole, but soon it spurted out anyway and hit her in the face. "Stop, please, stop," she hollered.

I started banging on the sides of my box in anger and frustration. "Stop it!" I yelled. "Why are you doing this to her?"

But Allan Witt kept his calm and never took any notice of me screaming at him or Camilla's crying and begging him to stop. It didn't take him very long to fill up most of the box with the Armagnac. Its sharp smell soon permeated the basement. Camilla was lifting her head trying to avoid getting it in her face, spitting, gurgling and crying at the same time. I felt so helpless, so frustrated for not being able to do anything. I growled and groaned and kicked the box in anger and desperation, but no matter what I did, I couldn't prevent Camilla's box from being filled. Soon she had only her face barely above the surface. More was pouring down through the hose, hitting her directly in her face, making it hard for her to breathe, when suddenly it stopped. Camilla gasped for air. She was holding her head above the surface of the liquid by lifting her torso a few inches with her arms. If she let go, her face would be covered.

I heard Allan curse and swear. "What the hell ...?" He was staring inside the box, then examining the funnel. Then he was cursing again. He tried to look through the hole in the barrel, then he cursed once again right before he stormed up the stairs.

He had run out of Armagnac.

52

Allan ran around in the kitchen while messing up his hair with his hands, opening cabinets, going through his collection of liqueurs.

"Just one more bottle," he mumbled frantically going through all of them, reading the labels, then putting them back. He found all kinds of very expensive alcohol, but no Armagnac. He speculated like crazy if it was possible to use something else. He pulled out a six-year old Calvados Pays D'Auge. Could this be used? *No*, he thought. *No, no, no*. The recipe explicitly said Armagnac. There was a difference. You couldn't just deviate from the recipe, could you? No, it had to be right. The bird was supposed to drown in the Armagnac so that its lungs and innards were filled with the tasty liquid. That was the way it was supposed to be, you couldn't just make up your own recipe. That wouldn't work. It had to be done right. It just had to. It had to.

Allan was circling himself in the kitchen, mumbling and rubbing his fingers against each other. His eye had an annoying tic that wouldn't go away. What now? he thought. What do I do? He looked at the watch. Still three hours left till the guests arrived. He still had time, didn't he? Could he drive to the store? Was there enough time to make it there and back and then prepare the rest? He shook his head. No, it was too late. The rest of the preparations took time. What else did he have to do? Oh yes, the woman. She needed to be cut open while still alive. Like the fish, like the Japanese fish, yes. He would serve that as an appetizer? But what about Sebastian? What was he going to do with him? Allan's fingers were hurting from tapping against each other while he was speculating. It was like he couldn't stop his mind, like his thoughts wouldn't stay calm.

Don't lose it now. Don't lose it.

The voices in his head were screaming at him, making it even harder to hear his own thoughts. Plus he had begun to hear a weird drumming sound inside his head that he couldn't escape. It sounded like a pulse, a heartbeat. He tried to shake his head, to get rid of it, he tried to tap the side of his forehead nervously to get it to stop. But nothing helped.

I'm not losing it. I'm keeping calm. I'm not going insane.

Then he looked at the clock again. Half an hour had gone by like this? How could it? He walked to the clock and looked at it. It shifted again. The numbers were shifting all the time! It was as if the minutes were running from him. He held his head between his hands while staring at it closely. Was this some cruel joke? Then he tapped at the glass. Was the clock broken? He turned and looked at another clock above the door. It said the same time. It wasn't the clock.

It was him. He was losing valuable time by speculating like this. This wasn't a time to be thinking, this was a time for action. He picked up the phone and called the store. He offered them a thousand dollars if they delivered three bottles of their finest Armagnac within an hour. He gave his address, then hung up without saying goodbye to the woman in the other end. He turned around a few times, trying to force the kitchen to stand still. Trying to make his mind stop spinning.

Everything is okay now. Disaster averted. The Armagnac will be here soon, and then you can move on.

Allan took in a deep breath to calm himself down. He held on to the kitchen table while forcing himself to breathe steadily. It was going to be alright. Everything was going to be fine. He couldn't let these little things get to him. With a project as big as this, some things were bound to go wrong; he couldn't expect everything to be perfect.

But that's what you do, isn't it? You demand perfection. It has to be impeccable or it isn't done right.

Allan clenched his fist and hit the kitchen table so hard he was certain he heard the bone crush inside of it. But he didn't mind. Just like he enjoyed the pain of others he also took pleasure in his own pain. He stared at the hand that was still clenched. The pain spread from his fist to the arm and into his entire body. He closed his eyes and enjoyed the waves of pleasure and pain going through him. When it was gone he opened his eyes, reached over and picked up his butcher's knife. He walked towards the door, then put his hand on the handle. Behind it he heard the girls crying. He paused and enjoyed the sound. Just before he turned the handle, he quoted another of his favorite horror movies, *The Fly*:

"Be afraid... Be very afraid."

53

I WAS FUMBLING with the lighter while Allan was gone. I tried to melt the plastic but ended up burning my fingers instead after a few minutes. It hadn't even left a burn mark on the plastic. I sighed and took a break. Allan Witt had been gone for a long time now and I wondered what he was up to. I talked to Camilla all the time, encouraging her to hold on, to keep her head up. But she was getting tired now. They were shaking.

"I can't hold on," she said. "I can't hold it anymore."

"Yes you can," I yelled back. "I'm getting us out of here. Hold on as long as you can."

"But I can't. My arms are hurting so badly. They are shaking now. It smells so bad in here. I can hardly breathe."

"You have to. Keep holding on just for a little longer now," I said while trying to melt the plastic with my lighter once again.

"It's armored," Camilla said. "The plastic is armored. It can sustain anything, bullets, fire everything. He told us."

"Crap." I sighed deeply and stared hopeless at the box,

feeling its edges, its sides. Everything has a weak spot, I kept thinking. Everything and everybody.

"My arms," Camilla cried. "They're caving in. My elbows are hurting."

"Your arms need to move to be able to pump the blood around in your body. You need to rest them, just for a little while. Can you dive under for just a few seconds, then come back up?"

"That's what I did when he filled the box with water, but this smells so bad. It smells so bad, Rebekka," she wept.

"I won't let you die in there," I said. "Neither you, nor Amalie. I will get you out of there. I promise. But for now you have to focus on staying alive. You have to rest your arms and then come back up. Move your arms while you're under, so the blood can circulate, and then come back up. It'll make you be able to sustain it longer. Trust me, okay?"

"O...okay," she stuttered. Camilla closed her eyes and held her nose as she dove under the fluid. A few seconds later she came back up, crying heavily, coughing, spitting.

"Are you okay?" I asked.

"I got some in my mouth, but I spat it out. It tasted so horrible!"

"I know. Just hold on."

The door opened and I hid the lighter in my hand with a gasp. In stepped Allan with a big butcher's knife in his hand. His hair was slightly messed up and his eye flickering with constant tics. He was smiling widely but seemed less controlled than earlier. If he was losing it, it could be both an advantage since he might be less careful, but it could also have the opposite effect since the crazier, the more dangerous he would be.

Camilla was gasping but holding on in the box next to me, while I had no idea how Princess Amalie was doing and it scared me that I hadn't heard a sound from her in a long time. All I heard was the sound of the pump constantly pushing more of that yellow mush inside of her. I had no idea how long a person could sustain that before the stomach would explode.

Allan Witt walked to Amalie's box, peeked in with a satisfied smile, then continued to Camilla. He looked at her while she struggled to keep her head above the surface.

"You'll give in soon," he said. "But I've ordered more just in case. It should be here soon."

Then he turned and looked at me. I gasped as our eyes met. He bent over my box and stared at me from above. Then he tapped it with his nail like I was an animal and he wanted to get my attention.

"You ready?" he asked.

I stared at the butcher's knife he was holding above his shoulder. Then I gulped. I knew what his intention was. "Please," I said. "Can't we find another way? Maybe I can help you with something. I know a lot of people, maybe I could get you out of the country," I lied. "There is still time. You could stop now. Do yourself a favor and stop before it's too late."

Allan Witt laughed loudly. "You don't know half the people that I know. I can get out whenever I want to. Don't you worry your pretty little head with that."

Allan Witt found a screwdriver and began unscrewing some of the screws in the box. "Now I could have sedated you with chloroform first," he said. "But that would be cheating, don't you think? No one sedates the fish when it's cut open." He smiled and looked into my eyes. "I want you to feel the pain."

I swallowed hard as the bottom of my box was carefully pulled off. I was completely still with my hand clenched on the lighter. Allan Witt removed the end wall and reached in to grab my legs. I kicked and screamed as he pulled me out. One kick hit him in the face, another in the chest. But still he managed to tie duct-tape around them and tie them tight together so I couldn't move them.

I grunted and tossed my body as he pulled the rest of me out and tried to catch my arms to tie them as well. I moved them constantly, throwing punches with my fists clenched, when he managed to grab my right wrist and restrain it on my back. I screamed in pain as he pulled it hard and I had to bend forward. I stared directly into the puddle of blood next to me. Allan Witt's expensive Italian leather shoes were in the middle of it. In the middle of the puddle of blood and Armagnac. I looked at my clenched fist as I felt Allan Witt's fingers on me, trying to turn me around and get my other hand. I lifted my head and looked him straight in the eyes, then I lit the lighter and set the small puddle on fire. I covered my face and threw myself backwards. In a matter of seconds the alcoholic drink exploded and caught Allan Witt's pants soaked in Armagnac.

54

"What the hell ...?"

Allan felt the fire lick his leg and burn the hair and skin on his shin. He jumped with a scream as the fire quickly moved to his apron and soon flames were close to his face. He sprang for the hose in the corner that he normally used to hose the blood off the floor. While screaming and patting the fire down from his clothes, he managed to grab the hose, and turned on the water. He yelled as he hosed it all down and managed to douse the flames.

Panting and gasping for breath he looked back. The woman was gone. The duct tape that had been around her legs was on the floor. The butcher's knife was gone.

Allan threw the hose on the ground. Soaking wet and with his shoes making sloshing sounds as he walked he hurried towards the stairs. With a grunt he stormed up to the door and opened it with a huge bang as it hit the wall behind it. He scanned the hallway and the open kitchen. He looked at the main entrance. No, it was locked and could only be opened by key. She couldn't have gotten out that way. Then he looked at the sliding doors leading outside. They were locked by key too. He wasn't that stupid. He knew that if he made a mistake and one of them came loose he would need to keep them inside the house. It was hermetically sealed. No one came in and no one got out. He heard a sound from the living room and reacted to it. With the speed of light he entered it and saw her. She hadn't gotten far. She was pulling all the doors and all the windows trying to open them. Frantically she was pulling, shaking the handles, banging on the glass as she saw him walk closer. Then she tried hitting it with the butcher's knife. She managed to crack the glass, before Allan grabbed it out of her hand.

Poor little thing, he thought. Just filled with hope and now it was all gone again. Sometimes life was just brutal that way, wasn't it?

"You can't get out," he said. "I have locks on all windows and doors. They can only be opened with a key." He put his hand in the pocket and pulled out his chain with his many keys. He dangled them in front of her, then pulled them away as she tried to grab them out of his hand. He put them back in his pocket.

"Nice trick with the fire by the way. I was completely startled. Very nice. But now we're done playing. You better come with me," he said and grabbed her arm.

She refused to move, so Allan lifted the knife. "Do you want me to cut you up in here, in the living room? I do prefer the basement since it tends to get so messy, don't you agree?"

He never did hear her answer before they were interrupted by the doorbell. Startled by the sound he turned his head. In a matter of a second the woman managed to plant a knee in his privates then put her fist in his face causing him to let go of her arm. For a few seconds Allan saw nothing but stars and the ceiling, he barely noticed that the woman stormed towards the main entrance. She was already at the door when he got back on his legs. She was fumbling with the lock trying to get the key in. Wow she was fast, Allan thought as he realized she had stolen the keys from his pocket. *But not fast enough.* Allan stormed towards her as she tried another key, then another, but he knew it would take her too long to find the right one. Only he knew his system, which color went to what door. No one, not even Sebastian could figure that out. She heard him and turned her head. Desperately she tried another key, fumbled with it, then realized that didn't fit either. Then she started banging on the door, trying to alert the person standing on the other side pushing the doorbell.

"HELP! I'm being held as a prisoner. Please help me!"

Now Allan was in a hurry to shut her up. He charged towards her, but as soon as he was almost there, she turned and ran towards the stairwell leading upstairs. Then she was gone. Allan cursed and snorted. Why did she have to make everything so damn difficult for him? Normally he enjoyed it when his victims were feisty, but today he didn't have the time for it. The doorbell sounded again and Allan slicked his hair back and checked that he looked decent. He pulled off the apron that had been burnt at the bottom. Then he put on his most charming smile, picked up the keys that the woman had dropped on the floor and put the right key in the lock.

"Yes?" he said to the teenage boy standing outside. He was holding a bag in his hand.

"Delivery?" he said. "From Hansen's Delicacies. You ordered three bottles of Armagnac."

Allan chuckled and smiled. "That's correct," he said. "I promised you a thousand dollars. He grabbed his wallet and pulled out a stack of bills. "Here take two."

The boy's eyes lit up. "Wow, thank you so much!" He was almost about to leave when he stopped. "Say. I thought I heard someone bang at the door just before and yell that they were being held captive or something?"

Allan laughed his aristocratic laughter. "That was just my daughter. She likes to play games, you know. Kids are like that sometimes. You know what it is like, don't you. You probably have a sister or a little brother, am I right?" Allan said while studying the kid. He took a step towards him, observing if there was any doubt in his face. If Allan detected any he would have to kill him. He held the bottle tight in his hand. He really didn't want to waste this last bottle of Armagnac on the young boy's pimply face. But he would if he had to.

"I guess," the kid said. Then he stared at the money in his hand and shrugged like he didn't care. "Thanks for the tip anyway," he said and waved goodbye.

"That-a-boy," Allan said and closed the door slowly while making sure the kid didn't come back. He went to the kitchen and put the bottles on the kitchen table. He debated within himself for a moment on what to do next. Should he go down to the basement and pour in the last Armagnac to finish his project with the girl or should he go upstairs and kill the woman right away before she found a way to get out or to alert more people? He wasn't sure what was most important right now. Time was running out, the guests would be here soon and he still hadn't even made an appetizer. On the other hand he couldn't leave the woman up there for long. She was smart and might find a way to get out or to expose him.

With the butcher's knife in his hands he started walking up the stairs quoting Jack Torrance in *The Shining*:

"*I'm not gonna hurt ya. I'm just going to bash your brains in. Gonna bash 'em right the fuck in! ha ha ha.*"

55

I ran up the stairs and through a hallway. It ended with two doors on each side, I ran into one, an office. It had books on many shelves from floor to ceiling and nice leather chairs and a desk with a big iMac in the middle of it. Desperately I searched the room for anything I could use to protect myself with. I opened the drawers hoping to find a knife or better yet, a gun. I went through the shelves and pulled down books, I went to the window and tried to pull it open, but that too was locked by key. I panted as I stormed around turning everything upside down, knocking over stacks of papers, tumbling to the floor.

Then I heard steps on the stairs and froze. I found a letter opener, and with my hands shaking picked it up and held it in front of me, ready to greet him if he entered, *when* he entered.

I held my breath as the steps came closer and I heard his voice close to the door. "Here kitty kitty," he said. "Here kitty kitty."

I looked at the letter opener in my hand. It was shaking heavily. My heart was pounding in my chest. I focused on keeping myself calm. My plan was to stab him with the knife as soon as he opened the door. A surprise attack. The voice came closer and now there was movement behind the door. Someone touched the handle and moved it. I went closer to the door holding the knife out in front of me. My palms were moist from sweating, my jaws trembling.

I stood with my back up against the wall next to the door, the knife ready in front of me as the door slowly opened, then was pushed up with a huge bang.

"Boo!" he said and jumped in front of me.

I lifted my hand with the knife and was about to stab him, when he grabbed my arm and held it back. It hurt so bad I dropped the knife. Then he slapped me across the face and I fell to the floor. "That's for kicking me," he said. "Now let's get to work."

He grabbed my legs and started pulling me, when suddenly the doorbell sounded again. Allan Witt let go of both of my legs. Then he sighed loudly. "Not again!" He looked at me, then he leaned over and slammed my head hard with the handle of the butcher's knife.

When I woke up I was alone. I opened my eyes and realized I was still in the office. I got up and tried the door. It was locked. The bastard had locked me inside the office while he answered the door. I heard loud music coming from downstairs and I heard ... could it be? I heard voices. Lots of voices! There were people in the house. People that might be able to help me, help us. I started banging hard on the door while screaming and yelling. Then I tried running into it with my shoulder like they did in the movies. But it didn't work. No one seemed to hear my pleas and cries for help; it was all drowned out by the loud music and many people talking at once. I sighed and slid down with my back against the door. I hid my face in my hands and cried thinking about Julie, Peter and Sune, thinking about Camilla and Amalie who probably were both dead by now. Was I ever going to see the people I loved again? Was I ever going to get out of here? I was beginning to lose hope. I looked around in the office. Then my eyes locked on the computer. I hurried up and ran to it. I could certainly use the computer for something!

I touched the space-bar and the screen lit up. Allan Witt hadn't shut it off properly when he left it. I touched the mouse and began looking at all the pages that were open. I opened the Internet, then logged on to my Hotmail account. I wrote an e-mail then sent it to Sune, Peter and the police in Karrebaeksminde where I assumed I still was. I told them where I was and where I was being held captive. I told them the Princess was here too, and her friend, but I didn't know if they were still alive. I pressed 'send' but the computer kept waiting, trying to send it. Then a note came up on the screen. Hotmail apologizing but *an error occurred*.

"No!" I said moving the mouse frantically. "Not now. Please work! Please send the mail."

But the webpage wouldn't reload. It waited and remained white for a long time. I sighed and bowed my head.

I decided to wait. Maybe there was something else I could do. I looked through his computer, looked at everything that seemed interesting. Then I found something. A folder on the desktop. It contained a lot of files, old articles, some of them I had written, some were financial statements and records for Allan and some of them were for Christopher III, Prince of Denmark.

56

They had been early. The guests had been early. Sebastian had invited them to come early, they told him. Come at five o'clock he had said. We'll surprise Allan.

Oh he was surprised alright when he opened the door and hundreds of people had screamed "Surprise!"

No doubt he was surprised. Especially since he wasn't ready with any of the food yet. Now he was walking around, mingling, talking to everybody, thanking them for coming while serving them the champagne Sebastian had bought before he died. Allan was shaking as he handed the glasses out.

"Now where is Sebastian anyway?" A woman with a big hat chirped. Allan wanted to pull the hat over her face and strangle her with it. He restrained himself and smiled charmingly.

"Just went out to get something. I'm sure he'll be here any moment," Allan answered. "You know how he is. Everything has to be perfect."

"That is true," the woman said and grabbed a glass.

Allan greeted another guest and handed him a glass,

Prologue

while looking towards the stairs. He had knocked the woman down and locked her in, but he was afraid she might wake up soon. He hadn't had the time to go to the basement either, but as soon as the guests were settled down a little he should be able to run off without them noticing anything.

"Did you see Sebastian's new collection at the show in Milan?" A man Allan knew as a very famous columnist for one of the big national newspapers said to him.

Allan shook his head.

"Oh you missed out. It was fabulous. A true masterpiece. I don't believe the world has ever seen as great a mind as his. He will do great things, I tell you. I predict that he will revolutionize the world of fashion." The people surrounding the man speaking all gasped in awe. "And you know I'm never wrong about these things."

"Well you might be about this," Allan mumbled and tried to wiggle his way out of the crowd. Everybody seemed to have a glass in their hand now. He had shown his face plenty to be able to disappear without being missed. It was after all Sebastian they all came here to see. Allan knew that perfectly well. To them Allan was only "the guy dating Sebastian." They hadn't come to celebrate his birthday, they had come to not miss out on being at one of Sebastian's great parties. Everyone knew you didn't miss out on those. They were always the social event of the year. The kind mentioned afterwards in the magazines with paparazzi pictures taken from the entrance and outside the house. Even if his parties often were very spontaneous, Sebastian always managed to gather a huge crowd because nobody wanted to miss out. You just had to be there.

Now why was it again that Allan had agreed to do this? Oh, yes, he thought as he turned around and looked into the face of no other than Prince Christopher III. He cleared his throat.

Allan smiled. "Welcome your Highness," he said and bowed slightly. The two bodyguards stepped backwards on the Prince's command.

Then the Prince signaled for Allan to come closer. He spoke to him with a low voice. "Cut the crap, Allan. You told me to be here, now I'm here. In case you don't know it, I'm having a family crisis at home; my daughter is missing, so if you don't mind please tell me right away what I am doing here?"

Allan smiled and kissed the Prince's cheek. Then he whispered. "Well you're here to party. Is there anything wrong with a man to want to see his own father?"

The Prince's face turned to stone. "I don't know what you're talking about. I'm not here to be ridiculed."

"Oh, but you have to dear father. Or I'll tell the entire party who my real father is."

"You must be deranged. I'm not your father. Yes I took you in when your mother died and took care of you till you were old enough to go to boarding school. Yes I have taken care of you ever since, but I am not your father. I don't know where you get these ideas from."

The Prince signaled his bodyguards that he wanted to leave and turned away.

"I got them from your wife," Allan said.

The Prince froze. Then he turned and walked back to Allan. The bodyguards stayed behind on the Prince's signal.

"What?" the Prince said.

Allan smiled. "Yes, Father. Countess Alexis told me. She told me that you are my father and that I am a rightful heir to the throne. You can't deny me my birthright. For all those years I should have been a part of the royal family. I should have been treated like a royalty instead of getting beat up and raped at a boarding school and never seeing my father. I should have received *apanage*, the funds, lifelong pay if you like - from the Danish state given to members of the royal families. I am entitled to be addressed properly, like royalty. I want all the perks, all the advantages that has been taken from me, that are rightfully mine. I want what is mine. I am royalty!"

The last part Allan said a little too loud. People surrounding them were looking in their direction. Allan smiled charmingly then lifted his glass to greet them. They nodded and greeted him back, then turned their heads. The Prince stared at Allan with wide eyes. He was shaking with fury.

"This is not the time nor the place for this," he growled.

"Well I think it is," Allan said calmly. "It's my birthday and I want my father to be here. So you better stay if you don't want all these people to know about your illegitimate son."

"I find it hard to believe that Alexis really told you all this," the Prince growled.

"Well she did. She contacted me right after she had left you. Guess she was in the mood for some revenge after you sent her lover-boy to the hospital."

The Prince growled again. Allan smiled perkily. "So you'll stay for dinner then?"

The Prince never answered. He turned his back to Allan and emptied his glass of champagne.

Allan shrugged. "I'll take that as a yes."

57

I WENT THROUGH all of Allan Witt's files on his computer and little by little all the pieces were put together for me to understand. An e-mail from the Countess Alexis, Princess Amalie's mother stated that Allan was the illegitimate child of Prince Christopher. In the mail she regretted her behavior back when he was a child and for the way they had sent him off to a boarding school and never even let him come back for weekends or holidays.

It was all my fault, she wrote. *I should have protected you. I should have demanded that you stay even if we had the baby in the house, but I didn't. When the Prince suggested that we send you away, I agreed. A decision I regret today. It wasn't fair to you. But the fact was that I was afraid of you. How could anyone be afraid of a 10-year-old child you might ask? Well you scared me. Ever since Amalie was born you had that look in your eyes like something had been taken from you, like your childhood had been deprived by the baby. I guess you knew she would somehow push you out of our lives which she finally did. One day I came into the nursery and found you standing next to the crib staring at the princess. At first I thought you were staring at her because you liked her, but then I looked at your hand and saw your clenched fist. It was bleeding. You had clenched it so hard your nails had penetrated the palm and caused it to bleed. You wouldn't stop staring at Amalie even after I called you to me. After that day I was afraid you might hurt the baby somehow. I kept you away from her and never left you two alone. I didn't know the Prince was your father. I didn't learn that awful truth until recently. I found your father's financial statements, his accounts and realized he was still paying you a huge amount of money even though you were old enough to take care of yourself. It had always been our agreement that we would pay for your education and for you to live until your eighteenth birthday, then it was supposed to stop. We would take care of you as long as you were still a child. So I confronted him, asking him why he had continued to pay for you every year even after that, and he finally confessed. He told me he was your father and that he had an obligation to take care of you. I realize now that he was paying to be discharged. He was paying you to not have to face the consequences of his actions in life. And I can't let him do that. I can't let him keep on lying to you and to the world. You are a rightful heir, you are part of the royal family and no one can take that away from you. You might never get the royal family to admit it publicly, but you are royal.*

With the best wishes for you in your future, Countess Alexis of Merchenburg.

I sat back in the chair while letting this new information settle in my head. It made sense, I guess, at least it explained Allan Witt's anger towards the Princess and her family. But it still left many unanswered questions.

A sound coming from the computer startled me. A message appeared in the side. I clicked on it and suddenly something appeared on the screen.

Any new pictures? I'm dying here. Let me in on what you're doing, a man named Cogliantry wrote. Cogliantry? I had heard that name somewhere before. Wasn't he a famous artist? Probably just a pseudonym I thought. He was talking about pictures. Maybe it was some sort of chat room for art lovers? Something about the chat made me continue reading. I went back to old messages, scrolled way back and skimmed what they had talked about. Then I froze completely feeling the blood leave my head. I started shivering as I scrolled through the messages. They were all so gross and despicable. They talked about women's private parts, about having vile sex with them, about forcing them, hearing them scream for mercy. All these messages that didn't go any further back than just a few days were all about killing people. Killing and torturing people. I gasped, my fingers trembling and shaking on the mouse while the realization found its way to my brain even if I tried to block it simply because it was too horrifying to even think it.

Allan wasn't alone. There were more like him out there. Many more, it seemed. And they were sharing their achievements on this chat room, sharing pictures and experiences, dreams and fantasies.

Afraid of what I would find next I scrolled back in Allan's messages and found one a few days old. Then I dropped the mouse on the floor. One of them had gone so far as to order a kill from Allan. A man who called himself Thomas De Quincey was specifically asking him to kill someone for him. It was the picture that made my heart stop. Underneath it said: *Her name is Rebekka Franck.*

58

Allan glanced through the crowd of people to make sure The Master wasn't among them. He probably wasn't far by now, he thought, maybe he was already here. Allan had never seen the Master in person, he didn't even know his real name. Part of him was looking forward to seeing him face to face. He was some kind of idol for Allan, well for all of them. And now he was coming here to claim Allan's kill. But it wasn't going to be with Allan's consent. Not willingly. Those were his kills and he had been looking forward to finishing them.

Allan glanced at the stairs leading to the rooms upstairs. He had to try and get away now. Besides people were beginning to get hungry now. It was time for the appetizer. Allan planned to run upstairs, kill the woman and cut her to pieces. Then bring the meat to the kitchen and prepare it. No one had to notice anything and he would get rid of the woman. That was part one. Part two was in the basement. The Armagnac-soaked girl and then the foie gras. Allan shook his head heavily to try and keep the voices down. They were screaming inside of him. They wanted a kill, they said. They needed the blood, they craved it. Allan knew he had to obey the voices or they would never leave him alone. They would keep yelling till he could take no more.

He had heard them the first time right after Amalie was born. They told him to go to her, that she was going to take his place, they had even warned him that he would be sent away. So he went to her room and stood next to her crib, staring at the small, ugly, wrinkled creature. The voices told him to kill her, to just put a pillow over her head and then leave her. But he refused. He restrained himself so much he hadn't noticed that he had hurt himself, that he had hurt his hand and was bleeding. That night the voices tortured him for not doing as told. They screamed all night and from that day on he promised himself to always listen to what they said, to always do as he was told. It was the only way he could experience peace within. It was the only way to shut them up. At least for a little while, at least until they came up with something new for him to do.

Everyone at the party seemed to be busy and enjoying themselves, so Allan thought it was time and walked to the kitchen. He grabbed a knife and walked towards the stairs.

"Hey Allan where are you going?" a half-drunk woman yelled behind him.

Allan closed his eyes, then took in a deep breath before he turned and smiled. "Just checking on the appetizer," he said.

"Oh, sounds good. I'm starving," the woman said.

"Well hopefully you won't be once this party is over," he said and turned towards the stairs while the woman went back to the living room. Allan had his foot on the first step when a voice came up from behind him.

"Going somewhere?"

Allan froze. There was something in the way the man

spoke, something in his voice that let Allan know that it could only be *him*.

With excitement and thrill he turned and looked at the man standing in front of him. He was tall and very muscular, just like Allan had imagined him. And good-looking, of course. Excessively handsome.

"Fred Einaudi, I presume?" the man said. He was flanked by two big men with bald heads.

Allan smiled. "You assume right, Thomas De Quincey."

"One of your partying guests was nice and let us in. I believe you have something that is mine?"

The two men stared at each other like dogs before a fight. It was all in the eyes who was the strongest. It didn't take long for Allan to realize he was defeated. This man had a glare that was even more coldblooded than Allan's. So Allan caved first. "Right," he said. "I was just going to get everything ready for you."

"We said alive, remember?" he said. Allan stared at the two bodyguards standing behind Thomas De Quincey. They glared at him, looking like they could swallow him in one bite.

"Sure," Allan said. "Make yourselves comfortable. Go get a drink and I'll be right back."

Barely had he finished his sentence and added an insecure laugh when Thomas De Quincey stepped forward and with one swift move grabbed the kitchen knife from Allan's hand and plunged it in his side. Allan bent over with a gasp and held on to the man's shoulder. The pain spread fast throughout his body as Thomas De Quincey pulled out the knife and wiped it off on Allan's clothes.

"Don't worry. I didn't hit anything vital," Thomas De Quincey whispered. "You'll probably survive. But now you know I mean business."

Allan moaned and gasped for air. His hand holding the wound turned red with blood.

"Now go and get me my package," he said and put the knife back in Allan's hand and pressed it against his chest.

Allan nodded, then turned and still while holding one hand to cover the wound he ran towards the stairs.

59

I HEARD SOMEONE in the hallway outside of the door and froze. Then there was moaning and a fumbling by the lock before the handle turned downwards. The door opened and I stared as Allan Witt tumbled in, his hand and shirt covered in blood.

In his hand he held a kitchen knife. Then he stared at the computer and saw all the files I had opened. He walked closer and glanced at the screen and looked at the article I had written called *When Greenland was supposed to be made Danish - the forgotten children*.

"What are you doing?" he asked.

"She was one of them, wasn't she?" I asked. "Your mother? She was one of those children from Greenland."

Allan shook his head. "I don't have time for this now ..."

"I wrote these articles, I know the story. In Nineteen Eighty-Two the Danish government sent thirty-three children ages six to ten from our colony Greenland to Denmark. They separated them from their families to bring them to Denmark to make them more Danish. The plan was to teach them the Danish language, Danish culture, Danish manners and have them bring it back home to Greenland where they could teach their families and grow up to be more "Danish." It was supposed to only be for a year but something went wrong and only a few ever returned. And when they did, they couldn't speak with their families anymore since they only spoke Danish and had forgotten their native language. Those who never returned were adopted by Danish families or simply taken in as hired help by rich people. Your mother was one of them, right? That's why you have those features, you look like you're Greenlander, but you're blond and have blue eyes. There is a reason for that. Your father is the Prince?"

Allan sighed deeply. He was in obvious pain from the wound. "Yes," he said. "But there is more to the story. The Prince didn't take her in to be kind to her or to help her out. He took her in because he and some associates from the Danish Movement wanted to do an experiment. He knew no one would ever miss my mother. Her family was all drunkards; half of them had shot each other. There was no one asking where my mother was. My mother was only thirteen when they came up with the experiment. I have all the files to prove it. That's how I learned. They're in the corner over there," he said and pointed at a stack of folders. "I broke into my father's office a few years back after I received the letter from the Countess. I knew my way around the castle, since I was a kid there. I found the folders in his safe. I knew the combination so it wasn't difficult. He always used the same combination to everything. That's where he hid them, the files that proved to me what kind of sick bastard he really is."

"He raped her, didn't he? I mean she had to have been young?"

Allan Witt growled then whimpered in pain. "It wasn't just a normal rape. He did it because he had a purpose. They wanted to take all the young girls from Greenland who had come here in 'Eighty-six and breed children with them. They wanted to make a new race, one that was more like Danes, who thought and acted more like Danes and thereby they thought they might solve all of Greenland's problems. They wanted to make Greenlanders with blond hair and blue eyes and send them back to change the population in time. That was their general plan."

"So they started with your mother?"

"Yes according to the records they tied my mother up in my father's castle and then he raped her all night while the others watched and took notes. They have it all written down in detail. I think they just liked the thrill of watching her suffer," Allan said and smiled. "Some people enjoy watching others in pain. They get a kick out of it."

"So what happened? Where is your real mother?"

"She killed herself right after my birth. Or maybe they killed her, I don't know. They told me she committed suicide by jumping out the window, but for all I know that might be a lie as well. I don't think I even care anymore."

"Why didn't they send you back like it was planned?"

"Something went wrong and they abandoned the project in Nineteen ninety-two. The prince was stuck with me, but luckily the countess whom he had just met, loved me and she was told she was barren."

"But then she had Amalie a few years later and there was no longer room for you at the castle."

"Well what do you know," Allan said. "That's my story. We all have a sad little story to tell, don't we?"

60

Allan closed his eyes and exhaled. The woman was annoying him terribly now. So were the three men waiting for him downstairs, waiting for him to deliver the package. To be honest he didn't know what to do next. He hadn't really thought it through. Should he simply deliver the woman as requested? But he had promised him the Princess as well. Never said it would be alive though, but now he wanted her alive. That was what he had said and he was used to being obeyed.

Allan inhaled sharply through his teeth in pain. The blood kept seeping out of his wound and his hand couldn't hold it back. He banged the backside of the hand holding the knife against his forehead to think more clearly. On top of it all the voices were screaming unbearably, demanding a kill. Maybe he could deliver the woman, then go to the basement and kill the girls? But that would leave him so unsatisfied. He didn't want the Master to win, he didn't want to obey him. Maybe he could kill the woman, then go downstairs and kill the three men? It was what he wanted the most, but it was such a dangerous path to take. The Master had killed more people than Allan ever had, he was known to be brutal, cruel even. Allan had admired him and read his stories on the chat with great joy, indulging in every moment and aspect of them. But it couldn't go on, could it? At some point the student had to become better than the Master. It was time for someone new to take the lead. It was time for Allan to shine and be admired.

The woman in front of him was staring at him as he lifted the knife and approached her. He had tried to kill her so many times now, he was beginning to wonder if he would ever succeed. He started wondering if it was even worth it, if she was worth the trouble now that he had all the other kills to make. But this woman had to be special since the Master himself wanted her. It was a strange coincidence that they had both wanted her. Allan had wondered a lot about that once he had seen the message from the Master with the woman's name and picture. Why was she so special? Allan knew why he wanted her, but why did the Master? Well the reason didn't matter. The very fact that Thomas de Quincey wanted her dead was reason enough to kill her on his own. Just to piss him off. To let him know who was in charge.

Allan stared at her as she walked slowly backwards. He kicked the chair aside. She was yelling, telling him to stop, to get out of here, but he didn't care. He wanted her dead now. He wanted to taste her skin, to smell her blood. This was it. It was now.

He let go of the wound and reached out his hand to grab her. She hit it, pushed it away, but it returned and now it was grabbing her neck holding it tight and pushing her up against the wall behind her. She was screaming and gasping for air. Just the way Allan liked it. He lifted her till her feet no longer touched the floor. Her throat was so tiny, so fragile between his fingers. He would only use the knife if he had to.

He preferred to strangle her, to feel the life ebb out of her just by the touch of his own fingers. He was strong; he always had strong hands and a strong grip, one that made people react when he shook their hand. Now he felt almost supernatural. Like a god or better yet, a vampire. Yes, that was it, he felt immortal, like he had the strength of the immortals.

But a kick too close to his wound planted by the woman reminded him that he was in fact very mortal and very much in pain. He groaned and bent forward in agony. Then the woman kicked him again, and again, always in the same spot. It hurt like hell. Allan whimpered. Then he felt the delightful feeling of anger rising, anger that gave him almost inhuman strength and capacity.

He growled at her and tightened his grip around her throat. Then he heard spurting sounds, the wonderful music of someone choking and he closed his eyes to better listen and enjoy the last breath, that exquisite sound of someone breathing for the very last time.

61

I was trying to fight him off. I was kicking and screaming but his grip on my throat became tighter and tighter the more I fought. It was like he gained strength from my fighting. I managed to kick him several times and hit him right in his wound, but somehow he still managed to keep up trying to kill me. Now he was seriously hurting my throat and I gasped for air. The feeling of suffocation was overwhelming and horrible. I started to see black spots and I had a tickling sensation in my arms and legs. I knew it was due to lack of oxygen in my body. I was scared and thinking only about Julie and getting back to her. No way she was going to grow up without a mother.

"Aaaargh," I sputtered and planted another kick directly in the wound. This time Allan Witt didn't sustain the blow. It hurt too bad for that. With a strange sound he bent over in anguish and fell to his knees. As he did he let go of my throat and I fell to the ground. I was coughing and sputtering, trying to get to my feet, crawling to get away from him and catching my breath when he grabbed my ankle and pulled me towards him. I put my nails in the carpet and tried to stop him from pulling me. I screamed and kicked my feet. He pulled me closer and closer while holding the knife in the air, ready to sink it into my flesh the first chance he got. In the distance I suddenly heard yelling. The music had stopped and the talking vanished. Suddenly someone screamed. There were sounds in the hallway, steps, someone running, doors opening. Then more voices and someone calling my name.

"Rebekka?"

"Yes!" I yelled and felt Allan Witt pull strongly. He grabbed my head and silenced me by putting his bloody hand over my mouth. I tried to scream, but it only became muffled sounds. I watched as Allan lifted the knife again ready to place it in my back.

The door to the room opened with a huge crash and someone entered. There was turmoil, I saw mostly feet and legs from where I was. Yelling, screaming, more turmoil and then Allan's grip on my feet loosened. Quickly I turned and stood up only to look into the face of someone I knew very well.

"Peter!" I screamed and threw myself in his arms. On the floor lay Allan Witt with his eyes staring empty into the air, his throat slit with the knife. "You got my email!"

I looked at his face and hugged him tightly never wanting to let him go again. "Yes," he said. "Yes I received your email and rushed to get here. Boy, have I been nervous. What the hell has been going on here?"

I sighed and held him closer, then I let go. I cried and cried, tried to talk but made no sense. Peter held me in his arms as he helped me down the stairs.

"Shh, shh," he said. "You can tell me it all later." I stopped and looked at him. "And the girls? They were in the basement."

"It's all been taken care of," Peter said. "They're safe. The police are here."

Finding it suddenly very hard to breathe, I stopped on the middle of the stairs. Everything was spinning. The room, the stairs, Peter, the people watching me as I walked down. I knew I couldn't stay conscious much longer and a few seconds later it all went black.

EPILOGUE

THEY BOTH SURVIVED. Princess Amalie and her friend Camilla were in bad condition when they arrived at the hospital, but they were alive and a few weeks later they were back home with their families. I had given the police my statement, but didn't contact them and they never contacted me. I was happy to read about their recovery in the papers and magazines. Shortly after coming home, Princess Amalie held a press conference telling the entire world that she was gay and she had found the love of her life and the world would have to deal with it any way they wanted. She was free and happy.

"One hell of a strong girl," I stated and put the paper down.

Dad looked back at me with a smile. "So are you," he said.

"Well I owe it mostly to Peter that we got out of there alive. He was there at the right time."

Julie looked at me while eating her pancake. "My dad is a hero," she said.

I leaned over and kissed her cheek. "He sure is."

I heard steps on the stairs and turned my head to watch

Peter come walking towards me with a smile. Then he leaned over and kissed me. Julie sighed. "Could you two please take it somewhere else? Someone's eating here."

Peter and I both laughed knowing that she didn't mean it. She really enjoyed us being together again and having her dad close all the time. I knew how important it was to her, that was why I wanted to give Peter a second chance.

Sune hadn't taken it well, though once I told him. Only a couple of days after I was discharged from the hospital I drove to his apartment and knocked on the door. He had of course heard all about what had happened to me and told me he was so sad and had been so scared once he heard it.

"So why didn't you come and see me in the hospital?" I asked.

"Well I did. But I saw your ex outside sitting holding hands with Julie. I believed it was more of a family moment for all of you. To be honest I think I was afraid you would blame me for not being the one to come to your rescue. I felt defeated."

"Well then you can probably understand why I'm telling you that I'm going back to be with Peter."

I saw the sadness in Sune's eyes and felt a pinch in my stomach. I really loved this guy, I did. We were just too different.

"I had a feeling this was going to happen," he said with a thick voice. A tear slipped from the corner of his eye and he hurried to wipe it away.

"I really love you. I do," I said and grabbed his hand. "It's just that I also still love Peter and I feel like I owe it to Julie to try and make it work with her dad."

Sune nodded heavily. "I know. I would die to give Tobias a real family as well. I would give up anything to have his mother with him again and give him what he has always longed for. It's just ..." He kicked the coffee-table next to him. "It's just so unfair."

"I know. But maybe it's the best for all of us. Now you can go out and find someone your own age. Maybe she can give you that second child you're dreaming of."

"But I don't want anyone else, Rebekka. I love you. You know that."

"That's just the way you feel right now. You'll feel different soon." I sighed. "It sucks having to break up with you, but I have to give this another try. I realized lately that my feelings for him never really died, they just kind of froze for a while. He reminded me of what we had together when he was himself again. Suddenly I remembered who I had fallen in love with."

Sune's eyes flamed up. "You slept with him, didn't you? You slept with him even though we were still together."

"Well ... yes. Okay. You and I were fighting and he was there, reminding me of everything, all what we had." I reached out my hand and stroked his cheek. "I'm so sorry, Sune. I never meant to hurt you."

He pushed my hand away and snorted. "Well it's a little too late for that now, don't you think?"

"I think that you're angry now and I'm going to leave. We'll talk some other time when you're calmed down."

I got up and walked to the door. Once in the hallway I heard Sune throw a plate at the wall and it shattering all over the floor. I exhaled deeply, feeling all kinds of guilt and condemnation. This was not at all how I had wanted things to be between me and Sune. But that was how it turned out and even if I wasn't proud of it, I had to realize I wouldn't be able to change it either.

Now I was with Peter again and he was sitting in my dad's

kitchen with all of us, eating breakfast, chatting and laughing. If there was one thing I learned from this experience it was to take one day at a time. Right now it was a Sunday morning and I was with the people I loved. This was how things were and how I wanted it to be.

THE END

AFTERWORD

Dear reader,

Thank you for purchasing *"Seven, Eight ... Gonna stay up late"*. Do not fear. This is not the end of Rebekka Franck's story. This is just part one. In part two you will get all the answers to why Thomas De Quincey wanted Rebekka killed and why he stole the remains of King Erik Klipping who was killed in Finderup Lade in 1286. (that is actually a real story). So fret not, it will all be explained in the next installment., *Nine, Ten ... Never sleep again.* It has just been released.

If you're into mysteries then don't forget to try out my other mystery-series the Emma Frost Mystery Series.

If you could leave a honest review of this book then that would make me very happy .

Take care,
Willow Rose

Connect with Willow online and you will be the first to know about new releases and bargains from Willow Rose

Sign up to the VIP email here:
http://eepurl.com/vVfEf

I promise not to share your email with anyone else, and I won't clutter your inbox. I'll only contact you when a new book is out or when I have a special bargain/free eBook.

Follow Willow Rose on BookBub:
https://www.bookbub.com/authors/willow-rose

BOOKS BY THE AUTHOR

MYSTERY/HORROR NOVELS

- In One Fell Swoop
- Umbrella Man
- Blackbird Fly
- To Hell in a Handbasket
- Edwina

7TH STREET CREW SERIES

- What Hurts the Most
- You Can Run
- You Can't Hide
- Careful Little Eyes

EMMA FROST SERIES

- Itsy Bitsy Spider
- Miss Dolly had a Dolly
- Run, Run as Fast as You Can
- Cross Your Heart and Hope to Die
- Peek-a-Boo I See You
- Tweedledum and Tweedledee
- Easy as One, Two, Three

- There's No Place like Home
- Slenderman
- Where the Wild Roses Grow

JACK RYDER SERIES

- Hit the Road Jack
- Slip out the Back Jack
- The House that Jack Built
- Black Jack

REBEKKA FRANCK SERIES

- One, Two…He is Coming for You
- Three, Four…Better Lock Your Door
- Five, Six…Grab your Crucifix
- Seven, Eight…Gonna Stay up Late
- Nine, Ten…Never Sleep Again
- Eleven, Twelve…Dig and Delve
- Thirteen, Fourteen…Little Boy Unseen

HORROR SHORT-STORIES

- Better watch out
- Eenie, Meenie
- Rock-a-Bye Baby
- Nibble, Nibble, Crunch

- Humpty Dumpty
- Chain Letter
- Mommy Dearest
- The Bird

PARANORMAL SUSPENSE/FANTASY NOVELS

AFTERLIFE SERIES

- Beyond
- Serenity
- Endurance
- Courageous

THE WOLFBOY CHRONICLES

- A Gypsy Song
- I am WOLF

DAUGHTERS OF THE JAGUAR

- Savage
- Broken

ABOUT THE AUTHOR

The Queen of Scream, Willow Rose, is an international best-selling author. She writes Mystery/Suspense/Horror, Paranormal Romance and Fantasy. She is inspired by authors like James Patterson, Agatha Christie, Stephen King, Anne Rice, and Isabel Allende. She lives on Florida's Space Coast with her husband and two daughters. When she is not writing or reading, you'll find her surfing and watching the dolphins play in the waves of the Atlantic Ocean. She has sold more than two million books.

Connect with Willow online:
willow-rose.net
madamewillowrose@gmail.com

HIT THE ROAD JACK

EXCERPT

For a special sneak peak of Willow Rose's Bestselling Mystery Novel *Hit the Road Jack* turn to the next page.

This could be Heaven or this could be Hell
~ Eagles, Hotel California 1977

PROLOGUE
DON'T COME BACK NO MORE

1

MAY 2012

She has no idea who she is or where she is and cares to know neither. For some time, for what seems like forever, she has been in this daze. This haze, in complete darkness with nothing but the sounds. Sounds coming from outside her body, from outside her head. Sometimes, the sounds fade and there is only the darkness.

As time passes, she becomes aware that there are two realities. The one in her mind, filled with darkness and pain and then the one outside of her, where something or someone else is living, acting, smelling and...singing.

Yes, that's it. Someone is singing. Does she know the song?

...What you say?

The darkness is soon replaced by light. Still, her eyes are too heavy to open. Her consciousness returns slowly. Enough to start asking questions. Where is she? How did she end up here? A series of pictures of her at home come to her mind. She is waiting. What is she waiting for?

...I guess if you said so.

Him. She is waiting for him. She is checking her hair in

the mirror every five minutes or so. Then correcting the make-up, looking at the clock again. Where is he? She looks out through the window and at the street and the many staring neighboring windows. A feeling of guilt hits her. Somehow, it seems wrong for this kind of thing to take place in broad daylight.

...That's right!

A car drives up. The anticipation. The butterflies in her stomach. The sound of the doorbell. She is straightening her dress and taking a last glance in the mirror. The next second, she is in his embrace. He is holding her so tight she closes her eyes and breathes him in until his lips cover hers and she swims away.

...Whoa, Woman, oh woman, don't treat me so mean.

His breath is pumping against her skin. She feels his hands on her breasts, under her skirt, coming closer, while he presses her up against the wall. She feels him in his hand. He is hard now, moaning in her ear.

"Where's your husband?" he whispers.

"Work," she moans back, feeling self-conscious. Why did he have to bring up her husband? The guilt is killing her. "The kids are in school."

"Good," he moans. "No one can ever know. Remember that. No one."

...You're the meanest old woman that I've ever seen.

He pushes himself inside of her and pumps. She lets herself get into the moment, but as soon as it is over, she finds herself regretting it...while he zips up the pants of his suit and kisses her gently on the lips, whispering, *same time next week*? She regrets having started it all. They are both married with children, and this is only an affair. Could never be anything else, even if she dreamt about it. The sex is great, but she wants more than just seeing him on her lunch break.

But she can never tell him. She can never explain to him how much she hates this awkward moment that follows the sex.

"They're expecting me at the office...I have a meeting," he says, and puts his tie back on. "I'd better..."

...Hit the road, Jack!

She finally opens her eyes with a loud gasp. The bright light hurts her. Water is being splashed in her face. She can't breathe. The bathtub is slippery when she tries to get up. Her eyes lock with another set of eyes. The eyes of a man. He is staring at her with a twisted smile. She gasps again, suddenly remembering those dark chili eyes.

"*I guess if you said so...I'd have to pack my things and go,*" he sings.

"You," she gasps. Breathing is hard for her. She feels like she is still choking. She is hyperventilating. Panicking.

The man smiles. On his neck crawls a snake. How does that old saying go again? *Red, black, yellow kills a fellow?* This one is all of that, all those colors. It stares at her while moving its tongue back and forth. The man is holding a washcloth in his hand. She looks down at her naked body. The smell of chlorine is strong and makes her eyes water.

"You tried to kill me," she says, while panting with anxiety.

I have to get home. Help me. I have to get home to my children! Oh, God. I can hear their voices! Am I going mad? I think I can hear them!

"I guess I didn't do a very good job, then," he answers. His chillingly calm voice is piercing through every bone in her body.

"I'll try again. *That's right!*"

2

MAY 2012

She had never been more beautiful than in this exact moment. No woman ever had. So fragile, her skin so pale it almost looked bluish. The man who called himself the Snakecharmer stared at her body. It was still in the bathtub. He was still panting from the exertion, his hands shaking and hurting from strangling the girl. He felt so aroused in this moment, staring at the dead body. It was the most fascinating thing in the world. How the body simply ceased to function. And almost as fascinating was what followed next. The human decaying process. It wasn't something new. Fascination with death had occurred all throughout human history, characterized by obsessions with death and all things related to death. The Egyptians mummified their dead. He had always wished he could do the same. Keep his dead forever and ever. He remembered as a child how he would sometimes lie down in front of the mirror and try to lie completely still and look at himself, imagining he was looking at a dead body. He would capture cats and kill them and keep them in his room, just to watch what would happen to them. He wanted so badly to stop the decaying process, he wanted them to remain the same always and never leave.

The Snakecharmer stared at the girl with fascination in his eyes. He caught his breath and calmed down again. He still felt the adrenalin rushing through his veins while he finished washing the girl. He washed away all the dirt, all the smells on her body. He reached down and cleaned her thoroughly between her legs. Scrubbed her to make sure he got all the dirt away, all the filth and impurities.

Then, he dried her with a towel before he pulled her onto the bathroom floor. His companions, his two pet Coral snakes, were sliding across her dead body. He grabbed one and let it slide across his arm while petting it. Then he knelt next to the girl and stroked her gently across her hair, making sure it wasn't in her face. Her blue eyes stared into the ceiling.

"Now, you'll never leave," he whispered.

With his cellphone, he took a picture of her naked body. That was his mummification. His way to always cherish the moment. To always remember. He never wanted to forget how beautiful she was.

He dried her with a towel. He brushed her brown hair with gentle strokes. He took yet another picture before he lifted her up and carried her into the bedroom, where he placed her in a chair, then sat in front of her and placed his head in her lap.

They would stay like this until she started to smell.

PART I

I GUESS IF YOU SAY SO

3

JANUARY 2015

He took the dog out in the yard and shut the door carefully behind him, making sure he didn't make a sound to wake up his sleeping parents. It was Monday, but they had been very loud last night. The kitchen counter was still covered with empty bottles.

At first, Ben had waited patiently in the living room, watching a couple of shows on TV, waiting for his parents to wake up. When the clock passed nine, he knew he wouldn't make it to school that day either, and that was too bad because they had a fieldtrip to the zoo today and Ben had been looking forward to it. When they still hadn't shown up at ten o'clock, he decided the dog had to go out. The old Labrador kept sitting by the door and scraping on it. It had to go.

So, Ben took Bobby out in the backyard. He had to go with him. The yard ended at the canal, and Bobby had more than once jumped into the water. Ben had to keep an eye on him to make sure he didn't do it again. It had been such a mess last time, since the dog couldn't climb back up over the seawall on his own, so Ben's dad had to jump into the blurry water and carry the dog out.

The dog quickly gave in to nature and did his business. Ben had a plastic bag that he picked it up with and threw it in the trash can behind the house.

It was a beautiful day out. One of those clear days with a blue sky and not a cloud anywhere on the horizon. The wind was blowing out of the north and had been for two days, making the air drier. For once, Ben's shirt didn't stick to his body.

He threw the ball a few times for the dog to get some exercise. Ben could smell the ocean, even though he lived on the back side of the barrier island. When it was quiet, he could even hear it too. The waves had to be good. If he wasn't too sick from drinking last night, his dad might take him surfing.

Ben really hoped he would.

It had been months since his dad last took him to the beach. He never seemed to have time anymore. Sometimes, Ben would take his bike and ride down there by himself, but it was never as much fun as when the entire family went. They never seemed to do much together anymore. Ben wondered if it had anything to do with what happened to his baby sister a year ago. He never understood exactly what had happened. He just knew she didn't wake up one morning when their mother went to pick her up from her crib. Then his parents cried and cried for days and they had held a big funeral. But the crying hadn't stopped for a long time. Not until it was replaced with a lot of sleeping and his parents staying up all night, and all the empty bottles that Ben often cleaned up from the kitchen and put in the recycling bin.

Bobby brought back the ball and placed it at Ben's feet. He picked it up and threw it again. It landed close to the seawall. Luckily, it didn't fall in. Bobby ran to get it, then placed it at Ben's feet again, looking at him expectantly.

"Really? One more time, then we're done," he said, thinking he'd better get back inside and start cleaning up. He picked up the ball and threw it. The dog stormed after it again and disappeared for a second down the hill leading to the canal. Ben couldn't see him.

"Bobby?" he yelled. "Come on, boy. We need to get back inside."

He stared in the direction of the canal. He couldn't see the bottom of the yard. He had no idea if Bobby had jumped in the water again. His heart started to pound. He would have to wake up his dad if he did. He was the only one who could get Bobby out of the water.

Ben stood frozen for a few seconds until he heard the sound of Bobby's collar, and a second later spotted his black dog running towards him with his tongue hanging out of his mouth.

"Bobby!" Ben said. He bent down and petted his dog and best friend. "You scared me, buddy. You forgot the ball. Well, we'll have to get that later. Now, let's go back inside and see if Mom and Dad are awake."

Ben grabbed the handle and opened the door. He let Bobby go in first.

"Mom?" he called.

But there was no answer. They were probably still asleep. Ben found some dog food in the cabinet and pulled the bag out. He spilled on the floor when he filled Bobby's tray. He had no idea how much the dog needed, so he made sure to give him enough, and poured till the bowl overflowed. Ben found a garbage bag under the sink and had removed some of the bottles, when Bobby suddenly started growling. The dog ran to the bottom of the stairs and barked. Ben found this to be strange. It was very unlike Bobby to act this way.

"What's the matter, boy? Are Mom and Dad awake?"

The dog kept barking and growling.

"Stop it!" Ben yelled, knowing how much his dad hated it when Bobby barked. "Bad dog."

But Bobby didn't stop. He moved closer and closer to the stairs and kept barking until the dog finally ran up the stairs.

"No! Bobby!" Ben yelled. "Come back down here!"

Ben stared up the stairs after the dog, wondering if he dared to go up there. His dad always got so mad if he went upstairs when they were sleeping. He wasn't allowed up there until they got out of bed. But, if he found Bobby up there, his dad would get really mad. Probably talk about getting rid of him again.

He's my best friend. Don't take my friend away.

"Bobby," he whispered. "Come back down here."

Ben's heart was racing in his chest. There wasn't a sound coming from upstairs. Ben held his breath, not knowing what to do. The last thing he wanted on a day like today was to make his dad angry. He expected his dad to start yelling any second now.

Oh no, what if he jumps into their bed? Dad is going to get so mad. He's gonna get real mad at Bobby.

"Bobby?" Ben whispered a little louder.

There was movement on the stairs, the black lab peeked his head out, then ran down the stairs.

"There you are," Ben said with relief. Bobby ran past him and sprang up on the couch.

"What do you have in your mouth? Not one of mom's shoes again."

It didn't look like it was big enough to be a shoe. Ben walked closer, thinking if it was a pair of Mommy's panties again, then the dog was dead. He reached down and grabbed the dog's mouth, then opened it and pulled out whatever it was. He looked down with a small shriek at what had come out of the dog's mouth. He felt nauseated, like the time when he had the stomach-bug and spent the entire night in the bathroom. Only this was worse.

It's a finger. A finger wearing Mommy's ring!

4

JANUARY 2015

"Hit the road, Jack, and don't you come back no more no more no more."

The children's voices were screaming more than singing on the bus. I preferred *Wheels on the Bus,* but the kids thought it was oh so fun, since my name was Jack and I was actually driving the bus. I had volunteered to drive them to the Brevard Zoo for their field trip today. Two of the children, the pretty blonde twins in the back named Abigail and Austin, were mine. A boy and a girl. Just started Kindergarten six months ago. I could hardly believe how fast time passed. Everybody told me it would, but still. It was hard to believe.

I was thirty-five and a single dad of three children. My wife, Arianna, ran out on us four years ago…when the twins were almost two years old. It was too much, she told me. She couldn't cope with the children or me. She especially had a hard time taking care of Emily. Emily was my ex-partner's daughter. My ex-partner, Lisa, was shot on duty ten years ago during a chase in downtown Miami. The shooter was never captured, and it haunted me daily. I took Emily in after her mother died. What else could I have done? I felt guilty for what had happened to her mother. I was supposed to have protected my partner. Plus, the girl didn't know her father. Lisa never told anyone who he was; she didn't have any of her parents or siblings left, except for a homeless brother who was in no condition to take care of a child. So, I got custody and decided to give Emily the best life I could. She was six when I took her in, sixteen now, and at an age where it was hard for anyone to love you, besides your mom and dad. I tried hard to be both for her. Not always with much success. The fact was, I had no idea what it was like to be a black teenage girl.

Personally, I believed Arianna had depression after the birth of the twins, but she never let me close enough to talk about it. She cried for months after the twins were born, then one day out of the blue, she told me she had to go. That she couldn't stay or it would end up killing her. I cried and begged her to stay, but there was nothing I could do. She had made up her mind. She was going back upstate, and that was all I needed to know. I shouldn't look for her, she said.

"Are you coming back?" I asked, my voice breaking. I couldn't believe anyone would leave her own children.

"I don't know, Jack."

"But...The children? They need you? They need their mother?"

"I can't be the mother you want me to be, Jack. I'm just not cut out for it. I'm sorry."

Then she left. Just like that. I had no idea how to explain it to the kids, but somehow I did. As soon as they started asking questions, I told them their mother had left and that I believed she was coming back one day. Some, maybe a lot of people, including my mother, might have told me it was insane to tell them that she might be coming back, but that's what I did. I couldn't bear the thought of them growing up with the knowledge that their own mother didn't want them. I couldn't bear for Emily to know that she was part of the reason why Arianna had left us, left the twins motherless. I just couldn't. I had to leave them with some sort of hope. And maybe I needed to believe it too. I needed to believe that she hadn't just abandoned us…that she had some stuff she needed to work out and soon she would be back. At least for the twins. They needed their mother and asked for her often. It was getting harder and harder for me to believe she was coming back for them. But I still said she would.

And there they were.

On the back seat of the bus, singing along with their classmates, happier than most of them. Mother or no mother, I had provided a good life for them in our little town of Cocoa Beach. As a detective working for the Brevard County Sheriff's Office, working their homicide unit, I had lots of spare time and they had their grandparents close by. They received all the love in the world from me and their grandparents, who loved them to death (and let them get away with just about anything).

Some might think they were spoiled brats, but to me they were the love of my life, the light, the…the…

What the heck were they doing in the back?

I hit the brakes a little too hard at the red light. All the kids on the bus fell forwards. The teacher, Mrs. Allen, whined and held on to her purse.

"Abigail and Austin!" I thundered through the bus. "Stop that right now!"

The twins grinned and looked at one another, then continued to smear chocolate on each other's faces. Chocolate from those small boxes with Nutella and sticks you dipped in it. Boxes their grandmother had given them for snack, even though I told her it had to be healthy.

"Now!" I yelled.

"Sorry, Dad," they yelled in unison.

"Well...wipe that off or..."

I never made it any further before the phone in my pocket vibrated. I pulled it out and started driving again as the light turned green.

"Ryder. We need you. I spoke with Ron and he told me you would be assisting us. We desperately need your help."

It was the head of the Cocoa Beach Police Department. Weasel, we called her. I didn't know why. Maybe it had to do with the fact that her name was Weslie Seal. Maybe it was just because she kind of looked like a weasel because her body was long and slender, but her legs very short. Ron Harper was the county sheriff and my boss.

"Yes? When?"

"Now."

"But...I'm..."

"This is big. We need you now."

"If you say so. I'll get there as fast as I can," I said, and turned off towards the entrance to the zoo. The kids all screamed with joy when they saw the sign. Mrs. Allen shushed them.

"What, are you running a day-care now? Not that I have the time to care. Everything is upside down around here. We have a dead body. I'll text you the address. Meet you there."

5

APRIL 1984

Annie was getting ready. She was putting on make-up with her room-mate Julia, while listening to Michael Jackson's *Thriller* and singing into their hairbrushes. They were nineteen, in college, and heading for trouble, as Annie's father always said.

Annie wanted to be a teacher.

"Are you excited?" Julia asked. "You think he's going to be there?"

"He," was Tim. He was the talk of the campus and the guy they all desired. He was tall, blond, and a quarterback. He was perfect. And he had his eye on Annie.

"I hope so," Annie said, and put on her jacket with the shoulder pads. "He asked me to come; he'd better be."

She looked at her friend, wondering why Tim hadn't chosen Julia instead. She was much prettier.

"Shall we?" Julia asked and opened the door. They were both wearing heavy make-up and acid-washed jeans.

Annie was nervous as they walked to the party. She had never been to a party in a fraternity house before. She had been thrilled when Tim came up to her in the library where she hung out most of the time and told her there was a party at the house and asked if she was going to come.

"Sure," she had replied, while blushing.

"This is it," Julia said, as they approached the house. Kids a few years older than them were hanging out on the porch, while loud music spilled out through the open windows. Annie had butterflies in her stomach as they went up the steps to the front of the house and entered, elbowing themselves through the crowd.

The noise was intense. People were drinking and smoking everywhere. Some were already making out on a couch. And it wasn't even nine o'clock yet.

"Let's get something to drink," Julia yelled through the thick clamor. "Have you loosen up a little."

Julia came back with two cups, and...Tim. "Look who I found," she said. "He was asking for you."

Annie grabbed the plastic cup and didn't care what it contained; she gulped it down in such a hurry she forgot to breathe. Tim was staring at her with that handsome smile of his. Then, he leaned over, put his hand on her shoulder, and whispered. "Glad you came."

Annie blushed and felt warmth spread through her entire body from the palm of Tim's hand on her shoulder. She really liked him. She really, really liked him.

"It's very loud in here. Do you want to go somewhere?" he asked.

Annie knew she wasn't the smartest among girls. Her mother had always told her so. She knew Tim, who was pre-med, would never be impressed with her conversational skills or her wits. If she was to dazzle him, it had to be in another way.

"Sure," she said.

"Let me get us some drinks first," Tim said and disappeared.

Julia smiled and grabbed Annie's shoulders. "You got him, girl." Then she corrected Annie's hair and wiped a smear of mascara from under her eyes.

"There. Now you're perfect. Remember. Don't think. You always overthink everything. Just be you. Just go with the flow, all right? Laugh at his jokes, but not too hard. Don't tell him too much about yourself; stay mysterious. And, whatever you do...don't sleep with him. You hear me? He won't respect you if you jump into bed with him right away. You have to play hard to get."

Annie stared at Julia. She had never had sex with anyone before, and she certainly wasn't going to now. Not yet. She had been saving herself for the right guy, and maybe Tim was it, but she wasn't going to decide that tonight. She didn't even want to.

"I'd never do that," she said with a scoff. "I'm not THAT stupid."

6

JANUARY 2015

Weasel was standing outside the house as I drove up and parked the school bus on the street. The house on West Bay Drive was blocked by four police cars and lots of police tape. I saw several of my colleagues walking around in the yard. Weasel spotted me and approached. She was wearing tight black jeans, a belt with a big buckle, a white shirt, and black blazer. She looked to be in her thirties, but I knew she had recently turned forty.

"What the...?" she said with a grin, looking at the bus. She had that raspy rawness to her voice, and I always wondered if she could sing. I pictured her as a country singer. She gave out that tough vibe.

"Don't ask," I said. "What have we got?"

"Homicide," Weasel answered. "Victim is female. Laura Bennett, thirty-two, Mom of Ben, five years old. The husband's name is Brandon Bennett."

My heart dropped. I knew the boy. He was in the twins' class. I couldn't believe it. I had moved to Cocoa Beach from Miami in 2008 and never been called out to a homicide in my own town. Our biggest problems around here were usually tourists on spring break jumping in people's pools and Jacuzzis and leaving beer cans, or the youngsters having bonfires on the beach and burning people's chairs and leaving trash.

But, murder? That was a first for me in Cocoa Beach. I had been called out to drug related homicides in the beach-side area before, but that was mostly further down south in Satellite Beach and Indialantic, but never this far up north.

"It's bad," Weasel said. "I have close to no experience with this type of thing, but you do. We need all your Miami-experience now. Show me what you've got."

I nodded and followed her into the house. It was located on a canal leading to the Banana River, like most of the houses on the back side of the island. The house had a big pebble-coated pool area with two waterfalls, a slide, and a spa overlooking the river. The perfect setting for Florida living, the real estate ad would say. With the huge palm trees, it looked like true paradise. Until you stepped inside.

The inside was pure hell.

It was a long time since I had been on a murder scene, but the Weasel was right. I was the only one with lots of experience in this field. I spent eight years in downtown Miami, covering Overtown, the worst neighborhood in the town, as part of the homicide unit. My specialty was the killer's psychology. I was a big deal back then. But when I met Arianna and she became pregnant with the twins, I was done. It was suddenly too dangerous. We left Miami to get away from it. We moved to Cocoa Beach, where my parents lived, to be closer to my family and to get away from murder.

Now, it had followed me here. It made me feel awful. I hated to see the town's innocence go like this.

My colleagues from the Cocoa Beach Police Department greeted me with nods as we walked through the living room, overlooking the yard with the pool. I knew all of them. They seemed a little confused. For most of them, it was a first. Officer Joel Hall looked pale.

"Joel was first man here," Weasel said.

"How are you doing, Joel?" I asked.

"Been better."

"So, tell me what happened."

Joel sniffled and wiped his nose on his sleeve.

"We got a call from the boy. He told us his mother had been killed. He found her finger...well, the dog had it in his mouth. He didn't dare to go upstairs. He called 911 immediately. I was on patrol close by, so I drove down here."

"So, what did you find?"

"The boy and the dog were waiting outside the house. He was hysterical, kept telling me his parents were dead. Then, he showed me the finger. I tried to calm him down and tell him I would go look and to stay outside. I walked up and found the mother..." Joel sniffled again. He took in a deep breath.

"Take your time, Joel," I said, and put my hand on his shoulder. Joel finally caved in and broke down.

"You better see it with your own eyes," Weasel said. "But brace yourself."

I followed her up the stairs of the house, where the medical examiners were already taking samples.

"The kid said his parents were dead. What about the dad?" I asked. "You only said one homicide."

"The dad's fine. But, hear this," Weasel said. "He claims he was asleep the entire time. He's been taken to the hospital to see a doctor. He kept claiming he felt dizzy and had blurred vision. I had to have a doctor look at him before we talk to him. The boy is with him. Didn't want to leave his side. The dog is there too. Jim and Marty took them there. I don't want him to run. He's our main suspect so far."

We walked down the hallway till we reached the bedroom. "Brace yourself," Weasel repeated, right before we walked inside.

I sucked in my breath. Then I froze.

"It looks like he was dismembering her," Weasel said. "He cut off all the fingers on her right hand, one by one, then continued on to the toes on her foot."

I felt disgusted by the sight. I held a hand to cover my mouth, not because it smelled, but because I always became sick to my stomach when facing a dead body. Especially one that was mutilated. I never got used to it. I kneeled next to the woman lying on the floor. I examined her face and eyes, lifted her eyelids, then looked closely at her body.

"There's hardly any blood. No bruises either," I said. "I say she was strangled first, then he did the dismembering. My guess is he was disturbed. He was about to cut her into bits and pieces, but he stopped. "I sniffed the body and looked at the Weasel, who seemed disgusted by my motion. "The kill might have happened in the shower. She has been washed recently. Maybe he drowned her."

I walked into the bathroom and approached the tub. I ran a finger along the sides. "Look." I showed her my finger. "There's still water on the sides. It's been used recently."

"So, you think she was killed in the bathtub? Strangulation, you say? But there are no marks on her neck or throat?"

"Look at her eyes. Petechiae. Tiny red spots due to ruptured capillaries. They are a signature injury of strangulation. She has them under the eyelids. He didn't use his hands. He was being gentle."

Weasel looked appalled. "Gentle? How can you say he was gentle? He cut off her fingers?"

"Yes, but look how methodical he was. All the parts are intact. Not a bruise on any of them. Not a drop of blood. They are all placed neatly next to one another. It's a declaration of love."

Weasel looked confused. She grumbled. "I don't see much love in any of all this, that's for sure. All I see is a dead woman, who someone tried to chop up. And now I want you to find out who did it."

I chuckled. "So, the dad tells us he was sleeping?" I asked.

Weasel shrugged. "Apparently, he was drunk last night. They had friends over. It got a little heavy, according to the neighbors. Loud music and loud voices. But that isn't new with these people."

"On a Sunday night in a nice neighborhood like this?" I asked, surprised.

"Apparently."

"It's a big house. Right on the river. Snug Harbor is one of the most expensive neighborhoods around here. What do the parents do for a living?"

"Nothing, I've been told. They live off the family's money. The deceased's father was a very famous writer. He died ten years ago. The kids have been living off of the inheritance and the royalties for years since."

"Anyone I know, the writer?"

"Probably," she said. "A local hero around here. John Platt."

"John Platt?" I said. "I've certainly heard of him. I didn't know he used to live around here. Wasn't he the guy who wrote all those thriller-novels that were made into movies later on?"

"Yes, that was him. He has sold more than 100 million books worldwide. His books are still topping the bestseller lists."

"Didn't he recently publish a new book or something?"

Weasel nodded. "They found an old unpublished manuscript of his on his computer, which they published. I never understood how those things work, but I figure they think, if he wrote it, then it's worth a lot of money even if he trashed it."

I stared at the dead halfway-dismembered body on the floor, then back at the Weasel.

I sighed. "I guess we better talk to this heavily sleeping dad first."

7

JANUARY 2015

"Who was that guy you talked to last night?"

Joe walked into the kitchen. Shannon was cutting up oranges to make juice. She sensed he was right behind her, but she didn't turn to look at him. Last night was still in her head. The humming noise of the voices, the music, the laughter. Her head was hurting from a little too much alcohol. His question made everything inside of her freeze.

"Who do you mean?" she asked. "I talked to a lot of people. That was kind of the idea with the party after my concert. For me to meet with the press and important people in the business. That's the way it always is. You know how it goes. It's a big part of my job."

He put his hand on her shoulder. A shiver ran up her spine. She closed her eyes.

Not now. Please not now.

"Look at me when you're talking to me," he said.

She took in a deep breath, then put on a smile; the same smile she used when the press asked her to pose for pictures, the same smile she put on for her manager, her record label, and her friends when they asked her about the bruises on her back, followed by the sentence:

"Just me being clumsy again."

Shannon turned and looked at Joe. His eyes were black with fury. Her body shrunk and her smile froze.

"I saw the way you were looking at that guy. Don't you think I saw that?" Joe asked. "You know what I think? I think you like going to these parties they throw in your honor. I think you enjoy all the men staring at you, wishing you were theirs, wanting to fuck your brains out. I see it in their eyes and I see it in yours as well. You like it."

It was always the same. Joe couldn't stand the fact that Shannon was the famous one...that she was the one everyone wanted to talk to, and after a party like the one yesterday, he always lost his temper with her. Because he felt left out, because there was no one looking at him, talking to him, asking him questions with interest. He hated the fact that Shannon was the one with a career, when all he had ever dreamt of was to be singing in sold out stadiums like she did.

They had started out together. Each with just a guitar under their arm, working small clubs and bars in Texas, then later they moved on to Nashville, where country musicians were made. They played the streets together, and then got small gigs in bars, and later small concert venues around town. But when a record label contacted them one day after a concert, they were only interested in her. They only wanted Shannon King. Since then, Joe had been living in the shadow of his wife, and that didn't become him well. For years, she had made excuses for him, telling herself he was going through a rough time; he was just hurting because he wasn't going anywhere with his music. The only thing Joe had going for him right now was the fact that he was stronger than Shannon.

But as the years had passed, it was getting harder and harder for her to come up with new excuses, new explanations. Especially now that they had a child together. A little girl who was beginning to ask questions.

"Joe...I...I don't know what you're talking about. I talked to a lot of people last night. I'm tired and now I really want to get some breakfast."

"Did you just take a tone with me. Did ya'? Am I so insignificant in your life that you don't even talk to me with respect, huh? You don't even look at me when we're at your precious after party. Nobody cares about me. Everyone just wants to talk to the *biiig* star, Shannon King," he said, mocking her.

"You're being ridiculous."

"Am I? Did you even think about me once last night? Did you? I left at eleven-thirty. You never even noticed. You never even texted me and asked where I was."

Shannon blushed. He was right. She hadn't thought about him even once. She had been busy answering questions from the press and talking about her tour. Everyone had been pulling at her; there simply was no time to think about him. Why couldn't he understand that?

"I thought so," Joe said. Then, he slapped her.

Shannon went stumbling backward against the massive granite counter. She hurt her back in the fall. Shannon whimpered, then got up on her feet again with much effort. Her cheek burned like hell. A little blood ran from the corner of her mouth. She wiped it off.

Careful what you say, Shannon. Careful not to upset him further. Remember what happened last time. He's not well. He is hurting. Careful not to hurt him any more.

But she knew it was too late. She knew once he crossed that line into that area where all thinking ceased to exist, it was too late. She could appeal to his sensitivity as much as she wanted to. She could try and explain herself and tell him she was sorry, but it didn't help. If anything, it only made everything worse.

His eyes were bulging and his jaws clenched. His right eye had that tick in it that only showed when he was angry.

You got to get out of here.

"Joe, please, I..."

A fist throbbed through the air and smashed into her face.

Quick. Run for the phone.

She could see it. It was on the breakfast bar. She would have to spring for it. Shannon jumped to the side and managed to avoid his next fist, then slipped on the small rug on the kitchen floor, got back up in a hurry, and rushed to reach out for the phone.

Call 911. Call the police.

Her legs were in the air and she wasn't running anymore. He had grabbed her by the hair, and now he was pulling her backwards. He yanked her towards him, and she screamed in pain, cursing her long blonde hair that she used to love so much...that the world loved and put on magazine covers.

"You cheating lying bitch!" he screamed, while pulling her across the floor.

He lifted her up, then threw her against the kitchen counter. It blew out the air from her lungs. She couldn't scream anymore. She was panting for air and wheezing for him to stop. She was bleeding from her nose. Joe came closer, then leaned over her and, with his hand, he corrected his hair. His precious hair that had always meant so much to him, that he was always fixing and touching to make sure it was perfect, which it ironically never was.

"No one disrespects me. Do you hear me? Especially not

you. You're a nobody. Do you understand? You would be nothing if it wasn't for me," he yelled, then lifted his clenched fist one more time. When it smashed into Shannon's face again and again, she finally let herself drift into a darkness so deep she couldn't feel anything anymore.

8

JANUARY 2015

"Hi there. Ben, is it?" I asked.

The boy was sitting next to his dad in the hospital bed, the dog sleeping by his feet.

"He won't leave his dad's side," Marty said.

Ben looked up at me with fear in his eyes. "It's okay, Ben," I said, and kneeled in front of him. "We can talk here."

"I know you," Ben said. "You're Austin and Abigail's dad."

"That's right. And you're in their class. I remember you. Say, weren't you supposed to be at the zoo today?"

Ben nodded with a sad expression.

"Well, there'll be other times," I said. I paused while Ben looked at his father, who was sleeping.

"He's completely out cold," Marty said. "He was complaining that he couldn't control his arms and legs, had spots before his eyes, and he felt dizzy and nauseated. Guess it was really heavy last night."

I looked at the very pale dad. "Or maybe it was something else," I said.

"What do you mean?"

I looked closer at the dad.

"Did you talk to him?"

"Only a few words. When I asked about last night, he kept saying he didn't remember what happened, that he didn't know where he was. He kept asking me what time it was. Even after I had just told him."

"Hm."

"What?" Marty asked.

"Did they run his blood work?" I asked.

"No. I told them it wasn't necessary. He was just hung over. The doctor looked at him quickly and agreed. We agreed to let him to sleep it off. He seemed like he was still drunk when he talked to us."

"Is my dad sick, Mr. Ryder?" Ben asked.

I looked at the boy and smiled. "No, son, but I am afraid your dad has been poisoned."

"Poisoned?" Marty asked. "What on earth do you mean?"

"Dizziness, confusion, blurry vision, difficulty talking, nausea, difficulty controlling your movements all are symptoms of Rohypnol poisoning. Must have been ingested to have this big of an affect. Especially with alcohol."

"Roofied?" Marty laughed. "Who on earth in their right mind would give a grown man a rape drug?"

"Someone who wanted to kill him and his wife," I said.

I walked into the hallway and found a nurse and asked her to make sure they tested Brandon Bennett for the drug in his blood. Then, I called the medical examiner and told them to check the wife's blood as well. Afterwards, I returned to talk to Ben.

"So, Ben, I know this is a difficult time for you, but I would be really happy if you could help me out by talking a little about last night. Can you help me out here?"

Ben wiped his eyes and looked at me. His face was swollen from crying. Then he nodded. I opened my arms.

"Come here, buddy. You look like you could use a good bear hug."

Ben hesitated, then looked at his dad, who was still out cold, before he finally gave in and let me hug him. I held him in my arms, the way I held my own children when they were sad. The boy finally cried.

"It's okay," I whispered. "Your dad will be fine."

My words felt vague compared to what the little boy had seen this morning, how his world had been shaken up. His dad was probably going to be fine, but he would never see his mother again, and the real question was whether the boy would ever be fine again?

He wept in my arms for a few minutes, then pulled away and wiped his nose on his sleeve. "Do you promise to catch the guy that killed my mother?" he asked.

I sighed. "I can promise I'll do my best. How about that?"

Ben thought about it for a little while, then nodded with a sniffle.

"Okay. What do you want to know?" he asked.

"Who came to your house last night? I heard your parents had guests. Who were they?"

9

APRIL 1984

Tim took Annie down to the lake behind campus, where they sat down. The grass was moist from the sprinklers. Annie felt self-conscious with the way Tim stared at her. It was a hot night out. The cicadas were singing; Annie was sweating in her small dress. Her skin felt clammy.

Tim finally broke the silence.

"Has anyone ever told you how incredibly beautiful you are?"

Annie's head was spinning from her drink. The night was intoxicating, the sounds, the smell, the moist air hugging her. She shook her head. Her eyes stared at the grass. She felt her cheeks blushing.

"No."

"Really?" Tim said. "I find that very hard to believe."

Annie giggled, then sipped her drink. She really liked Tim. She could hardly believe she was really here with him.

"Look at the moon," he said and pointed.

It was a full moon. It was shining almost as bright as daylight. Its light hit the lake. Annie took in a deep breath, taking in the moment.

"It's beautiful," she said with a small still voice. She was afraid of talking too much, since he would only realize she wasn't smart, and then he might regret being with her.

Just go with the flow.

"I loathe Florida," Tim said. "I hate these warm nights. I hate how sweaty I always am. I'm especially sick of Orlando. When I'm done here, I'm getting out of this state. I wanna go up north. Don't you?"

Annie shrugged. She had lived all her life in Florida. Thirty minutes north of Orlando, to be exact. Born and raised in Windermere. Her parents still lived there, and that was where she was planning on going back once she had her degree. Annie had never thought about going anywhere else.

"I guess it's nice up north as well," she said, just to please him.

Tim laughed, then looked at her with those intense eyes once again. It made her uncomfortable. But part of her liked it as well. A big part.

"Can I kiss you?" he asked.

Annie blushed. She really wanted him to. Then she nodded. Tim smiled, then leaned over and put his lips on top of hers. Annie felt the dizziness from the drink. It was buzzing in her head. The kiss made her head spin, and when Tim pressed her down on the moist grass, she let him. He crawled on top of her, and with deep moans kept kissing her lips, then her cheeks, her ears, and her neck. Annie felt like laughing because it tickled so much, but she held it back to not ruin anything. Tim liked her and it made her happy.

"Boy, you're hot," he said, groaning, as he kissed her throat and moved further down her body. He grinned and started to open her dress, taking one button at a time. Annie felt insecure. What was he going to do next?

Tim pulled the dress open and looked at her bra, then he ripped it off.

"Ouch," Annie said. She tried to cover her breasts with her arms, but Tim soon grabbed them and pulled them to her sides. He held her down while kissing her breasts. He groaned while sucking on her nipples. Annie wasn't sure if she liked it or not. He was being a little rough, and she was afraid of going too far with him.

Whatever you do, don't sleep with him. No matter what.

"Stop," she mumbled, when he pulled the dress off completely and grabbed her panties. Tim stopped. He stared at Annie. She felt bad. Had she scared him away? Was he ever going to see her again if she didn't let him?

No matter what.

No. She wasn't ready for this. She had saved herself. This wasn't how it was supposed to happen. Not like this. Not here.

"I want to go home," Annie said.

Tim smiled and tilted his head, then leaned over and whispered in her ear. "Not yet, sweetheart, not yet."

He stroked her face gently and kissed her cheeks, while she fought and tried to get him off her body. In the distance, she heard voices, and soon she felt hands on her body, hands touching her, hands slapping her face. She felt so dizzy and everything became a blur of faces, laughing voices, cheering voices, hands everywhere, groping her, touching her, hurting her. And then the pain followed.

The excruciating pain.

10

JANUARY 2015

Brandon Bennett was still out cold when I had to leave the hospital. I decided to wait to interrogate him till later. Ben had told me that he had been asleep, so he hadn't seen who was at the house, but there were two of his parents' neighbors who usually came over to drink with his mom and dad. I got the names and called for both of them to come into the station in the afternoon. Meanwhile, I had to drive back to the zoo to pick up the kids and get them back to their school.

"Daddy!" my kids yelled when I opened the doors to the school bus and they stormed in, screaming with joy. Both of them clung to my neck.

"How was the zoo?" I asked.

"So much fun!" Abigail exclaimed. She was the most outgoing of the two, and often the one who spoke for them. I had a feeling Austin was the thinker, the one who would turn out to be a genius some day. Well, maybe not exactly a genius, but there was something about him. Abigail was the one who came up with all their naughty plans, and she always got Austin in on them.

"Good. I'm glad," I said and smooched their cheeks loudly.

"You would have loved it, Dad," Abigail continued. "You should have come. What was so important anyway?"

I exhaled and kissed her again, then let go of her. "Just some work thing. Nothing to worry about."

The twins looked at each other. Abigail placed her hands on her hips and looked at me with her head tilted.

"What?" I asked.

"You only say for us to not worry if there is actually something to worry about," Abigail said. "Am I right?" She looked at Austin, who nodded.

"She's right, Dad."

I smiled. "Well, it is nothing smart little noses like yours should get into, so get in the back of the bus with your friends and sit down. We're leaving now."

Abigail grumbled something, then grabbed her brother's shirt and they walked to the back. The bus gave a deep sigh when I closed the doors and we took off.

The atmosphere on the bus driving back was loud and very cheerful. Loudest of all were my twins, but this time I didn't mind too much. After the morning I had spent with a dead body and a poor kid who had lost his mother, I was just so pleased that my kids were still happy and innocent. They didn't look at me with that empty stare in their eyes, the one where you know they'll never trust the world again. That broken look that made them appear so much older than they were.

"Grandma and Grandpa will pick you up," I said, as I dropped them off at Roosevelt Elementary School.

"Yay!" they both exclaimed.

I told their teacher as well, then parked the bus and gave the keys back to the front office.

"Thank you so much for helping out today," Elaine at the desk said. "It's always wonderful when the parents get involved."

"Anytime," I said.

I walked to my car, a red Jeep Convertible. I got in and drove to the station with the top down. I bought my favorite sandwich at Juice 'N Java Café, called Cienna. It had a Portobello mushroom, yellow tomato, goat cheese arugula, and pesto on Pugliese bread. I figured I had earned it after the morning I had.

The police station was located inside of City Hall, right in the heart of Cocoa Beach. I knew the place well, even though I was usually located at the sheriff's offices in Rockledge. Cocoa Beach was my town, and every time they needed a detective, I was the one they called for. Even if they were cases that didn't involve homicide. As I entered through the glass doors, Weasel came towards me. Two officers flanked her.

"Going out for lunch?" I asked.

"Yes. I see you've already gotten yours," she said, nodding at my bag with my sandwich from the café.

"I'm expecting two of the neighbors in for questioning in a short while. Any news I should know about?" I asked.

Weasel sighed. "The ME has taken the body in for examination. They expect to have the cause of death within a few hours, they say. They're still working on the house."

"Any fingerprints so far?"

"Lots. We asked around a little and heard the same story from most of the neighbors. The Bennetts were a noisy bunch. Nothing that has ever been reported, but the wife and husband fought a lot, one neighbor told us. He said they yelled and screamed at each other when they got drunk. He figured the husband finally had enough. I guess it sounds plausible. He killed her, then panicked and tried to dismember her body to get rid of it. But the dog interrupted him. He decided to pretend he had been asleep through the whole thing. When we arrived, the dad was asleep when Joel went up, but he might have pretended to be. Joel said he seemed out of it, though. Might just be a good actor."

"It's all a lot of theories so far," I said with a deep exhale. It was going to be a long day for me. I was so grateful I had my parents nearby.

I grew up in Ft. Lauderdale, further down south, but when I left for college, my parents wanted to try something new. They bought a motel by the beach in Cocoa Beach a few years after I left the house. The place was a haven for the kids. They never missed me while they were there. That made it easier for me to work late.

"I've cleared an office for you," Weasel said. "We're glad to have you here to help us."

I put a hand on her broad shoulder. "Likewise. I'll hold down the fort. Enjoy your lunch."

11

JANUARY 2015

"It all started when they lost their daughter."

It was late in the afternoon at the station. I had interviewed two of the neighbors who usually came to the Bennetts' house to drink with them, but hadn't gotten anything out of them. They didn't even know the Bennetts very well, they told me. They just knew that there was free booze. The Bennetts were loaded, and every drunk in the neighborhood knew that they could always find a party there. Only one of the two, Travis Connor, had been at the Bennett's house the night before. He told us he was the only guest at the time, but he hadn't stayed long. He had left the house at ten o'clock and gone to the Beach Shack to hang out with some buddies. I called, and they confirmed his alibi. The next-door neighbor, Mrs. Jeffries had told my colleagues that she had seen Laura Bennett walk onto the back porch at eleven to smoke a cigarette. So, I let the guy go. His hands were shaking heavily, and I guessed he was in a hurry to find a drink somewhere.

Around three o'clock, a woman had come to the station

and asked to talk to someone about the killing of Laura Bennett. Her name was Gabrielle Phillips.

The front desk sent her to me. Now, I was sitting across from her as she explained why she had come.

"They lost their child last year, and that's when it all went wrong," she continued. "I've known Laura since high school," she said. "She never used to drink. But when their daughter died in her bed at night, everything changed."

"Sudden Infant Death Syndrome?" I asked, and wrote it on a notepad.

"Yes. After that, they started drinking. Well, to be honest, Brandon has always drunk a lot, but she never did. Never touched a drop. It wasn't her thing. She didn't like to lose control."

"So, they drank and partied because they lost their child?" I asked.

"Well, Brandon always liked to party. Especially after Laura inherited all that money. He didn't have to work anymore. He had always liked to drink, but it got really bad. She was actually considering leaving him and taking the kids, but then the daughter died in her sleep, and she couldn't take it. She had a drink and then never stopped again. I tried to talk to her, but she shut me out and told me it was none of my business."

Gabrielle looked upset. I could tell she had loved her friend and cared for her. She was choking up, but held back the tears.

"I tried..." she continued. "I really did. But she wouldn't listen to me. I told her that guy was all wrong for her. He was trouble from the beginning."

I reached behind me and grabbed a box of tissues that I handed to her. She grabbed it and wiped her eyes, careful not to smear her make-up. I wrote on my notepad and tried to get all the details down.

"So, you say she inherited a lot of money? From her dad, right?" I asked.

"She inherited ten million dollars from him, and she never even knew him."

I looked up. "Excuse me?"

"She was born outside of marriage. Her mother was an affair that John Platt had once when he was on a book tour. They met in Tampa, where she lived at the time. Nine months later, Laura was born. John Platt refused to have anything to do with the child. He paid a good amount of money to the mother to keep her mouth shut and never tell the child who her real father was. Laura's mother later remarried when Laura was still a baby, and they decided to have the new husband be the father as well. To prevent any awkward questions. And to have Laura grow up with a real family. Her new father loved her, and she still looks at him like her real father. Both of her parents died two years ago in a car accident outside of Orlando."

"Sounds like Laura has suffered a lot of loss the last couple of years," I said.

Gabrielle sniffled and wiped her nose in a ladylike manner.

"So, her husband Brandon, tell me more about him?"

"He is the scum of the earth," Gabrielle hissed. "But, somehow, she loved him."

"How did they meet?"

"At a sports game. Can you believe it? A baseball game. UCF Knights were playing South Florida. Laura went to UCF; Brandon had just come to watch the game with some friends. He was an auto mechanic and smelled like oil and trouble, if you ask me. Smoked and drank too much. Liked to party. I was with her on the night they met outside the stadium. He just walked right up to her and told her she was gorgeous and that he would like to invite her out sometime. I was surprised to hear her accept. I couldn't believe her. But I guess she somehow wanted to rebel against her parents or something. They never liked him either, but she married him anyway. After four months of them dating, he proposed. Four months! I knew she was going to get herself in trouble with this guy. I just knew it."

"So, tell me some more about the inheritance. When did she realize she was going to get all this money?"

"It was right before the pig proposed. Go figure, right? He heard about the money, then wanted to marry her. I couldn't believe she didn't see it, but she told me she loved him, and I really think she did. I think all he loved was her money. Anyway, that's just my opinion."

"How did she learn about the money? From a lawyer?" I asked, thinking it must have been quite a shock...suddenly being a millionaire and suddenly realizing your entire childhood was based on a lie.

Gabrielle shook her head and wiped her nose again. She drank from the glass of water I had placed in front of her. It was hot outside. In the low eighties. She was wearing shorts and flip-flops. The state costume of Florida. Even in January.

"No, it was the strangest thing. He called her."

"Who?"

"John Platt. He called her right before he died. How he got her number, I don't know, but I guess when you're that big you have people working for you. He was sick, he said. Cancer was eating him and he wanted her to come. He didn't tell her why, only that he had something for her. At first,

Laura thought it was a joke, but he gave her an address and she looked it up and it turned out to be right. She called me afterwards and told me everything. She was freaking out. Said she had decided she didn't want to go, because it was too weird. But I convinced her to do it. I went with her, so she wouldn't be alone. Together, we were invited into his huge mansion on the beach in Cocoa Beach. He told her he was happy to see her. There were others there. I later learned they were her siblings. Two sisters and a brother. They had all grown up in the house, but were now living on their own, except for the youngest, who hadn't left the house yet, even though he was in his mid-twenties. They weren't very happy to see her, I can tell you that much. They weren't prepared to share their inheritance with some stranger, but they soon learned they had to."

"So, what happened?" I asked "What did John Platt tell her?"

"It was such an awkward scene. He was lying in bed, surrounded by nurses and family. He teared up when he saw Laura. It made her really uncomfortable. He wanted to hold her hand and started to cry. Then, he handed her a piece of paper. *Take this,* he said. *You deserve this more than any of the others.*"

"So, what was written on the paper?"

"It was a will. He had changed his will a few hours before we arrived. His lawyer had signed it and everything. It stated that she was going to inherit everything. All he had. The house, his money, everything."

I leaned back in my chair while the story came together for me. "So, the siblings didn't get anything?"

She shook her head. "Nope. Not a dime. They had grown up in luxury, so their father figured it was time for them to learn how to earn a decent living on their own. That's what he wrote in the letter. Laura had never known who her father was, never had any of his money, now he was giving her everything. I guess he tried to make amends for not letting her know he was her dad all those years. Laura was baffled, to put it mildly. She read the letter, but didn't understand. How could he be her father? She already had a father. She ran out of the house crying, and I ran after her. John Platt died shortly after, we later learned. Good thing for him, I think. Otherwise, the siblings would probably have started a riot. They tried to fight Laura with all their big lawyers afterwards, trying to declare that their dad was dying, and therefore not in his right mind when he made the will. After several months of going back and forth, the judge decided they didn't have a case and closed it. Laura was rich and, in time, came to accept the fact that she had been the result of an affair. Her mother confirmed it was true, and they didn't speak for a long time, but she forgave her eventually. Laura and Brandon bought the house in Snug Harbor and moved here shortly after they were married. She sold John Platt's old house, but wanted to stay in the town. She liked it here, she told me. I didn't see her much after she moved, since I live north of Orlando now, and I work full time, but every now and then, we would meet and catch up. But she was never really happy. She had Ben, and he was the joy of her life, but she kept talking about how Brandon was drinking and gambling her money away on the casino boats, acting like this big shot with her money. She wanted to leave him, but then she was pregnant again and decided to stay for the children. I met with her the week before the baby died. She said she was going to leave him, this time for real. That she was going back to the Tampa area and start over with the kids. Brandon's drinking had gotten worse, and he was still gambling a lot. In a few years, he had spent more than a third of her money. She was still certain he loved her, and maybe he does. I don't know him well enough to say he doesn't. But he also loved the money, and that's what went so wrong. After the baby died, I went to the funeral and Laura had a black eye. She told me in confidence that Brandon had slapped her, that he blamed her for the child's death. They fought about that a lot, she told me. He couldn't believe she hadn't checked on the baby during the night. It was her fault, he told her. And she believed him. She felt so guilty, she told me. So much it hurt. I said she should leave him, that now was the time to go, and she agreed, but she never did. Instead, she lowered herself to his level and took up drinking. The last time I spoke to her was three months ago, and she was so drunk on the phone I could hardly understand what she was saying. Now...I can't believe she's gone. What's to become of Ben?"

I shook my head with a deep exhale. I was starting to wonder that myself.

END OF EXCERPT...

ORDER YOUR COPY TODAY!

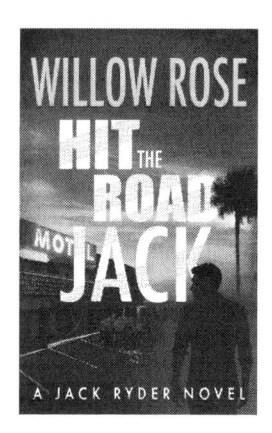

GO HERE TO ORDER:
https://www.amazon.com/Hit-Road-Jack-wickedly-suspenseful-ebook/dp/B00V9525BC

Printed in Great Britain
by Amazon